NO GOOD TEA
GOES UNPUNISHED

ALSO BY BREE BAKER

The Seaside Café Mysteries

Live and Let Chai

No GOOD TEA Goes UNPUNISHED

BREE BAKER

sourcebooks
landmark

Published by Sourcebooks Landmark, an imprint of Sourcebooks, Inc.
P.O. Box 4410, Naperville, Illinois 60563-4410
(630) 961-3900
Fax: (630) 961-2168
sourcebooks.com

Printed and bound in Canada.
MBP 10 9 8 7 6 5 4 3 2 1

To Judy and Craig Miller

CHAPTER

ONE

"Congratulations, Mrs. Miller," I said, embracing my childhood friend, Judy, who was still glowing from her recent exchange of wedding vows. "You look beautiful. Has anyone told you that today?"

"One or two people," she said, beaming back at me. "I can't thank you enough for doing all this, Everly. When you agreed to cater the wedding reception and be the local liaison, I never dreamed you'd manage all of this." She motioned at the crowded beach behind us, where half the town and a handful of her new husband's guests mingled and danced in bare feet on the sand.

I'd worked diligently for weeks with a local rental company to create the elaborate beach wedding of Judy's dreams, and I'd even petitioned the town council to close the portion of beach outside my home for the entire day to accommodate the big event. Everything had come together seamlessly. A blank check from Judy's new husband had definitely helped.

Judy had grown up in Charm with me. Her family lived on the more rural end of the island, near the maritime forest, and they'd struggled financially more than most. I hadn't been especially close to Judy as a child, but I remembered hearing her say in high school that she'd leave the island—and North Carolina—as soon as she graduated, and never worry about money again. Marrying Craig Miller, one of *Entrepreneur* magazine's Wealthiest Thirty Under Thirty, basically guaranteed she would accomplish that goal.

Judy smiled and bopped her head to a Beach Boys song rising from the DJ booth positioned outside my home and newly opened iced tea shop, Sun, Sand, and Tea. A salty summer breeze tousled the light-brown hair at the base of her neck. Her elegant chignon had loosened significantly during an enthusiastic round of the chicken dance. "I never thought a single day could be perfect, but this one really is. I've even eaten whatever I wanted since I got here Wednesday, and my dress still fits." She patted her perfectly flat stomach, which was currently wrapped in a designer white lace gown. Barefoot in the sand, under waning sunlight, she looked like an angel who might break into a graceful pirouette at any moment.

My fitted coral sundress, on the other hand, hugged all my many curves. I'd briefly considered a more flattering A-line, but Judy had insisted I looked like a shorter Jessica Rabbit in this dress, and I didn't hate that idea.

Judy's bright blue eyes sparkled as she watched her

new husband limbo beneath a striped pole several yards away from my iced tea tent. "Can you believe he's brilliant *and* silly? How did I get lucky enough to find both in one man?"

"Well," I said, handing her a Mason jar filled with crushed ice and my newest sweet tea creation, "he married you, so you don't have to convince me about the brilliant part."

She turned the full force of her smile on me and accepted the tea. I popped a coral-colored straw into the jar and folded my hands while I waited for the verdict.

"This is delicious." She took a long pull. The ice rattled as the tea line neared the jar's bottom. "Oh my goodness, what it this?"

"Hibiscus tea, cinnamon sticks, a dash of sugar to taste, lemon for garnish. I call it the Blushing Bride. It's a signature creation for your special day." I bobbed a goofy curtsy, then stood with a casual shrug. "Or the J. C. Miller, for Judy and Craig, if Blushing Bride seems like too much. What do you think?"

"I think this is the reason I heard about your shop all the way up in Massachusetts when you've only been open a few months."

My cheeks warmed with pride. "Thanks."

I'd left Charm several years ago to follow my dream of becoming a culinary mastermind—and also to chase a cowboy through the Midwest on a rodeo circuit. The cowboy had eventually broken my heart, and I'd hightailed it home to the island without finishing culinary school, but I was working to turn that unfortunate series of events into something good. For starters, I'd opened Sun, Sand, and Tea, a seaside café and iced tea shop, where I served recipes from my family's old cookbooks with my own unique flair. I might not have finished all my culinary classes, but I was happy, healthy, and home. What more could a lady ask for?

My superstitious great-aunts would say I was happy *because* I was home. According to them, my adventures couldn't have ended any other way. Aunt Clara and Aunt Fran harbored several outlandish beliefs about women in the Swan family. For starters, they believed we weren't supposed to leave the island. Our female Swan ancestors had helped found Charm, and we were therefore irrevocably tied to it, as was our happiness, health, and livelihoods. If that wasn't stifling enough, we were also, allegedly, cursed in love.

Personally, I'd never believed in my aunts' myths, so I did what I wanted, and I was certain that my heart was neither the first nor the last to have been broken by a cowboy, curse notwithstanding.

Despite the lost love, I was thankful the tide had turned and brought me back to Charm. My dream home had gone on the market almost immediately, at the exact asking price I could afford. Even better, the property was zoned for commercial use and ready for a business to be tucked into the first floor below the living quarters. These days, I was in love with a massive hundred-and-seventy-year-old estate on a cliff near the sea.

Judy set her empty glass down beside the pitcher. "Hit me again, bartender. It's hot as aces out here."

I refilled her jar with the hibiscus and cinnamon concoction and enjoyed the pretty red glow it cast over her hands as she lifted it to her lips.

Craig made his way through the sand in pale gray suit pants, a white dress shirt unbuttoned halfway down his chest. The tie and jacket had been abandoned pre-limbo. He kissed his bride and enveloped her in his arms. "I love you."

"Tea?" I offered, passing him a jar of Blushing Bride.

"Thank you." He accepted the drink without releasing Judy. "For everything," he said, smiling. "I doubt any amount of money could have accomplished all this without you at the helm. This party is unbelievable. I don't think an army could have pulled this off, and you did it all by yourself."

Judy laughed. "If we'd asked my mom to be our local liaison, we'd be eating fish off paper plates next to Daddy's backyard grill right now and fighting mosquitos."

I gave the twenty-foot buffet of finger foods a long, prideful look. The dishes were displayed under little mesh screens on long tables covered in white linens and manned by the rental company's staff. Each recipe had come from one of my family's ancient, crumbling cookbooks. "Have you had a chance to eat anything?" I asked Craig.

He nodded. "I've eaten everything. I'd eat at your café every day if I could. Have you thought of opening a satellite location in Martha's Vineyard?"

"No." I shook my head. Possible curses aside, I liked Charm, and since I'd come home I couldn't imagine ever wanting to leave again. Plus, the shop had only been open a few months, and I was still working to establish a predictable income—preferably one that would pay the bills and rebuild the savings account I'd drained to make my iced tea dreams come true, not to mention the endless maintenance and improvements needed for a house as old as mine. The small amount of money I'd accepted for my work on the Millers' wedding was already set aside for aesthetic improvements to the café and a membership at one of those big-box stores where I could buy supplies in bulk. "I love that you decided on a Friday wedding," I said. "I hope your out-of-town guests will stay and enjoy Charm through the weekend."

Craig set his empty tea jar aside. "We chose today because it's the six-month anniversary of our first date."

"Wow." I dragged the word into several syllables. "I knew it was a short engagement, but I had no idea you'd just started dating that recently."

Judy curled her fingers under the collar of Craig's shirt to tug him closer. "I was so distraught when I lost my teaching job in Boston that I drove to Martha's Vineyard, rented a cottage, and just sat by the sea contemplating what to do with my life. I thought it was over. I thought I'd have to move, start over. Look at school districts in need of educators, maybe even come back to Charm and bait hooks for Dad and my brothers' fishing crew. Then I ran into Craig while we were waiting in line for shrimp tacos, and here we are."

Craig kissed her nose.

"Did you find a teaching job in Martha's Vineyard?" I asked.

"Nope." Judy didn't take her eyes off her husband. "Craig asked me to move in with him a few days after we met, and I've just been hanging out with him ever since."

I tried to imagine a man who could make me want to stop working and move into his house less than a week after meeting him, but my imagination wasn't that good.

"Wait until you see our room," Judy told Craig. "It's amazing. I almost felt guilty staying in it without you last night."

Craig looked at me with gratitude. "You aced that too, I guess."

"I did my best," I said. I might've gone a little crazy giving my largest guest room a wedding-themed makeover: white eyelet lace duvet, pillow shams, and bedding, fluffy white rug, white pillar candles. Heirloom crystal vases and silver candlesticks. Roses on the nightstand, vanity, and every flat surface I could fit them on. Judy had spent her last night as a single woman in there, and she would spend her first night as Mrs. Miller in there as well. I wanted the space to be worthy of creating the highest caliber of memories.

She turned her cheek against his chest, catching my eye. "I still can't believe you bought this old place."

"My house?" I glanced at the historic beauty with satisfaction.

"I've heard so many stories about it over the years,"

she said. "My brothers used to tell me it was haunted. I always ran past it whenever I came to this part of the beach or boardwalk, even as a teen."

"Haunted?" I asked. "I love this place." Though if she'd asked my great-aunts, they would've heartily agreed with Judy's brothers.

The wedding coordinator cut through the crowd at the buffet and made a beeline for my tea tent. "Time to cut the cake," he called.

A woman holding a big camera followed along behind him, sliding and sinking in the soft white sand with every step. "I'd love to get a photo of Craig and Judy cutting the first slice together," she said. "The sun's setting fast, so we have to hurry if we want the good light. Then I'd like to relocate to the bay for a few shots at twilight."

The planner opened his arms to herd the happy couple along. "We're arranging transportation to the bay as soon as the cake is cut," he said, "but we've got to keep moving."

The bay was just across the island from my home, not ten minutes by car. Charm was part of North Carolina's barrier islands, the long narrow strips of land separated from the mainland by channels, also known as the Outer Banks. The sun rose over the Atlantic outside my back door and set over the bay. The lighthouse-like tower that rose from the top of my old Victorian made views of both possible—and perfect.

I followed the foursome through the soft, warm sand to the cake table and waited while the photographer clicked away. Judy gripped the cake knife, then Craig slid his hands gently over hers. They smiled. They cut. It was adorable.

The photographer checked the screen of her camera and frowned. "Can we try that again? This time, tug your sleeve over the bracelet."

She mimed the act, and Craig obeyed, dipping his chin and blushing slightly as he stuffed the edges of a braided hemp band beneath the cuff of his dress shirt. "Sorry."

Judy's face paled. She stared at Craig's wrist for a long beat, then dragged her attention back to the photographer without making eye contact with her husband. Her smile was suddenly hollow and staged.

I jumped in to help the waitstaff finish cutting the cake. Nearly three hundred slices later, all fifty of Craig's guests and more than two hundred of Judy's were enjoying a light almond torte covered in edible beach-themed bling.

Craig's brow pinched as he pulled his phone from his pocket. "It's Pete," he said softly, then turned and paced away.

"Pete is the business partner?" I asked Judy. I was doing my best to remember names, but I'd heard a hundred new ones since breakfast.

"Yeah," she said with a frown. "I was sure I saw him here." She turned in a small circle, peering at the crowd. "What did he do? Leave after the ceremony?"

"Would he do that?"

"Maybe," she said. "Who knows with Pete. He and

Craig have been buddies since college, but Craig's the only one who grew up. Pete is as irresponsible now as he was ten years ago, which makes him a millionaire mess. Bad investments, tons of debt. He drives Craig batty, but Craig's too nice to ever say so." She stopped and wrinkled her nose. "I'm sorry. That was such a downer. What's important is that Craig is wonderful, and I'm happy."

My best friend, Amelia, emerged from a group of nearby guests and headed our way. Her sleek blond bob danced in the wind and over her shoulders. "Congratulations!" She wrapped Judy in a big hug and rocked her back and forth before stepping away to admire her. "You look absolutely stunning."

"Thank you," Judy said. "So do you."

Amelia always looked amazing in her vintage pinup ensembles. Today's aquamarine sequined sheath, which enhanced the color of her already bright blue eyes, was no exception.

"I can't believe you're really here," Amelia told Judy. "It's just like old times, except now you're married!"

Judy's smile widened. "I know you had a huge hand in this amazing party too, so thank you. Words aren't enough, but seriously, thank you so much. I can't stop smiling."

"*That* is enough," Amelia assured. "Besides, friends do things for each other. Sometimes Everly helps me stock my Little Libraries with books, and sometimes I help her make two thousand hors d'oeuvres and fifty gallons of iced tea."

I laughed. Amelia wasn't a chef, but she was loads of fun, a great listener, and an incredible friend. She'd been by my side through every quiche and kabob that made this dinner possible. I owed her about a month of trekking around the island with wagonloads of books to fill the Little Libraries she maintained, where townspeople could pick up free books to read or leave some behind for others to enjoy.

"You picked the perfect weekend for a party," Amelia told Judy. "Summer Splash starts Sunday, so some folks are literally painting the town."

Summer Splash was Charm's annual arts festival. Local vendors and artists came out in droves to display and sell their wares.

"We picked today for the wedding because it's the anniversary of our first date," Judy said, her smile slipping slightly as she scanned the area where Craig had disappeared. "I'll be right back. Too much nerves and tea, I think."

"Do you think we might be the ones in a fancy white dress one day?" Amelia asked as Judy walked away.

I tried to imagine myself in Judy's narrow, custom-designed gown but couldn't. Not just because I'd left for college in a size six and returned in a twelve, but mostly because the idea I might really be cursed in love sometimes got the better of me.

"Are you setting up a booth at the festival for Charming Reads?" I asked, changing the subject.

"Right outside my shop," she said. "Are you going to be there?"

"I hope so. I plan to see Craig and Judy off tomorrow morning with a massive breakfast before their flight to Maui. After that, I'll be helping my aunts brainstorm ideas for a video they want to shoot. Apparently a honeybee advocacy group called Bee Loved is accepting video applications from beekeepers across the country for a chance to appear in their upcoming documentary on the plight of the American honeybee."

Amelia raised her brows. "That's going to be interesting."

"Tell me about it."

Amelia laughed. "Your aunts are the bee's knees. They have this in the bag. Maybe next you can reach out to some ghost hunters about filming in your house."

"My house isn't haunted," I said. "Unless you count Lou." Lou was the seagull who seemed to have come with the place. He often appeared on my deck out of nowhere and made me scream.

"I don't know how you grew up in your family without believing in curses and ghosts and legends."

"Oh my," I said with a smile. "And I'm not sure how you grew up in a normal family and believe everything my aunts tell you."

"It's safer this way," she said.

I rolled my eyes.

The wedding planner and photographer darted through the crowd in our direction, eyes wide and mouths gaping. "Have you seen the happy couple?" the planner panted as he stopped to catch his breath.

"The groom took a call a little while ago," Amelia said.

"And Judy just went inside to freshen up," I added. "Why? What's going on?"

The planner turned a dirty look on the photographer at his side. "She spent too much time trying to catch candids in the crowd, and now we've missed the opportunity to get the couple to the bay before the natural light has completely gone."

"It's okay," the photographer assured him, though her voice wasn't very convincing. "Twilight can be beautiful for reception photos, and I found a place about three hundred yards up the beach where we can get some unique shots with a giant sandcastle."

Amelia rocked onto her toes. "Summer Splash arts festival saves the day."

It was true. Charm had some unparalleled talent in the sand-sculpting arena, and they always went big for Summer Splash.

I patted the photographer's shoulder. "I'll check on Judy and be right back." I hurried up the hill of sand and seagrass toward my home, hoping Judy had just needed a break from the chaos of her day and wasn't feeling ill from too much sun.

I crossed my rear deck and followed the wide wrap-around porch to my front door, then let myself inside. "Judy?" The space was eerily silent as I dashed from room to room, peeping into open doors and knocking on closed ones.

Finding no one inside, I hurried back, moving faster now as twilight threatened to disappear like the sunset. I followed the porch again, this time to my backyard, where a picket fence–wrapped garden and small greenhouse overlooked the sea. Warm, salty scents rose from the food at the reception below, mixing pungently with the sweet magnolias and crepe myrtle growing thick and wild in my garden.

Hundreds of heads bobbed on the beach at the base of the jagged hill, dancing, laughing, and chatting around tall bistro tables arranged in the sand. I used my vantage point from the garden's edge to seek the only two people I was in charge of keeping happy today but had somehow lost.

Amelia jumped up and down in the distance, waving one arm overhead. I couldn't be sure from this range if she was flagging me, but I hoped her enthusiasm meant she'd found Judy or Craig, or preferably both. I hustled back over the hill and across the sand to her side. "Did you find them?" I bent forward at the waist to catch my breath from the run. "Tell me the happy couple is already on their way to the giant sandcastle for some twilight photos."

"I'm not sure," she said, hooking her arm in mine and towing me down the beach, away from the party. "The planner called Craig's phone, and I heard it ringing."

We stopped near a six-foot-tall sandcastle with four elaborately detailed walls with turrets and corner towers. The wall facing away from the water had a narrow arched opening where children could wander in and out.

The photographer and planner stood shoulder to

shoulder a few feet away, staring at the patches of sea-grass near the boardwalk. The path, made of weathered wooden planks, ran parallel to the beach and covered the perimeter of the island, breaking only occasionally for a park, forest, or cove. Here, the boardwalk was only a few yards from the sand, but it stretched farther inland as it climbed the hill toward my house, to the point that my house stood between it and the sea.

"Try again," the photographer said, nudging the planner's elbow. "I'd swear it was right there." She pointed to a patch of tall, bushy grasses.

I squinted through the falling darkness and ran a wrist across my damp forehead. Hopefully the sweat running down my back and cleavage wouldn't stain my dress. Much as I'd enjoyed being compared to Jessica Rabbit, I couldn't wait to take the stifling number off.

The planner tapped his phone screen, and the wedding march sounded nearby. "I love that Craig made that my ringtone," he said, tromping into the grasses.

The photographer sighed, casting a wayward look overhead at the vanishing light. Judy and Craig might've missed their chance for wedding photos at twilight, but nowhere on earth rivaled Charm for its perfect night sky. No smog. No high rises or mountaintops to block the magical view. Just the endless, inky darkness and billions of twinkling white stars above.

"There's no one over here," the wedding planner called. "Just his phone. Why would he leave his phone?"

A new thought occurred to me, and I turned to face the water. I wasn't sure what kind of people would ditch their reception for a skinny dip at twilight, but it would explain the absence of both our bride and groom.

I inched closer to the water's edge and scanned the glittering surface for signs of a couple so caught up in one another they hadn't noticed a search party had formed on the sand. I didn't see a couple in the distance, but something caught my eye in the surf several yards away.

"Amelia," I called over one shoulder.

She headed my way.

"Do you see that?" I asked, moving quickly toward the large object as it drifted into focus. "Is that a man?" Goose bumps rose on my skin, and I kicked off my sandals and ran for the body being pulled further away with each sweep of the tide.

"Call 911," I yelled as I realized why I couldn't make out the man's features. He was floating face down! I dove for him, clutching his arm and wrenching his face out of the water as I rolled him onto his back. My heart clenched painfully as recognition dawned. "It's Craig!"

I staggered out of the water, bending forward and feeling the full weight of him as we emerged onto the beach. The undertow of retreating waves tugged and pulled at his body, nearly dragging him from my grip.

Amelia trudged through the water to catch his feet. "I'm here!"

"Call 911," I hollered again, this time at the photographer and wedding planner, who were standing motionless and clearly in shock. "Now!"

"I did," Amelia said. "I think I heard the photographer call too."

We positioned Craig on his back and checked for vitals. "I don't feel a pulse," Amelia said, moving her fingers from his wrist to his throat.

I tilted his head back and opened his mouth, hoping she'd missed the heartbeat. Five summers of lifeguard training were immediately present in my mind. "He's not breathing." I checked his airway. "No obstructions." His skin was cool to my frantic touch. "Is there a doctor here?" I called into the night. "A medical professional?" No one stepped forward.

Amelia rose to her knees and fit her hands against his chest. "We've got this, and the ambulance is on its way. Ready?"

I blew into his mouth, inflating his lungs. Amelia pumped his silent heart.

Heavy shadows fell over us as guests began to gather round. "Look for Judy!" I yelled, my vision blurring with tears. "Check the water!" I covered Craig's mouth with mine again, taking my turn in the work to revive the unrevivable. My heart ached and my mind scrambled in fear and grief and shock. Had my childhood friend become a widow just hours after her wedding? Or was it even worse? Was she in the water somewhere too?

I rested again while Amelia took over. This time, I dared to look at the black waves rolling in, dark and ominous in the waning light.

A bright light flashed over us as the photographer

pointed her camera's flash in our direction. "What is that?" she asked, pointing first to his waterlogged and deeply stained dress shirt, then my dress and Amelia's hands.

"Blood," Amelia said, falling back on the sand.

I froze, confused and terrified. Her palms were dripping water and slick with blood, as were my chest and torso.

Craig's shirt was soaked in red, and his shirt was torn.

"What happened?" the photographer asked, keeping her distance as she swept the light from Amelia's face to mine.

"I don't know," I said. Before I could process the possibility that Craig had been murdered at his own wedding reception, a theater-worthy scream rent the night.

Judy staggered forward, parting the gathered crowd and clutching the silver cake knife to her ruined white gown. The knife was covered in blood.

CHAPTER

TWO

Cops and EMTs peppered the beach within minutes, pushing us away from Craig's body and corralling all the guests, including Craig and Judy's families, behind a flimsy line of yellow crime-scene tape, where they would speak with interviewing officers. Amelia, Judy, and I went inside the sandcastle and huddled together, tears rolling and hearts broken. I kept watch through the small, arched windows.

A policeman had taken the knife from Judy and dropped it into an evidence bag before instructing us to stay put. The detective was on his way. Staying close wasn't a problem. The sandcastle was as far as Amelia and I could coax Judy from Craig's side. Giving our formal statements to the detective would be more complicated, at least for me. It had only been four short months since Detective Grady Hays had considered me a possible murderer, and I could only imagine what he'd think of me finding yet another body.

Judy sobbed into her palms, her knees pulled

tightly to her chest. "I was looking for Craig when I saw a glint of light on the ground," she whimpered. "The party lights were reflecting off the crystal handle of our cake cutter, so I picked it up. I couldn't understand how the knife had gotten so far from the cake or what was smeared all over it—it was something dark, but our cake and frosting were both white. Then I heard the commotion, and I saw the crowd gathering near the water. People were saying Craig was hurt." She peeled strands of tear-soaked hair from her cheeks. "And I knew it was his blood on the knife." Judy burst into tears again.

I rubbed her back and exchanged helpless looks with Amelia over Judy's bowed head.

The world outside our sandcastle was a flurry of lights and activity. Guests had been divided into groups for interviews and dismissal. Little plastic numbers were set on the sand and in the grass for evidence collection. The medical examiner hunched over Craig's body.

My great-aunt Clara's silhouette moved through the chaos in our direction, the wispy material of her silver gown flowing behind her on the night's breeze. "Knock knock," she said softly, stooping to poke her small face through the sandy archway. Moonlight shone on her flawless ivory skin and long blond and white braid. "I thought I'd find you all in here."

"Do you need me?" I asked. She and her sister, my great-aunt Fran, had been left to assist and oversee the waitstaff in my absence. Guilty as I felt about that, I couldn't bring myself to leave Judy, and I wasn't sure how far away I was allowed to go, anyway.

"No, no," she said. "Fran and I have everything taken care of, but it's getting late and the wind is chilly, so I brought you these." She handed us a stack of beach blankets. Since the sun had gone down, the temperature had dropped by fifteen degrees, and my sopping clothes and hair seemed to grow colder with each gust of wind.

I passed the blankets to Judy and Amelia before wrapping my shoulders with the last one. "Thank you," I told Aunt Clara. "I'm sorry I'm not out there helping."

"Don't you worry," Clara cooed. "Fran and I have the help of the rental company until midnight, and there's plenty of food and drinks to keep folks satisfied while they wait to be interviewed." She gave us a warm smile, turned on her heel, and was gone.

Aunt Clara and Aunt Fran had worked alongside my grandma to raise me after my mother died when I was small. I didn't remember my mother, but Grandma had been my world until she'd passed away while I was off chasing the cowboy. Thankful as I was to be home now, I wished more than anything that I'd come home soon enough to tell her how much I loved her one last time.

Judy pressed the corner of the blanket to her eye. "I just can't understand how this happened."

"Me either," I said, speaking figuratively, of course. The bloody knife she'd had in her hands earlier was likely the literal explanation.

"Everly," a familiar voice called through the doorway. Detective Grady Hays crouched just outside the castle, his steel-gray eyes searching. "You mind coming out here to talk to me?"

Detective Hays was a former U.S. Marshal who'd moved to Charm from Charlotte in search of a fresh start for himself and his young son, Denver, after they lost Grady's wife to cancer. He'd arrived just a few months after I'd returned to Charm, and we'd met at a crime scene like this on his first official day as Charm's sole investigator. We'd become friends during the last investigation, but hadn't spoken much since the case closed, and I realized I'd missed him.

He tipped his cowboy hat at Amelia, then Judy. "Ladies, I'd like to speak with each of you once I've finished with Miss Swan."

My shaky knees wobbled as I ducked beneath the doorway of the sand castle. "Hey."

Grady pressed a warm hand to the small of my back to steady me. "You okay?" he asked, tempting me to break down and bawl. Being strong for Judy was almost more than I could bear, and knowing Grady's shoulders were tough enough to handle my worst made the thought extremely appealing. The zip of electricity passing between us was nice too.

I forced my chin up, refusing to fall apart when I still had the strength to keep it together. "Good as I can be, I guess."

He looked me over, slipping his fingers under the blanket to lift it and examine the blood-stained dress beneath. The scents of cologne and shampoo wafted from his black leather coat, and I shivered hard. "Let's get that dress off," he said, steering me toward my house.

"What?"

"I'd like to have it sent to the lab. Meanwhile, it'll do you good to get into something clean and dry. Where'd you get the blanket?"

"Aunt Clara just brought a stack of them out," I croaked, feeling a tidal wave of emotion take hold. My weak noodle legs wobbled again, and I stopped.

"I don't want the dress back," I said. "Can you have the lab destroy it when they finish whatever they're going to do to it?" I never wanted to see the thing again. The memories of this night would haunt me for the rest of my life.

"Sure." Grady looked down at me and held my elbow more securely. "Need to sit a minute?"

I nodded, and he helped me to a massive piece of driftwood where partygoers had been snapping selfies with disposable wedding cameras all day.

I took a seat, certain my wobbly knees wouldn't hold me upright any longer. "I can't believe this is happening," I said.

Grady lowered himself onto the log beside me, stretching long jean-clad legs and worn-out cowboy boots. "It's awful. A wedding ought to be a day to cherish. I'm sorry."

"Thanks," I said, wondering if he was remembering his own wedding as we spoke. Grady kept plenty of secrets behind his carefully built walls, and I respected that. I imagined it was especially important to him as a lawman and father, but as his friend, I wished he'd let me in a little more. Then again, friends usually stayed in touch between murders. "How are you doing?"

He rubbed his forehead. "Better than you, I think. Better than Craig Miller." He dropped his hand to his side with a sigh. "Charm's police force isn't prepared to handle this. There are six of us. *Six.* Normally, that's more than enough, but trying to carefully screen three hundred people at ten o'clock at night? We'll be lucky to talk to half of them before midnight."

My teeth chattered, and I wrapped my arms tight around my middle. "We tried to save him before I saw the blood," I said. "Amelia and I were doing CPR. She was pressing on his chest."

"Well, I heard he was face down in the ocean," Grady said. "I'm not sure anyone would've thought to look for a secondary cause of death."

"What if we killed him?" I asked, shaking from head to toe.

"You didn't." Grady shook his head. "Coroner says he died instantly. The knife went right through his heart."

My eyes filled with unshed tears as the weight of his statement settled over me. "Who would kill a groom at his wedding?"

"Bride had the murder weapon," Grady said. His voice was flat and devoid of emotion. "We'll start there, run prints."

I wiped my eyes.

"How well do you know Judy?" he asked.

"She went to school with Amelia and me," I said. "Her family is from Charm."

"When was the last time you spoke with her? Before she contacted you about catering the reception, I mean. Were the two of you close when you were younger? How well do you know her today?"

I pulled my chin back, mind reeling from the sheer number of questions. "We weren't close, and we didn't really keep in touch. Why?"

"How would you describe her?"

"Why?" I repeated, more slowly.

"She was a fisherman's kid," he said. "Came from a family with consistent financial struggles."

"So?"

"So, Judy just married one of the wealthiest young entrepreneurs in America, and the minute he died, everything he had probably became hers."

"That's ridiculous," I said. "She loved him, and why would she kill him at their wedding? Why not wait a few months and arrange for a plausible alibi, or at least not show up at the crowded crime scene with the murder weapon in hand?"

"Crime of passion?" he suggested. "Not every crime is premeditated."

"That possibility ruins your theory that she killed him for his money." I tugged the blanket more tightly over my shoulders, feeling the fine layer of salt and sand scrape against my icy skin. "It doesn't matter, anyway. She didn't do this."

"Tell me what happened," he said, sincerity in his pale gray eyes. "Anything you can remember or that you think is significant."

I filled him in on everything from Craig's phone call from Pete to the wedding planner finding Craig's phone in the grass right before I spotted the body floating in the water.

"So then you went in and pulled him out," Grady said, a look of mild exasperation in his eyes.

"Amelia helped," I said. "Judy showed up a few seconds later, right after we noticed the blood. The first responders were here in minutes."

Grady turned his attention to a passing deputy. "Tom," Grady called.

The deputy changed direction, greeting me with a nod. "Yeah?"

"Do you have a copy of the guest list?"

Tom flipped the pages of his clipboard and pulled one free. "The wedding planner struck lines through the guests who RSVP'd but didn't show. I've put checks next to everyone I've interviewed. Two checks if I think we should talk to them again." He handed the page to Grady.

"How many more guests need to be interviewed?"

Tom looked at his clipboard. "I've spoken with twenty people, but there are hundreds more. I'll check with the other officers and see what kind of progress they've made."

"Appreciate it."

Grady ran a finger down the guest list, tilting the

clipboard toward me. "Can you tell me which of these are Judy's family members?"

I took his pen and underlined the ones I knew for certain. "There could be more," I said. "Extended family or women whose last names are different than what I knew them as before."

"Every little bit helps," he said, scanning the changes I'd made to his list. "I want to talk to Judy at the station where she can think more clearly. I'll need her gown too." He cast a glance in the direction of the sandcastle where we'd left Judy and Amelia. "Do you want to talk to her about that before I do? Maybe coming from you it will sound less official and frightening than it would coming from me."

"Sure, and I can drive her to the station whenever you're ready for her. She was planning to spend the night here, so she has everything she needs to change inside."

"She can't go to Maui in the morning," he said gently.

"I know." I struggled not to ask him what kind of bride would trot off on her honeymoon twelve hours after her husband had been murdered. I rubbed the knotting muscles along my neck and shoulders and counted silently to ten. "She's not going anywhere. Amelia and I couldn't drag her any further from Craig than the sandcastle. That's why we were sitting in there."

"All right." Grady motioned me to my feet. "Are you feeling steadier yet?"

"A little."

"Then let's get moving."

Cool, salty air whipped my blanket into a frenzy around my legs as I followed Grady back to the sand-castle. I mentally prepared myself to find Judy in a heap, tipped over Amelia's lap crying, and I racked my brain for the right words to convince her to leave the beach, shower, and give up her wedding gown to a crime lab. But as we got close, a short burst of laughter stopped me in my tracks. The low rumble of a man's voice followed.

Grady narrowed his eyes as he crouched in the doorway of the sandcastle.

I butted my way in beside him, eager to see who had infiltrated our private girl space.

A man I recognized as Jasper Vaughn sat where I had been a short while before, his arms wound protectively around Judy. Her head rested on his shoulder.

Amelia sat next to them, looking as confused as I felt.

"What's going on here?" Grady asked.

Jasper had lived in Judy's neighborhood when we were young, and he'd opened a fishing company out of high school. This was the first I'd seen of him since high school. He'd filled out well, grown into his crooked nose and square jawline. As a kid, he'd been a gangly set of knees and elbows, but approaching thirty, with ten to fifteen years of hard labor under his belt, Jasper looked pretty good.

"I'm Jasper Vaughn, officer." He stretched a lean-muscled arm out to shake Grady's hand.

"Detective Hays," Grady corrected. "Were you a guest at the wedding, Mr. Vaughn?"

"Please, call me Jasper, and yes, I'm a guest of Judy's. We go way back. Probably to diapers, but I don't remember the exact year we met."

"Friends, then?" Grady asked, his blank cop face in place. "Family? Exes? Lovers?"

Judy's jaw dropped and her cheeks flushed red.

"Friends," Jasper said, "and I know you've got a job to do, but I'd appreciate it if you don't make suggestions like that about Judy again."

Grady let his sharp gaze travel over them. "Forgive me, but you've got her all wrapped up like you might try to make off with her."

Jasper's jaw clenched and popped. "You're suggesting she'd cheat on her fiancé," he said, "and Judy isn't like that."

"Husband," Grady corrected. "She's a married woman now."

Jasper's eyes flashed hot. "Widow," he corrected.

Judy gasped at the word *widow* and wiggled free of Jasper's grasp. "I asked Jasper to stay with me tonight, if that's all right with you, Everly. I don't want to be alone, and I don't want to go home to my folks' house or back to Martha's Vineyard."

Grady slid narrowed eyes in my direction.

"Whatever makes this easier on you," I said.

Grady shifted his weight, knocking against me in the crowded little doorway. "I'm going to need official statements from both of you, preferably given at the police station and in writing. Also, I don't want you or Mr. Vaughn to leave the island until I give you the okay, all right? So, that means Martha's Vineyard is off the table. So is Maui."

Judy's eyes bulged. "I'm not going anywhere without my husband, and I don't plan to fly him to Maui like this in case you think that's a possibility."

"Of course not." Grady checked his watch. "It's going on eleven. Let's get off the beach for the night. Mrs. Miller, you can take a few minutes to get cleaned up if you'd like, and Everly can escort you to the station. I'll follow." He turned to me. "I'll be out here helping however I can as soon as I finish speaking with Mr. Vaughn. Come find me when you're ready to go."

Amelia exited the castle, followed by Jasper, then Judy.

"There she is," a man called from the cluster of guests still in line for questioning. "What happened today, Judy?"

I frowned. "Who is that?" I asked her. I didn't recognize him from the island. "Is he someone you know from Massachusetts?"

"I don't know," she said.

"Have some respect, man," Jasper barked. Amelia and I closed ranks in front of Judy. If this guy wasn't a friend, he needed to go.

"Come here," Grady said, marching toward the man, who eagerly met him halfway.

"Yes, officer?"

I gave Grady another look. His badge was on his belt, covered by the jacket. How had this man recognized him as anything other than a guest or random local? Maybe he was from Charm.

Grady looked the guy over and raised an eyebrow. "Reporter?"

His mischievous eyes twinkled. "Very good. I guess you really are a detective." He extended a hand. "I'm Ryan O'Malley, wedding columnist for the *Times*."

"The *New York Times*?" Amelia asked with a hint of awe.

He produced a set of credentials from his pocket and flashed them at Grady. "That's the one."

"You've come a long way for a wedding," Grady said. "Are you a friend of the bride or groom?"

"Neither, but it's not every day a young power-house millionaire like Craig Miller gets married."

Grady gave the press badge and photo ID a thorough once-over, then returned them to Ryan. "All right, New York reporter," he said. "Have you spoken to one of the officers yet? Are you cleared to go?"

"No." He made an inauthentic-looking sad face and shook his head. "I've just been talking to all these nice people and letting them go ahead of me in line."

"I bet," Grady said. "Learn anything good?"

"Quite a bit, really. Did you know that most of these people are from Charm or have been a part of this community in one way or another for a very long time?" Ryan turned his eyes to me. "They're all very fond of you, Everly Swan," he said. "Seems you're a bit of a legend in the flesh around here. The Swan who got away." He paused to pin me with a bright smile. "You surprised folks when you left, then you came back and brought two murders with you." He raised two fingers. "Two people dead in four months. Pretty unusual for a town this small."

I felt the intense gaze of every person in my little group heating my chest, neck, and cheeks.

Only Grady kept his eyes on Ryan. He moved to the side, effectively blocking my view of the reporter. "So, you've been working the guests this whole time and haven't learned anything about who would want to hurt Craig Miller?" he asked.

Ryan laughed. "Oh no. Investigating murders is your job, I believe. I'm just here to write about the food, drinks, and atmosphere. Maybe note who the bride is wearing and where she and the unlucky groom were going on their honeymoon."

Somehow I didn't believe that any reporter lingered behind at the scene of a murder to ask people what they thought of the food, drinks, and atmosphere.

Grady scoffed. "You're a fluff reporter."

"A wedding columnist."

Grady shoved two fingers in his mouth and whistled so loudly I half-expected a horse to come running. "Listen up," he hollered.

The world stilled.

"It's half-past eleven," he began. "I know you're all tired and want to go home, but we need statements from everyone at the reception. If you're planning on leaving the island tonight, then I'd appreciate it if you could stay until we talk to you. If you'll be in town through the weekend, one of the officers or I will be in touch with you tomorrow to complete the interviews.

We'll finish on Sunday, if we can't get through them all tomorrow."

"Sunday?" Ryan asked. "That's seventy-two hours. Detective Hays, are you holding these wedding guests as suspects?"

"Only until I've had a chance to speak with them."

Ryan raised his thick, dark brows. "What do you think, Miss Swan?" he asked. "Got any room at the inn?" He nodded at my house, standing tall above the beach.

I studied his face, which was round and youthful with an easy grin. "No. All full."

"Come on," he sang. "There must be a dozen places a guy like me could get comfortable in a big house like that."

"Knock it off," Grady said. "You're not getting comfortable anywhere near her."

I eyeballed Grady. Had I imagined the protective snap to his voice?

"I'll get you a room on Bay View and speak to you first thing in the morning," he said.

"There's no rush," Ryan said, his fashionably cut hair lifting lazily on the breeze. "I'm in no hurry to go. In fact, if you need me, I'll be sticking close to these ladies." He swept a pointed finger from me to Judy, then stopped on Amelia with another wink.

My great-aunts marched through the sand, waving their arms overhead. "We can help," Aunt Clara called out to the masses. "We've moved all the food and drinks inside. If you need a place to stay while you make arrangements for the night, come inside. We'll send you off with a doggy bag and something sweet." They led a group toward my home like a couple of Pied Pipers.

"I guess I'd better go with them," I said, watching the guests stream up the boardwalk to my house. "Aunt Clara and Aunt Fran are going to need help, and the wait staff is officially off the clock in twenty-five minutes." I hugged Judy, then squeezed her hands. "Why don't you come with me? I can take you upstairs to shower and change, then we'll come back out and find Detective Hays."

She nodded. "Okay."

A flash of bright light pinned us in place as a white minivan with the Beach Cab logo stenciled on the side pulled up. The silhouette that climbed out was long and lean. Whoever it was dragged two suitcases from the back seat and headed our way in a hurry.

I squinted against the light, unable to see clearly until the cab reversed out of the way.

"Craig!" a woman's voice called frantically. "I'm here!"

Judy went rigid and gripped my arm with ice-cold fingers.

"I hope it's not too late!" the woman cried, her British accent almost comically out of place in the Carolinas. "Craig! I love you. Don't do this! My plane was late! I would've been here sooner if I could have!" She ran for the beach, dragging her luggage over the hill and through deep and bumpy grass.

"Whoa," Grady said, pulling his badge from his pocket and holding it out. "Stop right there."

Her eyes were wild and dark as she spotted Judy, Amelia, and I, taking in the bloodstains covering our dresses. "What happened?" Her gaze locked on Judy, and she began to tremble. "Where's Craig?"

Judy covered her face with both hands and her beach blanket fell away, revealing the full extent of her ruined gown. Broad strokes of her husband's blood crisscrossed the white lace where she'd tried frantically to wipe her hands clean.

Jasper pulled her to his chest as she began to cry.

"What's this about?" Grady asked. "Who are you? Why are you arriving for a wedding at nearly midnight?"

"My plane was late," she repeated. "I came to stop Craig from making a huge mistake, and I know he plans to stay here tonight." Tears began to pour down her cheeks as she stared at Judy's blood-soaked gown. "What did you do to him?" she screamed.

Judy sobbed.

Grady spread his arms wide, acting as a barrier between the woman and Judy. "Slow down. Who are you?"

The woman squared her shoulders and lifted her chin. "I'm Cynthia Ophelia Preston. Craig Miller is the love of my life, and I am his. I've come to intercede before it's too late for an annulment. Where is he?"

"Dead!" Judy shouted. "Craig is dead!"

Cynthia's eyes went wide. Her mouth fell open. "What did you do?" She dropped her luggage and launched herself at Judy, colliding instead with Grady, who stepped into her path. He held Cynthia fast with no visible effort. Despite her impressive height, she was rail thin and far too emotional to do more than scream and flail.

"How did you know Craig was planning to stay here tonight?" Grady asked as she thrashed in his arms.

"Because he told me! He loved me! He knew I didn't want this. I wanted him, and he wanted me too." Cynthia's knees buckled, and she flopped onto the ground in tears.

My mouth opened, and air swept from my lungs. Craig had a mistress? And she came to stop the wedding? I dragged my gaze from her to Judy, mired in grief and shock. Someone had murdered her new husband, and now she had to deal with a supermodel British mistress? Did life get any worse?

A sob escaped Judy's lips, and she made a run for my house.

"You did this!" Cynthia screamed at Judy's back. "You took everything from me! You killed him! You killed the love of my life!"

CHAPTER

THREE

Grady stood over Cynthia, broad palms covering narrow hips. "You got her, Swan?" he asked, flicking his gaze to Judy's fast-disappearing shadow.

"Yep," I said. "Good luck with that." I dropped my gaze to Cynthia as Grady lowered himself into a squat beside the late-arriving lunatic.

His stern voice was audible behind me as I hurried after Judy. "I think you should start from the beginning, Miss Preston."

I followed the last guest through my front door and across the foyer toward Sun, Sand, and Tea. The space that was now my café stretched through the entire south side of the first floor, and with luck, one day it would fill the entire level. My living quarters were private, located on the second floor and guarded by a locking door at the base of an interior staircase. I gave the knob a jiggle on my way past. *Locked.* Either Judy hadn't gone up to her room, or she had locked the door behind her.

Ahead of me, the café was bursting with displaced wedding guests. The previous owner had strategically knocked out walls between the kitchen and formal dining area, creating a large space for entertaining, and I'd added twenty seats for service—five at the counter and fifteen scattered across the wide-planked, whitewashed floor. The seating options ranged from padded wicker chairs around low tables to tall bistro sets along the perimeter, and at the moment every seat and nearly every square inch of space was occupied. Even the deck off the back of the room was now teeming with people.

I hoped to replace the current seating with something equally casual but more cohesive one day, and there was another thousand or so square feet available beyond the kitchen just waiting for renovation and expansion, which had once been a ballroom for the original occupants of the house. I was waiting for time and funds to begin tackling that project. In the meantime, the ballroom had served well as a staging area for all things wedding-related.

I threaded my way to the counter, where my great-aunts smiled warmly at guests and dished out the finger foods, appetizers, and snacks I'd made for the reception. Even the row of Blushing Bride tea dispensers had been lined up alongside the food. "Have you seen Judy?" I asked Aunt Fran as she arranged mini quiches, stuffed mushrooms, and coconut shrimp skewers onto a plate.

She glanced at me, confused. "No. Is she missing?"

"Not missing," I said. "I think she just needed a minute."

A woman in high heels and a size zero sundress set her tea aside with a grunt. "Honey, that girl needs more than a minute," she drawled. "She needs a lifetime of therapy." She dropped her gaze to my dress. "And you need a change of clothes before you come any closer to this food."

I recognized her as a neighbor of Judy's parents, but couldn't recall her name. And she wasn't the only one staring at my ruined dress: horrified faces surrounded me. My head ached. Not everyone had seen what I had. Some of these folks had only been told the groom had died, or was found in the water, and here I was covered in his blood. "I'm sorry," I whispered.

Aunt Clara lifted a hand to stop me. "Why don't you go upstairs to shower and change? Fran or I can look for Judy."

"I'll go," Amelia said, weaving through the crowd to my side. "Most of these people are calling cabs and will be out of here soon. I'll find Judy and let her know the masses are preparing to move on. She might come out of hiding then."

"Thanks." I turned back to my aunts. "Any chance you found my silver beaded clutch while you were moving the contents of the tea tent?"

Aunt Fran reached below the counter and pulled out a small bag. "Did it look like this?"

I heaved a sigh of relief. "Yes." I couldn't imagine going back to the beach until I'd changed. Now I wouldn't have to. "Bless you." I fished my key from inside the zippered pocket, unlocked the door to the stairway, and took the stairs up two at a time.

Although I took the world's fastest shower, most of the guests were gone by the time I came back downstairs. My freshly shampooed hair was wound into a messy bun at the nape of my neck. I'd stuffed my ruined dress into a plastic shopping bag and put on black capri-length yoga pants and an off-the-shoulder tunic.

Ryan the reporter was lazing on a stool at the counter, paddling ice around in his full jar of tea with a straw, and flirting shamelessly with my aunts.

"What are you doing?" I asked.

"Learning things," he said with a grin.

I frowned at Ryan. "What did you learn?"

He spun his cell phone on the counter so I could see the screen. "It seems that one of today's guests is either the secret author of your local gossip blog, or a mole reporting back to the blogger."

The *Town Charmer* was a blog that had popped up while I was away at culinary school, written by an anonymous and very well-informed author. It covered every hint of island scandal, conspiracy theory, or news. Locals also used it for weather updates and tide schedules. The fact that the blogger had been at the wedding was interesting, but not terribly surprising given the number of locals on Judy's guest list. I lifted the screen and read the headline. "An Enchanted Wedding Day Ends in Murder for One Former Charm Resident." Well, if anyone in town hadn't heard immediately via texts and the gossip grapevine, they knew now.

I felt Aunt Clara's eyes on me as I skimmed the article recapping basic details about the evening, which were clearly from an onlooker's perspective. Whoever had written the article did a nice job describing the scene from afar. What they lacked in actual details was made up for by an abundance of focus on the confused and frightened guests. "Who do you think the blogger is?" Aunt Clara asked.

"I don't know, but there's nothing useful in here. This person doesn't know anything specific about the crime."

"The writer knew you pulled Craig from the water," she whispered, "and that Amelia helped with CPR."

"I was soaked. Anyone could see I'd gone in the water, and by the time we started CPR, there was a crowd forming." I cast an appraising gaze around the room. Amelia and Jasper were perched on the bar stools beside Ryan, arms folded on the counter and looking as exhausted as I felt.

"Did anyone find Judy?" I asked.

"Yeah," Amelia answered. "She's in the gazebo, and she wants to be alone."

"Okay, thanks." I'd have to check on her soon. "What about these other guests?" I asked, scanning the handful of remaining faces but recognizing none. "Are they all Craig's guests?"

Jasper flicked his gaze in their direction. "I don't know them."

Ryan smiled. He rolled up the sleeves of his dress shirt, drawing my attention and creating an obvious dramatic pause. He had taken off his jacket and his tie was undone, draped over his shoulders like a scarf. "The big guy in the pink tie is Warren Granger. He owns Granger Automotive in Corolla, and he's one of Craig and Pete's newest clients. That's his wife in the matching pink gown. The cluster of folks on their cell phones by the windows are all richy up-and-ups from New England society."

I nodded, impressed and slightly unnerved by the amount of information he had on complete strangers.

Corolla was another Outer Banks town, not far from Charm. Mr. Granger had probably driven to the wedding and would likely be on his way back once he finished the pile of chicken skewers and mound of molten chocolate brownies in front of him. Hopefully none of the others would look to me for somewhere to stay tonight. I had my hands full already.

"What about Craig's family?" I asked. What would they do in a situation like this, so far from Martha's Vineyard? Could they even begin making funeral arrangements or whatever personal things were necessary when they were hundreds of miles from home?

"I spoke to his cousins while I was in line outside," Ryan said. "Craig's mom rented two massive homes in town, and the entire Miller clan is staying together until the body is released for a funeral in Martha's Vineyard."

My stomach caved and twisted at the words *body* and *funeral*.

Amelia stroked my arm. "How are you holding up?"

"I've been better," I said. "But I should check on Judy. Detective Hays will want to talk to her soon."

When I turned toward the door, I found Mr. Granger staring at me. He smiled and offered me his hand. "I'm Warren Granger," he said. A black belt fixed his navy suit pants at his belly button, and black leather loafers poked out beneath the too-short pant legs. "You were the one who found Craig, weren't you?" His round, red face was screwed up with concern, and a pair of bushy salt-and-pepper eyebrows formed a sharp V between his eyes.

"Yes." The word came out more breathlessly than I'd intended. My fingers began to shake with memories of towing Craig ashore. I dropped Mr. Granger's hand and knit my fingers together. "Did you know him well?"

"Not well. We met a few times to talk about what he could do for my company," he said.

Ryan edged closer and cocked a brow. "And what was that, exactly?"

Granger rocked back a half step, putting a little distance between himself and Ryan. "Craig was a data scientist. He's been going through all the data on my servers and analyzing it for patterns. He's been known to find links between seemingly unrelated traits that companies can use to make more sales or target new customers."

"Or identify fraud and embezzlement," Ryan muttered, pushing the straw in his tea between his lips.

I shoved his elbow off the bar stool backrest and gave him a warning look.

"I don't understand," Mr. Granger said.

"It's nothing," I said. "This is Ryan. He's a rude reporter. You were saying?"

"Ah." He fumbled with his tie a moment. "Well, sometimes information we don't even think is being stored can turn up a new way of saving time or money. I'd had high hopes for the results. I hope they'll still be available."

"Do you mean he'd finished the analysis?" I asked.

"A few weeks ago, yes. We were going to chat tonight over drinks at the reception, but that never happened." He cast a wayward look through the widows facing the beach.

"Are you heading home tonight?"

"I hope so. I would've left sooner, but my wife got to talking with the folks from Massachusetts. Seems she'd like to vacation there again soon."

Ryan made a show of setting his tea back on the counter. "Well, I am definitely staying," he announced. "This is opportunity gold."

"Gross," I said. "Turning a man's murder into your career move? Really?"

"Hey, I wasn't always a wedding columnist. I'm an investigative journalist at heart."

"You gave that up to cover weddings?" Mr. Granger asked.

"I like to investigate," Ryan said, "but I also like to pay the bills and eat more adventurous meals than instant noodles and black coffee." He turned a charming smile on Amelia. "I don't suppose you have an extra room or a couch I can keep warm for a night or two? Save my budget a hit?"

Amelia's cheeks flushed red. "My apartment is very small."

Ryan grinned, clearly amused with himself. "The town is probably flooded with wedding guests. I'm sure they've booked all the decent housing," he said to me. "Your home seems a bit like overkill, doesn't it? Surely you have a room to spare."

"I do not."

He puckered his brow. "There must be a dozen guest rooms in this old house."

"Seven," I said, "but I'm not in the habit of letting strangers sleep over, especially when there's a murderer on the loose."

"Hmm. Is the detective any good at his job?" Ryan asked.

"Very," I answered without hesitation. "He'll get to the bottom of this fast."

"Do you think he'll need your help again like he did with the murder in April?"

I froze. How had Ryan found out about that?

"You solved another local murder?" Mr. Granger asked.

"Not really." I'd poked around and gotten myself knocked over the head, then poisoned. Not exactly a textbook definition of *solved*.

"I should go see Judy," I said.

"Maybe we can partner on this one," Ryan called after me.

I walked outside, ignoring his offer. I peeked out at the beach, where Grady and the other policemen still combed the scene. Cynthia and the coroner's van had gone, though presumably not together. I headed around the opposite side of my home toward the gardens.

Judy was still in the gazebo, stroking the white cat that had shown up and started following me around after I bought the house in the spring. I'd named the cat Maggie after Magnolia Bane, the mistress who'd supposedly thrown herself off the widow's walk at the top of the house. My aunts had always believed that Magnolia's restless spirit was reincarnated in a white cat, and here one was. I figured, *why not?*

"Hey," I said, stepping through the tall grass.

"Hey."

I sat beside Judy and gazed at the moonlight falling over the ocean. "Ready for a hot shower? Maybe get out of that dress?"

Maggie blinked bright green eyes at me, then peeled herself off of Judy's lap and slunk away to stand guard on the gazebo's opposite ledge.

Judy threw her arms around me and sobbed. "I can't believe she showed up here," she cried.

I patted her back and struggled to make sense of her words. "Cynthia?" That was the part about tonight that she couldn't believe?

Judy nodded and sniffled. "I hate her so much."

A thousand thoughts jockeyed for position in my

mind and on my tongue. "Wait. You know her?" The knots in my stomach tightened with betrayal on Judy's behalf. That woman had come to wreck their wedding, and Judy knew her!

She pulled back to wipe her face. "Craig met her in college. They both belonged to the rowing teams, and they dated before Craig and I met, but she's never been completely out of his life."

I studied her face. "You knew he was cheating?"

Judy turned puffy red eyes to meet mine as tears rolled down her cheeks. "Yes."

I leaned back. "That's not good." Judy knew her fiancé was cheating but married him anyway, then went missing at the reception and reappeared clutching his murder weapon. All just a few hours after his multimillion-dollar estate became hers. *Not good at all.*

"I probably look even more suspicious now," she said. "As if finding the knife wasn't enough."

"You have to tell Detective Hays."

"He'll arrest me. Everyone will know I married a cheater. My family will be so disappointed."

I set a hand on hers. "This isn't a secret you can keep anymore. You knew about the affair, and you need to say so. After all, it could be connected to the murder in some way. Detective Hays will figure everything else out, but you've got to be honest with him. That's the only way this works."

"No." Judy rose to her feet, her puffy red eyes going hard. "I've been through enough. I don't need to be humiliated too."

Someone cleared their throat in the shadows nearby, and Judy and I jumped.

"Mrs. Miller," Grady said, stepping into view. "Everly."

Judy gasped. "You were listening to us? You can't do that!"

"How much did you hear?" I asked.

Grady moseyed forward to the gazebo. "I just arrived, but I heard enough to know it's time we head down to the station to talk."

"I haven't showered," Judy said, stepping back.

"You can bring your things and change there. I won't keep you long tonight, but it's best we talk now, while the night's events are fresh in your mind."

Her frame stiffened. "Am I under arrest?"

"No, ma'am," he said, his expression a mix of apology and resolve. "It's just procedure."

Judy crossed her arms and lifted her chin. "Then I don't have to go." Her voice cracked with desperation.

Grady lowered his voice and dipped his head, presumably attempting to look less intimidating to a thoroughly traumatized woman. "No, ma'am, but it would be nice if you did."

I suddenly felt like we were being watched, and I scanned the darkness around us. Maggie hissed. The hair on her back rose, and she began to pace the gazebo, complaining low in her throat.

I peered into the night, begging my eyes to see more than reaching shadows.

"Detective?" a woman's voice chirped in the opposite direction, and I spun, clutching my chest. A woman in a navy-blue windbreaker strode to Grady's side, an evidence bag dangling from one gloved hand. "You wanted the victim's phone?"

"I did," he said. "Thank you."

"Pete called," I said, struck by a flash of memory. "After Craig and Judy cut the cake, he walked away to take a call from Pete." I looked to Judy. "Where is Pete?"

Judy studied her feet. "I don't know."

"I didn't see him inside with the others," I told Grady. "Have you spoken with him?"

"Not yet." He looked at the other cop, and she nodded.

"I'll locate Pete," she said before striding away into the night.

A moment later, something glowed and buzzed beneath the gazebo's slatted wooden floor.

Judy whimpered.

"Is that your phone?" I asked. Why was it under the gazebo? Had it fallen? Or had she tried to hide it?

"Let me get that for you," Grady said, moving to retrieve the phone.

Judy bent to reach for it, but he beat her to the punch.

Grady turned the device over on his palm, and the screen lit with a stream of incoming notifications, presumably from worried family members and friends. "May I see your recent calls?" he asked Judy.

She tapped the phone screen several times, and handed the phone to Grady, crying quietly.

I craned my neck for a better view of the little screen. "You called Craig?" I asked Judy.

She nodded, wiping her eyes and nose frantically with the backs of her hands.

"When? Did he answer?"

Had she called to say she loved him, or had she asked him to meet her down the beach, away from the DJ and festivities so she could lash out over his infidelity?

I shook the harsh thought from my head. It wasn't like me to assume the worst in people, but the ache I'd carried after last spring's murder had returned to my chest and settled heavily on my sternum. I sipped the salty ocean air in and forced it back out in long, calming streams.

"It was just dead air," Judy said. "I called to see where he was. He wasn't at the house. Not in the gardens. I called and someone answered, but all I could hear were the waves. Whoever it was didn't say anything."

"Mrs. Miller," Grady said flatly, reaching a hand in her direction. "It's time to go."

Judy's shoulders drooped. She moved reluctantly toward him, head bent in regret or heartbreak. Maybe both.

Grady shot me a pointed look that I couldn't interpret.

"What?" I mouthed. My aunts always said I had a sixth sense about people. They said it was a gift to be cultivated, but where Grady was concerned, I was usually at a loss.

Judy followed meekly after Grady. The fight had drained from her pale features, and the tears had stopped coming as she let him lead her away from the gazebo.

My heart broke impossibly further. "We'll figure this out," I promised their retreating forms. "I know almost everyone on this island. Someone saw something that will clear this up, and I'm going to talk to everyone until we have answers." My heart soared with each word of my vow.

"No," Grady called over his shoulder, never losing pace. "You absolutely will not."

"I'm a resource," I shouted. Asking a few questions was the least I could do for someone who was hurting so badly, and I truly wanted to right this. "I can help."

"Don't start with me again, Swan." Grady disappeared with Judy, and without further discussion.

I was alone again. Something rustled at the back of the garden, making me jump. I sucked in air and stared into the night, the hairs on my arms and neck rising to attention. I imagined someone lurking in the dark grasses beyond the cliff's jagged edge, to the left or right where patches of earth still stood against the odds in a series of plateaus I'd used as steps more than once already this summer, when taking a shortcut from the beach to the garden.

"Hello?" I called, heart hammering in my chest.

The world was silent again, save for the continuous roll of waves against the shore below.

Maggie arched her back and hissed, followed by a seething growl rumbling deep in her core. My heart rate spiked at the sound. She tore from the gazebo with a wail and bounded out of sight, over the cliff's edge with practiced grace.

I ran in the opposite direction with exactly zero grace, and I didn't stop until I'd locked the front door of my home behind me.

CHAPTER

FOUR

I watched shadows drift across my ceiling until the sun crested the horizon around six. Then I shuffled out of bed to start a fresh pot of coffee. Thanks to my home's history as a boarding house, I had a service-able second-floor kitchen in addition to the larger one in the café below. The cabinets and fixtures were all older than me, but there were newish appliances courtesy of the previous owner, and workspace galore. I pulled my backside onto the outdated laminate countertop and inhaled the bitter scent of liquid enthusiasm as it brewed.

Jasper was sprawled over an armchair in my living room, having dozed off before Judy's late return from the police station. Our inability to connect or make small talk had surely helped him fall asleep, and I'd been thrilled when I'd heard his first snore. Grady had brought Judy back to my place from the police station around 2:00 a.m. She hadn't wanted to wake Jasper, but she and I had talked quietly until after four when she'd fallen asleep midsentence on my couch. She couldn't spend another night in the room I'd made up for her and Craig, so I covered her with a quilt and went to stare at my bedroom ceiling until dawn.

I poured a mug of coffee, careful not to disturb Judy or Jasper in the adjoining living room, and let my hazy mind wander back to the eerie feeling I'd had in my garden. I'd double- and triple-checked the locks on all my windows and doors, but I couldn't shake the notion I was being watched until Judy had come home and redirected my thoughts.

My rubber fitness band beeped on the counter beside *Beach Home* magazine, and I smiled. I'd worn the little pink-and-white number faithfully since its purchase five months back, and I'd become somewhat hooked on knowing how many steps it took me to get places. I couldn't bring myself to wear a rubber bracelet with my fancy coral dress, so I'd abandoned it twenty-four hours ago. Funny, because the groom hadn't worried about his ugly hemp bracelet clashing with his suit. Maybe when you're the star of the show, you can make those kinds of bold fashion choices. As unofficial coordinator of all the moving parts, I'd felt I had an image to uphold.

I plucked the pink band off the counter and secured it to my wrist. Three words flashed on the screen.

BE MORE ACTIVE.

"Yeah, yeah," I told it. "First, coffee." I sipped my introductory cup while committing mentally to a morning walk and fanning through the dog-eared pages of my magazine. I had dreams of jazzing up the décor at Sun, Sand, and Tea, specifically with a seating ensemble I'd found in the magazine featuring the casual appeal I loved and a color scheme that tied it all together. In the magazine, the pieces began in a well-appointed sunroom and spilled seamlessly onto a million-dollar veranda with outdoor kitchen. My spread wasn't nearly as fancy as all that, but the furniture was perfect for my café and rear deck, if only I could bring myself to part with the cash. Or if only I had the cash to part with.

I drank my first refill while wondering how I could possibly open for business today with a killer on the loose in Charm and Judy cloaked in grief on my couch. Closing for the day would mean losing much-needed income, and running the café was what made my mortgage payments possible. Not to mention that being open today would give me a chance to talk to folks about what they'd heard or seen last night, if they'd been at the reception—and what was churning in the gossip mill if they hadn't. Even Grady couldn't fault me for making conversation with my customers.

I swallowed the dregs of cup number three and went to put on my exercise gear.

The morning heat was a shock to my system after a night spent in the cool world of air conditioning. My skin was slicked from the humidity before I'd hit the boardwalk outside my back door and sweat beaded across my forehead moments later. It was the delicious, invigorating heat only available at the seaside.

I pulled it deep into my lungs and, despite my heavy heart, smiled. It was my first summer at home after far too many summers spent away.

I hit my stride early, pleased with the progress in my performance these last few months. When I'd returned home, I could barely make half the ten thousand daily steps my fitness band demanded of me. These days I cleared eight thousand regularly, and my pants fit better. I was still a size twelve, but I was holding tight to the adage that size didn't matter. What mattered was that I could run up my stairs without seeing spots now.

Heat hovered over the sand in the distance like an apparition. Crime scene tape roped off the entire section of beach where Craig and Judy had been married, where they'd had their reception, and where he'd been found in the surf. Even the sandcastle where Amelia, Judy, and I had taken refuge was off limits to anyone without the proper credentials.

I followed the boardwalk as it curved away from the beach and shifted closer to town, passing through the overgrown marsh on its way. A great blue heron cocked its head at me, and I smiled. Small fish fled at the sight of him, racing along in the shallow water beneath the boardwalk. I breathed in the briny air, the scents of earth, sand, and sea, the faint aromas of sunblock and waffles being served at a local family restaurant. My heart unfurled. No matter how I tried to escape, Charm always pulled me back in.

The path curved again, and Ocean Drive, the road

that ran along the boardwalk, became visible through increasingly sparse flora. Shops and locals walking around downtown came into view a few steps later, but my attention was fixed on Amelia, crouched in front of a Little Library on the boardwalk up ahead.

"Good morning," I called, a fresh smile blooming on my lips.

"Hey!" She waved a book overhead as I approached.

Amelia had erected several Little Libraries in town. They were often repurposed furniture pieces like chests, cabinets, or hutches that now held books, and island readers were encouraged to help themselves to the books inside. Amelia had set up two on the boardwalk, but this was my favorite of them all. Some of the Little Libraries were custom-made and designed to look like giant birdhouses or big wooden tomes, and all were whimsically painted by Amelia herself. This one had previously been a brown curio cabinet, but now it was an Amelia Butters Original. Painted light blue and trimmed in white, a seascape motif was stenciled down the sides with seashells and starfish, seahorses and mermaids. She'd traded the curio's glass for something equally transparent but infinitely more durable and stocked it with a great selection of books from her store. The Little Library concept worked on a leave one/take one premise, and I both left and took from the shelves regularly.

"How did you sleep?" she asked.

"Awful. You?"

She shook her head. "I didn't. I almost came over,

but I figured you had your hands full with Judy. How's she doing?"

I thought back to the restless lump on my couch. The little sounds she'd made in her sleep as I'd finished my morning coffee had been a heart-wrenching mix of grief and fear. "She's sleeping," I said. I glanced back in the direction of my home, as if I might be able to check on her somehow from there. "I still can't believe any of this is happening. And for the record, you could've come over. You're welcome anytime. If I had been asleep, I would have gladly gotten up to talk with you."

"Thanks." She pulled in a deep breath and let it out with a sigh. "I don't think I'll ever stop thinking about pulling Craig from the water or performing hopeless CPR only to realize he'd been stabbed." She put a hand over her heart. "It's unthinkable."

I did my best to squelch the horrific images that sprang to my mind. "I just hope whoever killed him is caught quickly. Murderers shouldn't get one extra minute of freedom, and Judy is in desperate need of peace and closure." I closed my eyes briefly. "I promised Judy I'd ask around to see if anyone saw something that might explain what happened to Craig. Maybe someone with information will be more comfortable opening up to me than Grady."

My watch beeped. The screen flashed: **BE MORE ACTIVE.** "Let's walk," I suggested.

"I'll help you," Amelia offered. "Between the two of us, we'll probably see half the island come through our shop doors by the end of the week, and the rest of the town will turn up at Summer Splash."

I hadn't even considered the fact that Charm's residents would be in the streets all week for the arts festival. I wouldn't need to go door-to-door. Most islanders fancied themselves an artist of some sort, or a connoisseur, so Summer Splash was a widely attended event. People set up display tables, dance troupes and bands performed, and the town council always brought in a group of North Carolina cowboys and ecologists to talk about the history and preservation of our wild horses.

The cowboys had always been my favorite part.

We stepped off the boardwalk and onto the grassy area beside Ocean Drive, then headed across the street to the nearest row of shops.

"What's going on at your place, exactly?" Amelia asked. "Is it just you and Judy, or did Jasper sleep over?"

"Jasper's there," I said. "It's weird, right?"

"Yeah." Amelia fiddled with her bracelet. "Did Ryan stay with you last night?" she asked softly.

I stopped to stare at her. "The reporter?"

She smiled.

"Oh my goodness," I said. "No, he didn't. Why do you ask?" Based on her goofy expression alone, I probably didn't want to know.

"Just wondering." Her cheeks turned pink, and I shook my head.

We crossed the grassy median onto Main Street. Everywhere I looked, Summer Splash preparations were underway. Shops had posted their display schedules in the front windows. Announcement banners hung from light posts on every corner. Food and drink vendors had rolled their wagons into place behind us along the sea side of Ocean Drive.

The seven-day festival began on Sunday and went through the following Saturday night. I'd hoped to set up a table with tea samples, but I wasn't sure what would happen now. How long would the coroner keep Craig's body? Judy surely wouldn't leave Charm without it, and she wasn't interested in staying with her family, so she and Jasper would probably be at my place for the duration of her stay.

"Are you doing any special events or activities at Charming Reads this week?" I asked.

"My dad's face-painting and doing a few how-to demonstrations with oil and watercolor on canvas. I was going to hold a write-in for locals interested in writing a novel, but now I'm not sure. What about you?"

"I don't know if I'll be able to get away."

Amelia pushed her bottom lip out. "I can give away your samples at my table, if you want."

A wave of relief hit my chest. Getting my tea samples into the hands of the masses was an opportunity not to be missed, but I wanted to stay with Judy while she needed me. Thanks to Amelia's generous offer, I could do both. "I could hug you," I said. "Thanks." We slowed in front of her shop. "Did you say you were going to have a write-in? Are you thinking of writing a book now? Selling and reading them isn't enough for you?" I teased. "You're such an overachiever."

She shot me an impish smile. "It's crazy, I know, but sometimes I get so caught up in reading a story that I think about how great it would be to write one that does the same thing to someone else. Maybe I could give another reader the kind of escape my favorite authors give me."

"Sounds incredible," I said, "and right up your alley. What will your story be about?"

"I don't know. Until last night I was going to write about a small-town murder and the two best friend amateur detectives who fight for truth, justice, and the American way. I'd planned to use my experience helping you with Mr. Paine's murder as the foundation."

I nodded approvingly. "I like it. Write what you know, right?"

"Yeah, but I know some scary stuff and now I think writing about it might be too much like reliving it for me."

I could understand that. Writing about the ugly and harrowing events of April sounded like my personal nightmare. I preferred the calm and safety of my usual days to those filled with mysterious attacks and death threats.

The sudden shriek of a woman sent my heart into my throat. "Good grief," I gasped.

Amelia grabbed my arm. "What was that?"

Across the street, a woman I recognized from the wedding was standing in front of Grady, who was out of uniform and holding his hands in the air, palms out.

"Isn't that Craig's mom?" Amelia asked.

"Yep." I looked both ways and stepped off the curb. "Let's go see what happened. Why do you think she screamed?" The woman didn't look injured, and there was no one else with them. I turned to grab Amelia's hand and pull her across the street, but she wasn't there.

Amelia still stood on the sidewalk outside her store. "I'm going to stay here," she said. "I don't think I'm ready to face his mom, and Detective Hays intimidates me," she added more quietly.

Grady's rigid stance and signature no-nonsense expression, combined with the ever-present sidearm and badge, gave the impression he was perpetually on the verge of performing an arrest. Or delivering a fatal wound. "Understandable," I said. "I'll report back."

We traded thumbs-ups, and I hurried across the street before I missed anything else.

Grady made a sour face as I hopped onto the sidewalk beside him. His low-key blue jeans and gray T-shirt were simple and unassuming—in other words, completely misleading. Nothing about Grady Hays was simple, and he was never unassuming.

"What's going on?" I asked, looking from Grady to Mrs. Miller. "Everything okay?"

"No!" she wailed. "I can't leave this blessed island to plan a proper funeral for my boy."

"As soon as the autopsy is complete…" Grady said.

Mrs. Miller shook a finger in his face. "I'm willing to be patient. All I ask is that you let me mourn."

"I'm so sorry, Mrs. Miller," I said. She'd been so full of joy when I'd met her at the rehearsal dinner and again at the wedding. Seeing her this way broke my heart. "Is there anything I can do to help?" She looked to be in full mourning already, if the black pantsuit, tears, and puffy face were any indication. I couldn't make sense of her accusation. How exactly was Grady keeping her from mourning?

Mrs. Miller dabbed a handkerchief to the corners of her red eyes. "I asked to have a nice vigil in remembrance of my Craig, but your town's selfish, lunatic council said no, and this man won't help me."

Grady shifted his sympathetic gaze to me. "She wants to light paper lanterns and set them off over the water, but the town council wouldn't approve it."

Mrs. Miller sniffled into her hanky. "It would be beautiful. A friend of mine lost her husband last year, and she had a paper lantern vigil back home. It was written up in the paper and everything. Martha's Vineyard cares about people's losses."

Grady rubbed a heavy hand over his forehead. "The council doesn't want the lanterns landing in the water, and they won't fast-track the application anyway, which apparently takes seven to ten days to approve."

"They were all there today," Mrs. Miller snapped. "All of them, but they wouldn't just sign the damn request!"

I gave a knowing groan. The town council was notoriously stiff on the rules. Aunt Fran was the newest council member and it drove her crazy. She said the group seemed to think that without the overabundance of unnecessary protocols and redundant procedures Charm would descend into a state of anarchy.

"It's ridiculous," Mrs. Miller muttered, seeming to have shocked herself back to reasonableness with her four-letter outburst.

"I'm sorry," I said. "Is that why you screamed?"

"She screamed at me," Grady said. "She wants me to do something to override the council or force them to change their minds." He turned back to Mrs. Miller, clearly exasperated. "I wish I could. I really do, but my hands are tied."

I nodded. "It's true. Local police have no authority over council matters."

Mrs. Miller swiped the handkerchief under her drippy nose. "I lost my son." Her tears began to flow again, and Grady went pale.

"How about a small compromise?" I offered. "Maybe you can hold a candlelight walk on the beach in his memory. You can use my café as a gathering point before and after the vigil. Maybe walk a while, stop when you're ready and say a few heartfelt things about Craig, then go back to my café for refreshments."

"Really?" she asked. "You would do that?"

"Of course. If that sounds like something you'd be interested in, I'm happy to make the arrangements."

Her face reddened and pinched. "Thank you," she whispered.

"It's no problem," I said, feeling a portion of my heart ache with hers.

Grady's phone rang, and he practically turned the pocket of his jeans inside out getting to it. "Detective Hays," he answered. His eyes went cold. "I'll be right there." He put the phone back in his pocket and turned to Mrs. Miller. "I'm sorry, ma'am, we've got to go. Do you have Everly's number to coordinate the arrangements?"

"Yes," she said. "I believe so."

Grady curved strong fingers under my elbow. "Let's go."

I waved goodbye to Mrs. Miller with my free hand as I hurried to keep up with Grady. "What's going on?" I asked, once we'd landed on the boardwalk headed toward my home. "Who was on the phone?"

"Judy. Someone was in her room. She says whoever it was went through all her things and left the place a mess."

"*My* place?" I squeaked.

"That's the one."

CHAPTER

〜

FIVE

Judy and Jasper were sitting on the front steps when we arrived.

"Everyone okay?" Grady asked, resting both hands on his hips and giving the couple a serious once-over.

Judy nodded a little too quickly, chewing the skin alongside one thumbnail, her hand trembling.

Jasper had a steady arm looped over her shoulders. He curled his fingers more tightly against the curve of her bicep and tugged her closer to his side—whether to protect her or assure she wouldn't escape him, I wasn't sure.

I rubbed goose bumps from my arms as memories of a previous break-in knotted my stomach. My café had been trashed, the cupboards and pantry unloaded and rifled through, a threat carved into the chalkboard that I used to post my daily menu. I could only image the mess that awaited me upstairs now. I shoved the thoughts back into the mental lockbox where I stored unpleasant things and took a seat beside Judy. "What happened?"

"I don't know," she whispered, wiping her puffy red eyes, one knee bobbing furiously.

"Tell us whatever you can remember," I said. "Any detail could be significant."

Judy dropped her hand from her face and looked up at Grady. "I was in the shower, getting ready for the day. I thought I heard someone rustling around while the water was running, but I assumed it was Jasper, tidying up or looking for the television remote or something. I didn't give it too much thought because I was having a hard time pulling myself together, and I need to visit my family and Craig's today. They'll show up here to check on me if I don't go to them, and that's worse. At least if I'm the visitor, I can control when I leave."

"Do you need a ride?" I asked.

"Jasper offered to drive me."

Of course he did. Jasper had been by Judy's side at every turn since I'd found Craig in the water, and his presence at a break-in felt extremely unsettling. Though, to be fair, upsetting Judy seemed counter-intuitive to his apparent goal of becoming her hero. Unless he was one of those goons who caused trouble so they could sweep in and rescue the girl.

"Where were you when this happened?" Grady asked, eyes narrowed on Jasper as he headed for my front door.

"I was on the beach," Jasper said.

"Judy thought you were in the next room," Grady said. "You didn't tell her you were going out?"

"No. I could hear her crying in the shower, and I figured she needed some time alone. So I went down to walk on the beach."

Grady frowned. "And you left the door unlocked behind you?"

Jasper rose his feet to face off with Grady. "I don't have a key. I would've been locked out. Besides, I wasn't far, only a hundred yards or so up the beach. I could still see the house."

A lot of good that did. I pressed my fingertips to the dull ache forming in my temple.

Grady jammed the doorbell and it echoed loudly inside the house.

"She was in the shower," Jasper said. "She wouldn't have heard the doorbell."

Grady closed his eyes briefly. "You thought she was going to be in the shower longer than you'd be out walking on the beach?"

Jasper bristled. "I don't know what you're getting at, but why don't you just come out and say it?"

"All right," Grady said. "I think your story's not so good."

I formed a tiny O with my lips as Jasper curled his hands into fists at his sides.

Judy stood and walked to the door. "Let's just go see the mess. How about that?"

Grady stepped back, allowing the three of us inside. "Did you touch anything after you realized what had happened?"

"Not much," Judy said. "I got dressed and called

for Jasper, and when he didn't answer, I went looking for him. I found him outside, told him what happened, then waited on the porch while he went upstairs to take a look for himself."

Grady considered that for several long beats. "Have you been outside since you called?"

"Yes," Judy said. "Jasper was back in less than a minute. We stayed put until you got here."

My kitchen and living room were neat and tidy, exactly how I'd left them. I peeked into my bedroom and found the same to be true in there. The guest room where Judy and Craig were supposed to spend their wedding night, however, was a disaster. Judy's bags had been overturned and tossed aside. The bed she hadn't slept in was stripped, the sheets and blankets thrown into a heap. The mattress and box spring were askew. Feathers lay everywhere. I struggled to process the mess before me. Who would do something like this, and why? All the time and money I'd spent transforming the previously empty room was thrown out the window. My heart broke selfishly over the loss of my pretty little guest room.

Grady picked his way through the space, keen eyes roaming. "Was anything taken?"

Judy moved into the doorway. "I don't think so."

"How can you tell nothing was taken just by looking at this?" Grady said. He made a show of scanning the awful scene. "I can barely tell what everything is."

My heartbeat quickened. Grady posed a good question. "You thought Jasper was the one making all this noise?" I asked.

Judy nodded. "Yes. Between the running water and my crying, I had no idea this was happening."

I looked at the wall shared by the guest room and bath. The intruder would have heard the shower running. He or she would have known someone was in the room next door, not to mention the moment the water shut off and it was time to run. Still, what was important enough to commit a crime in broad daylight with a potential witness only a few feet away?

Grady pulled a pair of rolled blue gloves from his pocket and snapped them on. "Why don't you all wait in the living room while I sort through this mess?"

Judy crossed the living room to the couch where she'd slept and pulled a pillow into her lap. Jasper sank down next to her. "The only things of value I brought with me are in my purse and on my ring finger," she said. "I had my rings with me in the bathroom, and my purse was emptied onto the nightstand. Everything is there. I could even see the cash and credit cards poking out of my wallet."

"How about some hot tea?" I asked, noticing the pasty tone of her skin. "Maybe something to eat?"

"I can't eat," she said.

"Just some toast. I've got honey from my aunts' beehives and freezer jam from their garden." I rounded the island separating the living room from the kitchen. "You should get something in your stomach or you'll be sick."

I set a kettle on the stovetop and slid a few slices of bread into the toaster while Grady finished dealing with the crime scene. Since nothing was taken, he was done before I'd delivered the food to Judy. "So, what do you think?" I asked Grady when he emerged from the guest room.

"And you have *no* idea who could have done this?" He looked at Judy, ignoring my question. "Not even a guess?"

"You think I know?" Her voice quivered, and her eyes glossed with unshed tears. I was no detective, but Judy didn't look like someone who was hiding a secret to me. She looked like a woman whose world had been turned upside down when the man she loved was found stabbed to death.

I plated a stack of buttered toast triangles, then positioned them on a tray with little pots of honey and jam. I ferried it all to the coffee table along with two mugs of hot tea, struggling for air as the silence in the room pressed heavily on my lungs. "I thought I heard someone in the bushes when you left last night," I blurted.

Three stunned faces turned in my direction.

"What?" Grady asked. "Where?"

"Near the cliff behind the garden. I heard the grasses rustling, then the cat went gonzo and took off in that direction. I ran inside and locked the doors. I looked through all the rear windows for signs of the cat or an eavesdropper, but I never saw anyone." I wrapped my arms around my middle, more than a little freaked out by the recollection. "It might've been nothing. Maybe just another cat, but it was scary, and I haven't seen Maggie since."

Judy looked aghast. "You think something happened to your cat?"

"She's not mine," I said. "I feed and house her, but she does what she wants, and normally I wouldn't worry, but…" I let the sentence trail off as my chest constricted. Maggie had appeared out of the blue in April, then followed me around until I'd given her a bath and invited her inside. After that she'd made it clear that she wasn't mine, but I was absolutely hers, and she protected me from sandpipers on the beach, sparrows in the gardens, and all species of insect.

Grady started for the stairs. "Show me where you heard the sounds."

I followed after him. "What about the guest room? Are you finished in there? Can Judy straighten her things?"

"Yeah. There's not much I can do beyond write up a vandalism report. No one broke in, and nothing was stolen." Grady stopped at the top of the steps and looked past me to Judy. "If you notice something's missing when you start sorting out the mess, let me know."

Grady and I made a pass through the gardens, then along the cliff and rear of my property. There was nothing to see, no telltale shoe imprints, incriminating threads caught on a bush, or other crime drama-worthy clues lying around. As we finished the search, he excused himself to take a call from his mother-in-law, waving as he climbed behind the wheel of his truck.

I didn't know his mother-in-law, but I hadn't gotten a very good impression of her from afar. She lived hundreds of miles away in DC, and still managed to set him on edge with every call.

I gave the area one last sweep of my gaze. Anyone could've been watching me from the shadows, but a few people had more reason than others to be there, in my opinion. Craig's crazy ex-lover, Cynthia, for example. She might've been creeping around to get details Grady hadn't given her, or maybe she wanted an opportunity to yell at Judy. Who knew? The reporter, Ryan, was another possibility. He'd said he could use this story for the scoop of a lifetime. Even Jasper had reason to lurk. He seemed determined to stick close. Maybe I'd heard him sneaking off last night when Judy left with Grady. There were probably other suspects too, but those three were at the top of my list of likely listeners.

When Grady left to do whatever he had planned for today, I let Judy know I was going out, then I headed back into town. I still needed to check in with my aunts about their video application to Bee Loved and tell them about the candlelight vigil I'd offered Mrs. Miller, then open Sun, Sand, and Tea in time for lunch.

I moved double-time down Main Street. My heart rate was up, and I'd lost my battle with heat and humidity—I swore I could feel my hair getting poofier with every passing second. Thankfully, I was still in my exercise gear, and a little sweat was sure to make me look more athletic.

My aunts' honey shop, Blessed Bee, came into view

a few doors down in a yellow clapboard building with stenciled honeybees buzzing a curlicue path over the large front window. The shop was bookended by identical buildings, one pink and one blue, which originally had been homes for long-ago Charm residents. The pink shop sold ice cream, and the blue one was Charming Reads, Amelia's bookstore.

I hurried across the straw welcome mat and enjoyed the blast of chilly air over my shoulders. The shop's interior walls were painted a softer yellow than the exterior clapboard and loaded with white shelves. Crown molding outlined a sky-blue ceiling painted with fluffy cloud shapes.

Blessed Bee sold everything from lip balm and face scrub to suckers and soap, all made with pure, organic honey drawn straight from my aunts' personal hives. They'd hoped I would join them in their beekeeping business someday, but my near-paralyzing fear of bees had kept that possibility from taking flight. I was sincerely thankful for the Bee Loved opportunity, though. Helping my great-aunts with their video application finally gave me a chance to bond with them about bees while staying safely out of sting range.

I wove my way through the store, nodding and smiling at shoppers as I approached the counter. "Good morning," I said to Aunt Clara as she hotglued the last of a dozen fuzzy yellow pom-poms to a display board with black stenciled letters. GET THE BUZZ ON BEES. Each pom-pom had been given black stripes and a set of pipe cleaner antennae. "Cute."

"Thanks! It's for Summer Splash, but it turned out so nice, we might be able to use it in the Bee Loved video." She set the glue gun aside and admired her work. "I love bees," she said, her bright smile showing both rows of pearly white teeth. "And I love you. How are you doing this morning?" She rounded the desk to pull me into her arms. "How's Judy?"

"We're both okay, I guess," I said, pulling back to study her smiling face. "How's the script writing coming along?"

"Not great." She played with the ends of my hair, flipping them around before tossing them off my shoulders. "Fran and I have some differences of opinion on how to best use the limited time, and there's an awful lot to cover in just three minutes."

I gauged the set of her lips and lift of her brow to mean they were looking to me for a ruling on the matter. "How can I help?" I asked, hoping I could do whatever it was without being trapped in the middle of one of the no-holds-barred battles my only-child mind couldn't possibly understand.

Aunt Clara and Aunt Fran were sisters by two different fathers. According to the legends they insisted on repeating, the men who loved Swan women tended to die suddenly and young, and Aunt Clara's father passed away shortly after she was born. My aunts were opposite in appearance, personality, and nearly everything except their passions for beekeeping, Charm, and me. Where Aunt Clara was fair-skinned, blue-eyed, and blond, Aunt Fran had an olive complexion, dark eyes, and salt-and-pepper hair. Differences aside, they moved in tandem through life and seemed to speak a silent language that only they understood. The slight lift of a brow or flick of a gaze was sometimes all it took to send them into motion for one another.

I looked more like Aunt Fran than Aunt Clara. My aunts said I'd inherited my snub nose and giant owl eyes from my dad, but I'd never met him. He'd died before I was born. Sudden massive heart failure at age thirty-six. A total coincidence, I was sure.

"I think we need to submit a hard-hitting application that focuses on the grim statistics of the endangered American honeybee. Fran thinks we should tape something light and pithy to garner votes. She says online voters want flashy and silly instead of sincere and educational."

I nodded, agreeing heartily with both opinions. People needed to know the facts if they were going to be moved to action, but if my aunts' video didn't win the contest, then someone else would be featured in the documentary, and I didn't need to see the other applicants to know my aunts were the best beekeepers for this film. So, Aunt Fran's idea to do whatever it took to win people's hearts held a lot of water too.

"Whatever we do, it has to be perfect," Aunt Clara said. "We think Bee Loved is using video applications instead of paper ones so the applications can double as screen tests, since the winners will be followed and taped for several days during filming." Aunt Clara winked. "*Screen test* is a term they use in Hollywood."

"Why don't I look at both scripts?" I offered. "Maybe I can combine your approaches into something that will hit all the necessary notes and engage internet voters."

She passed a stack of papers to me with a cheerful smile. "We hoped you'd say that."

Aunt Fran finished helping a customer and came over to hug me. "We've been sick with worry. Tell me you were able to sleep." She looked away before I could answer, locking Aunt Clara in a meaningful stare. "She didn't sleep. I told you."

"I'm okay," I said, "but I could use a little help with something. Mrs. Miller wants to have a memorial for Craig, and I offered up my café as a gathering point before and after." I smiled bigger and tried to look as sweet as possible. "I was hoping you might be available to help."

"Of course," Aunt Clara said.

Aunt Fran motioned for us to follow her into the stockroom. "I was at that town council meeting," she said. "I can't believe the council rejected her request for a vigil. It was shameful. That group has no compassion. No humanity." Aunt Clara patted her sister's arm in sympathy.

Aunt Fran had filled the empty seat on the town council after Mr. Paine, a previous member, was murdered. Unlike most islanders, Fran loved to keep up on, and complain about, town politics, so when the seat opened, she'd nominated herself and run unopposed. It was a foot in the door for bigger things.

She'd been thinking of running for mayor since Mayor Dunfree took office years ago and made a bunch of changes that peeved her off. So far, the idea of running for mayor was more a topic of conversation than anything she had a real plan for, but I had a feeling a peculiar stint as campaign manager was in my future.

"I motioned to make an exception to the rules," she said, "but they were so worried about breaking protocol that no one would vote with me. No one wants to rock the boat. Heaven forbid any of them be seen as a troublemaker. It's horrible the way they'd all rather hold on to their rules and regulations than comfort a grieving mother."

"I suggested Mrs. Miller have a candlelight vigil on the beach instead of sending off paper lanterns," I said. "If we go out after sunset when the beach is empty anyway and we use battery-operated candles, we won't need to request the area be temporarily closed or worry about contaminating the beach or ocean. Basically, we can skip running the event past the council."

Aunt Fran nodded. "Sneaky. And it's for a good cause. I like it." She tapped her toe, still clearly miffed at the situation. "I'm going to have a talk with the mayor one-on-one. Maybe I can reason with him about the paper lanterns. The woman lost her child, for goodness' sake. If she wants lanterns, she should have lanterns. If that doesn't work, we'll do the vigil, but I want to try to get her what she wants if I can."

"Thanks," I said. "I know she and Judy would both appreciate the effort if they knew."

"Well, don't tell," Aunt Fran said. "I don't want to disappoint anyone if I hit a wall."

"Got it," I said, my heart softening as I looked into my aunts' sincere faces. "Thank you for everything you guys do for me. I don't tell you as often as I should, but I appreciate you both. Very much."

"It's what we do," Aunt Fran said. "One day when a younger Swan comes along, your job will be to help her."

"Okie-dokie," I said, taking a big-girl step away from that nightmare of a conversation. As far as I knew, the Swan line ended with me, so any "younger Swans" would have to come from my loins, and considering my terminally single status and the family's alleged curse, I wasn't in a good place for continuing that particular chat right now.

I hooked a thumb over my shoulder. "I'd better get moving. I'm going to open the café for lunch today, and I'll see what I can do with these scripts."

"Maybe we can do a dry run tonight," Aunt Clara suggested. "We can meet back here to see what you've come up with, then talk set and costume design."

I paused. "What?" I'd agreed to tape a one- to three-minute application video, not a feature-length two-woman play. "I don't think you need all that."

Clara let out a tinkling laugh. "Silly. Of course we do!"

"Seven o'clock?" Fran asked.

I nodded woodenly, not wanting to think about the size of the mess I'd accidentally volunteered for. "See you at seven." I strode out of the shop and into the blinding sunlight with purpose. I had plenty of time to worry about what to do with my aunts. But I only had an hour to get my shop open if I wanted to hear what folks were saying about last night.

CHAPTER
SIX

E verly!" Judy's voice cracked through the air as I
headed down the sidewalk. She waved to me from
her place in line at the ice cream shop.

I changed directions and went to say hello. The
prickles of feeling someone's gaze on the back of my
neck went with me as I moved into line beside Judy.
I scanned the area, but didn't see anyone looking my
way. *Residual heebie-jeebies*, I told myself. After finding Craig's body last night and knowing someone
had broken into my home this morning, a few creepy
aftershocks were probably par for the course.

"What are you doing?" she asked. "I thought you
were opening Sun, Sand, and Tea for lunch today."

"I am. I just needed to talk with my aunts. I ran
into Craig's mom this morning. She wants to hold a
candlelight vigil, and I suggested she use my shop as a
meeting ground."

Judy ran the pads of her thumbs under her eyes,
which filled with tears. "I know. I talked with her after

you left. You've already done too much, you don't have to be involved anymore. You know that, right? I can figure this out. My family can help, or I can try to pull something together myself that will honor Craig." Her voice and composure cracked on her husband's name. She struggled visibly to regain herself, but it was too late. A few deeply shuddered breaths later, her pretty face collapsed in pain.

I rubbed her arm, certain a full-fledged hug would be her complete undoing. "It's no trouble. I want to help. How did everything go after I left?" I asked, forcing a change of subject. I hadn't meant to make her cry in public, and it was almost her turn to order. "Was anything missing once you started cleaning up?"

"No. Not that I can tell." She took a few silent beats to compose herself and bat the tears from her eyes before speaking again. "I guess it was a crime of passion, and that could only mean Cynthia."

I'd thought that too at first, but the longer I'd let the idea roll in my mind, the more I'd begun to wonder if I was being too narrowly focused. Maybe the mess was made for another reason. "What if whoever did that was actually looking for something?" I asked. "Maybe nothing was taken because the intruder didn't find what he or she was after."

We shuffled forward with the line. "Like what?" she asked. "It's not as if Craig or I brought anything of value, since it was a destination wedding. Just clothes, toiletries, and wedding rings."

"It's only a theory." But honestly, if I knew my

fiancé was cheating on me, I'd have assumed the same thing she had.

From outside the terrible love triangle, however, it seemed possible that there was another reason for the break-in. I gave the crowd a careful look. "What happened to Jasper?" I asked, turning in a small circle in search of the slender towhead. "Wasn't he driving you to see your family today?"

"That was before the break-in," she said. "Now all I want is ice cream and a nap. Jasper's cleaning up the mess and letting everyone know I'm resting." She swallowed audibly, and fear flashed through her pale blue eyes. "I keep wondering what would have happened if the nut who tore up the room had walked in on me in the shower. It's not like I could have defended myself in there. I could've been killed."

I hooked an arm over her shoulders. "Better get two scoops," I said. "It has been a bad couple of days."

"Yeah." Judy wiped her eyes again, this time with trembling fingers, and took a deep breath. "I'm thinking mint chocolate chip with chocolate sauce, whipped cream, and a warm brownie."

"Good choice," I said. "Let's make it two, and it's my treat."

We collected our heavenly sweets, then chose a table slightly removed from the rest of the patrons where we could talk. A pickup towing a black and silver horse trailer rolled down Main Street and my dumb heart flipped at the sight of it.

"Cowboys," Judy whispered, watching the truck

roll by. "I wanted to learn to rope and ride so badly as a kid, but Dad was only interested in teaching me to fish, and Mom was busy grooming me to be a princess." Judy gave a dark chuckle. "When I was old enough to date, Mom told me to go out and find a prince who'd love, honor, and protect me. Someone who would make sure there was always enough money to pay the electric bill and mortgage. She didn't want me to have to worry the way she does."

I stuffed a spoonful of whipped cream between my lips. What could I say to that? Especially now.

I let my gaze follow the horse trailer as it grew small in the distance, hating myself for the familiar ache in my heart and gut that still accompanied the thought of my own cowboy. I forced Wyatt's image back into my mental vault and changed the subject. "Jasper seems a lot clingier than I remember from high school," I said, testing the water on a potentially touchy subject.

Judy pushed a wad of whipped cream around the mint chocolate chip soup left in her bowl. "I never told anyone this, but Jasper and I dated in secret before I left for college. It wasn't supposed to be a big deal, so we kept it to ourselves. I guess he held on to the flame a little more tightly than I did. I feel guilty for leaning on him so heavily right now, but it's nice to have someone I can trust to hold me together. I'm glad to have him."

"I get it," I said. "I'm one hundred percent behind whatever gets you through this right now." Though I couldn't help wondering if Judy's former secret boyfriend had spent the better part of a decade pining for her, and perhaps took the recent opportunity to remove another man from her future. Permanently.

Judy dragged her attention from the road where the horse trailer had since vanished and refocused on the big plastic sundae bowl before her. "Whatever happened to that cowboy you ran off with?" she asked, her eyes landing briefly on my bare ring finger.

"Nothing, really," I said. Wyatt had been in town for Summer Splash, studying the wild horses and healing from a recent rodeo accident, when we met. I'd spent the next few years following him across the United States while he chased his dream, but even after being so severely injured that doctors didn't think he'd ever ride again, he'd refused to stay in Kentucky with me while I finished culinary school. He'd never chosen anything over rodeo before, and he wasn't about to start with me.

"What's that mean," Judy asked, "*nothing, really*?"

"I guess it means he did what cowboys do. He broke my heart."

⤝⤞

Back at home, I showered and dressed in my usual uniform for a day at my seaside iced tea shop: cut off shorts, a light blue V-neck T-shirt with the Sun, Sand, and Tea logo printed on it, and flip-flops. The T-shirt was part of a campaign to promote my brand. I'd gotten the idea from a book on sales and marketing that I borrowed from one of Amelia's Little Libraries. I'd already painted my wagon and bicycle light blue, so buying a few shirts with the Sun, Sand, and Tea insignia for myself seemed smart.

The dining area was bright with late morning sun streaming in through my rear wall of windows and sliding glass doors to the patio. A cloud of dust motes hovered in the air, then vanished when I flipped the lights on. I turned the CLOSED sign to OPEN, put my favorite station on the radio, and got busy prepping for lunch.

Within minutes, I'd danced a broom around the room and stopped back where I'd started, in front of the massive chalkboard anchored to the wall behind the counter. I pushed my step stool into place and erased the outdated list of dishes, but left the twenty flavors of iced tea alone. Those were already neatly divided into caffeinated, decaffeinated, and sugar-free, and further grouped by tea types: green, black, herbal, etc. The tea list didn't change as often as the food menu.

Prepping for Craig and Judy's reception had left my refrigerator and pantry heavy on fruit and nuts, so I brainstormed the possibilities. The fruit wouldn't last long, so it was going to be the official side dish of everything. I tapped a yellow stick of chalk against the blackboard and then printed a fresh menu in neat block letters beneath the words "Daily Selections."

Pineapple Chicken Wraps
Spicy Shrimp and Avocado Tacos
Cherry, Blueberry, and Goat Cheese Salad

I set a pot of water on the stove, plopped a block of

chocolate into a bowl, and picked up a piece of pink chalk to script *Chocolate Covered Strawberries* under "Sweet Treats." I added *Blueberry Cheesecake Bites* and *Red Velvet Ice Cream Sandwiches* to that list.

Next, I had to deal with the all the leftover Blushing Bride tea. I chose bright orange chalk and made chubby bubble letters: *Free Summer Splash Special with any purchase*. Unfortunately, any Hibiscus Mint I still had at the end of today would have to be dumped. I had a strict twenty-four-hour policy on my brews.

The precious sound of my seashell wind chimes put a smile on my face. "Welcome to Sun, Sand, and Tea," I said, turning to greet my first customer of the day.

Craig's business partner, Pete, climbed onto a stool and slouched over the counter.

My jaw dropped at the sight of him. I tried not to stare, but I'd only ever seen him in a tuxedo, and he looked completely different in his white short-sleeved button-down and flamingo-pink shorts.

The spaces between his shirt buttons gaped from his awful posture. "I'm glad you're open. There's nothing to do in this town, and I'm depressed." He pushed mirrored aviator sunglasses up onto his wavy brown hair and sulked openly.

"Where have you been?" I asked. Pete looked awful, his skin red and eyes glassy. Where had he been throughout everything that had happened? I couldn't believe he was still on the island. "Are you sunburned?"

He rolled tired blue eyes up at me. "I fell asleep on the beach."

I poured a jar of the newly relabeled Summer Splash Special and slid it in his direction. "The southern summer sun isn't to be taken lightly," I said. "A little aloe and some tea will help."

He lifted the drink to his lips and sipped. "I was supposed to be in Maui today," he said. "*Maui*. Instead, I'm stuck here in some tiny town in the Carolinas, I don't even remember where. I shouldn't have to. This place was supposed to be a pit stop. It wasn't supposed to matter."

I considered taking my tea back, but reminded myself he'd recently undergone a major personal loss. "You're in Charm, North Carolina," I said, letting the full weight of my Southern drawl drip all over the words. "It's a lovely town with plenty to see and do. Why were you tagging along on Judy and Craig's honeymoon, anyway?"

"I wasn't going on their honeymoon," he groaned. "I wanted to see the island. They were going. Why not travel with friends?" Pete puffed air through his nose and tapped his phone. He turned the screen to show me an ad for a Hawaiian resort. "Craig reserved some private beach bungalow for him and Judy. I made reservations for this place." There was a hotel in the background of the ad, but the main image was a line of bikini-clad twenty-somethings drinking cocktails and looking thrilled.

I opened my junk drawer, liberated a tiny umbrella toothpick, jammed it through a chunk of pineapple, and balanced it on the rim of his jar. "Look, instantly tropical. Better?"

He put his phone in his pocket. "No."

I rinsed a head of lettuce and began chopping it for the salad, trying to decide what to ask Pete first. "So, are you stuck here because you're waiting for the wedding party to go back to Martha's Vineyard together, or are you still waiting to talk to the police?"

Pete tossed the little umbrella aside and popped the pineapple into his mouth. "Your town's only detective is holding me hostage here. He asked me not to leave. I don't even know if that's legal."

"I think the police can hold a suspect up to seventy-two hours without making an arrest," I said. "That's what they always say on my crime shows."

"An arrest for what?" he said, balking. "I didn't do anything. I wasn't even around when you pulled Craig out of the water, and this isn't a television show. I can't be a suspect. This is my life." He dragged the words of his final sentence like a heartbroken teen.

"He's not holding you," I said. "You aren't in custody." I tapped my fingernails on the counter. "Where did you go after the wedding ceremony? I never saw you at the reception."

"I was walking on the beach." He finished his tea and thumped the empty jar on the counter. "I'd had enough faux romance and forced merriment, so I lifted a bottle of champagne from the bar and went to clear my head before I had to watch Craig hunt for Judy's garter and a bunch of dressed-up women go head-to-head for a chance to catch the bridal bouquet. When I got back, the champagne bottle was empty, and so was half the beach."

I mulled over his explanation and refilled his jar to keep him talking. I didn't like the words *faux romance* used to describe my friend's wedding, or the fact Pete had no alibi at the time of Craig's death. Add that to his apparent indifference about the loss of his partner and it was easy to see why Pete hadn't received his get-out-of-Charm-free card yet. "What made you call Craig while you were off drinking and clearing your head?" I asked.

Pete puckered his brow. "I didn't call anyone."

"Yes, you did," I countered. "I was with Craig when he got your call. I watched him walk away to answer it. Were the two of you fighting?"

"No, and my phone was dead last night, so there's no way I called him or anyone else until I got back to the Millers' beach house." He wiggled his tea jar, sloshing the liquid over the ice cubes, then turned a concerned expression on me. "How's Judy doing?"

"She's strong," I said. "She'll be okay in time." I searched his eyes for signs of guilt. Had Craig lied about who'd called him, or was Pete lying now? I couldn't guess why either man would want to lie, but Grady would have the phone records soon enough. "Are you and Judy close?" I asked. She hadn't seemed like his biggest fan.

Pete took a long drink and frowned. "I like her," he said begrudgingly. "She deserved better than Craig, and she definitely didn't deserve this."

"You didn't like Craig?" I asked, hoping to sound more casual than accusatory, but failing miserably.

Pete snorted. "Let's just say I wasn't his biggest fan lately. Now I'm trapped in a rented beach home with his family for the foreseeable future, and I think his mother is planning to nominate him for sainthood."

I leaned closer, catching him in my pointed stare. "Which of his choices didn't you like, specifically?"

Pete frowned. "What?"

"Business choices? Life choices? Financial choices? People make a lot of choices."

Pete waved a dismissive hand. "Can we drop this, please?" he asked. "I came in here to get out of the sun and maybe tell Judy I'm sorry this happened to her. I'm going to pass on your weird inquisition."

The chimes on the door sounded again, and Ryan and Mr. Granger walked into the café. Ryan had traded his suit and tie for a pale-green T-shirt with *Charm* emblazoned across it and a pair of tan shorts. He'd stuffed his bare feet into leather boat shoes and looked exactly like any tourist I'd ever seen. Mr. Granger looked as if he was on his way to work in dress slacks, a long-sleeved button-down, and a jacket that I imagined either covered enormous sweat marks or Mr. Granger was impervious to the heat.

I filled two more canning jars with ice cubes and drowned them in Hibiscus Mint tea. "Summer Splash Special," I said delivering one to each man. "Tea's on the house today. Can I get you something to eat?"

Mr. Granger frowned. "I think I'll need to see a menu."

"Sure thing." I pointed to the chalkboard behind me.

"That's it?" he asked. "The board says you have twenty kinds of iced tea, but only three lunch items and three desserts?"

"That's right," I said. "The food menu changes daily. Sometimes with the tide. Is there anything you'd like to try?"

Ryan patted the counter. "We'll take one of everything," he said. "On me, Mr. Granger. We can enjoy the ocean view without the searing heat, share a smorgasbord of good food, and chat."

"All right," Mr. Granger agreed, his gaze stuck on Pete, who hadn't looked up from his empty tea jar.

I gave Pete another refill and went to work prepping plates with mini tortillas—soft for the chicken wraps and hard for the tacos. "Pete and I were just talking about how much he likes our town," I said, turning to my stove to heat a pan.

"You're Pete?" Mr. Granger asked. "Craig's business partner? I'm Warren Granger. I've been trying to reach you."

Pete didn't make eye contact or bother to look in his direction. "Sorry. My phone's dead and I lost my charger." My mouth fell open, shocked by the blatant and seemingly unnecessary lie.

"Perhaps we can talk now," Granger said. "Seems like a serendipitous encounter."

"Seems like a tiny island," Pete grumbled.

Mr. Granger cleared his throat. "The last time I spoke with Craig, he said he'd found something interesting in my data and he wanted to talk to me. Even made plans to discuss it at his wedding reception. That must mean something, right? Can you clue me in on what he found? Was it bad?"

Pete sighed, slid off his stool, and tossed a wad of cash on the counter.

"The tea was free," I said, catching a twenty before it slid onto my tacos.

He ignored me, addressing Mr. Granger. "I'll be in touch as soon as all this"—he lifted his palms into the air—"is over."

"Of course," Mr. Granger said. "I'm sorry if it was crass of me to bring up work at a time like this."

Pete walked out without another word. Ryan watched him go, then turned to me with tented brows. I forced a smile and got busy lining thin strips of chicken in a pan. While the chicken browned, I prepped and served two Cherry, Blueberry, and Goat Cheese Salads and slid them across the counter. "Salad starters." I smiled. "The wraps and tacos will be up in a few minutes, then I'll get the desserts plated."

Mr. Granger dug in.

Ryan smiled, keen eyes trailing my every move. "I ran into Mr. Granger at the ice cream parlor. Can you believe it?"

Based on the chocolate smudge on Mr. Granger's shirt, I could. "No kidding?" I asked. "I was there today too."

And I'd felt eyes on me. Could it have been Ryan watching me? Mr. Granger?

"Did you spend the night in Charm, Mr. Granger?"

I held my breath in anticipation of the answer. Had the police also asked him not to leave town?

"I'm waiting for my interview with the police," he said, "so my wife and I rented a place on Bay Street. She went shopping when the stores opened, and I went for ice cream. I felt bad, at first, having something so sweet that early in the day, but then I ran into Ryan."

"Great minds think alike," Ryan said, his voice filled with satisfaction. I turned away, rolling my eyes.

More people trickled in as it got closer to noon, and I stole time between customers to research a few of my new acquaintances online. I started with the duo before me. Mr. Granger was no social media guru. He had an outdated Facebook page and no other online presence. A quick run of his name through the local court records showed he hadn't had any recent traffic violations or arrests. Ryan, on the other hand, had a robust online presence, having written dozens of articles on high society weddings and various New York City events. His social media overflowed with update posts and self-ies taken with B-list celebrities and folks he'd labeled "up-and-coming" thises or thats. I would need at least a week to read through half of the information available on Ryan, but none of it seemed very useful. You only had to know him for a few minutes to see what kind of guy he was—self-satisfied and a little obnoxious.

I fell down an internet rabbit hole when I typed the words *Bee Loved documentary* into a search engine. I'd wanted to watch past application videos, find out if the organization had ever run this contest before, and check out current submissions, in other words, the competition, if possible. It seemed smart to know what my aunts were up against before I compiled their ideas into one winning script. Pages of results came back instantly. It seemed as if the entire North American beekeeping community had been waiting for this moment on pins and needles. The official website's chat room's activity was pulsing like a ticker tape. Dozens of video applications had already been uploaded to the Bee Loved documentary page, and the comments were rolling in. "Good grief," I whispered. This was a lot of pressure. Not to mention, Aunt Clara was so tender-hearted and Aunt Fran was so competitive that the experience was bound to end either in extreme victory or eternal flames. I watched all the available video applications before closing my laptop. The online polls would open for voting in a few days, and we needed to come up with something extraordinary before then if we didn't want to end up beekeeping laughingstocks.

By two o'clock, I'd made a lot of notes and very little progress on combining my aunts' scripts, the lunch crowd had vanished, and I was alone with a mess to clean up. I considered shirking my duties in favor of a few more internet searches on Craig's possible killers before the next round of customers arrived, but my heart wasn't in it anymore. Running a busy café on my own had wiped me out, and I still needed to come up with something to present to my aunts.

I grabbed a rag and headed to the deck to wipe

down tables and chairs. The patio door slid easily under my hand, and I paused for a moment to bask in the obliterating heat. A stout gray-winged seagull paced the railing, his white breast puffed, head cocked and beady black eyes focused on a few dropped shrimp beneath the tables.

"Hey, Lou," I said, kicking shrimp into the clear for him. "Enjoy." He swooped onto the deck and gobbled up the shrimp.

I dragged my wet rag in big circles over each table top and chair seat.

"How far do you travel around here?" I asked him. "All over Charm or just onto my roof and back to the deck?"

He spread his wings and puffed to twice his size before returning to normal.

"Nice," I said, nodding appreciatively. "Do you know Jasper?" I asked. "Ever see him while you're flying around?" Who had Jasper become in the years since high school? I hoped he'd become a good guy, but how could I be sure? Lou nabbed another fallen crustacean, and I narrowed my eyes on him. "I bet you can see everything from the rooftop—the beach, the gardens, the boardwalk. You'd tell me if someone was following me, right?"

Lou flew back to the railing and pointed his beak toward the ocean. He wasn't a big talker, but he was a great listener.

"Think about it and let me know," I suggested, wiping the last table. "See you later, Lou."

Back inside, I loaded the dishwasher and stared at the seats where Mr. Granger, Ryan, and Pete had been. The talk with Lou had gotten my adrenaline going again. Pete had been in a terrible mood. He'd lied to Mr. Granger about his cell phone, then pretended to be mourning after he'd just told me he was sad because he wasn't in Maui. I opened my laptop and typed in *Pete Fiduccia*.

Pete's social media was like a stream of advertisements for expensive brands. He'd tagged the selfies with words like Armani, Rolex, and Ferrari. His car's doors opened skyward. His closet was the size of my entire bedroom. I couldn't help recalling Judy's opinion of him: She said he'd never grown up. That he had debt. Made bad investments.

What if Craig had finally told him to shape up or ship out? What if Pete decided that eliminating Craig would give him full ownership of a company he could sell for millions? That seemed like a solid motive for murder to me.

The café was silent, aside from an Eagles song playing on the radio and the gentle hum of air conditioning overhead. My gaze darted back to the photos of Pete on my laptop, and my heart rate climbed. When it came down to it, Pete had more to gain than anyone from his partner's death, and he was complaining the loudest about wanting to get out of town.

Maybe he was trying to escape an arrest for murder.

CHAPTER
❧

SEVEN

Jasper and Judy arrived with the early dinner crowd around four. Judy's hair was slicked into a tidy ponytail, and her face was no longer splotchy. Her eyes were clear, and she'd chosen an apricot A-line sundress that gave her pale cheeks the illusion of color. Jasper was in his usual cargo shorts and T-shirt. My online searches for him hadn't turned up anything I didn't already know. He was a fisherman who owned his own boat and sometimes rented it out for private excursions. His social media was updated mostly during football season, and he kept an excessive number of high school photos, considering he was thirty. Judy could be found somewhere in nearly all of them.

"Hey," I said, stopping at the small table where they sat. "What can I get you? I put up a new menu today, but if there's something else you'd like"—I smiled at Judy—"I can talk to the chef."

"I think I'll try the salad," she said. "It sounds

amazing, and I'm craving a glass of your grandmamma's Cucumber Mint Tea."

"On it." I beamed, wholly warmed by the fact Judy had known my grandmother. Grandma had been everything to me when I was growing up, and our family recipes meant the world to both of us. I turned to Jasper. "Anything for you?"

"Shrimp tacos," he said, "and Iced Chai."

"I'll be right back with the drinks." I turned and nearly ran into Ryan. "What are you doing?" I gasped. "You can't sneak up behind people like that. It's terrifying."

"Calm down. I just walked in." He hiked one brow toward his thick, dark hairline.

I released a heavy breath and hurried behind the counter. "What happened to your sidekick, Mr. Granger?"

Ryan followed me as far as the counter and leaned a hip against it. "He had things to do. Like me."

I scooped ice into two empty jars. "And what are you doing?"

"I'm back for more of your delicious tea," he said. "I figure while I'm here, I might run into some more people I know from the wedding, and maybe they'll need someone to talk to. You can plan on seeing me around quite a bit for the next few days."

I made a gagging sound. "You're using my shop as a place to snoop."

"What?" He tried to look offended and failed. "Okay, so what? So are you."

"Am not. I'm only here to serve people and

hopefully pay my mortgage." I gave him a glass of my Summer Splash Special, ignored my guilt over lying about snooping, then filled Jasper and Judy's jars.

"My offer stands, you know?" he said, "I bet if we partner up on this, we can have the case closed in no time. Solve the crime. Bag the killer. Win friends and influence people."

I set the jars back down. "Did you actually learn anything from Mr. Granger?"

A sly smile slid across his face. "I knew it! I saw you on your laptop every chance you got, probably googling every person who walked in here today. What did you find out?"

"You first."

His grin widened. "I got an earful about how rude Pete was for walking out when Mr. Granger wanted to talk to him. I didn't think he'd ever stop, and he wouldn't let me change the subject, so I steered him into a store his wife had just walked inside of and she took him from there."

I ferried Jasper and Judy's teas to their table, then darted back to Ryan. "So you learned nothing. Nice work." I pulled clean plates from the dishwasher and fresh veggies from the fridge. "Do you think Pete could have done this?" I lowered my voice and ducked my head, using Ryan as a shield between myself and Jasper and Judy's table. "Would he kill his partner for full owner-ship of the company? Does he have a temper? All I know about him is that he's more concerned with not getting his trip to Maui than having lost his friend to murder."

Ryan leaned over the counter on his elbows as I prepped the salad and tacos. "I've read articles on Craig and Pete since they first hit the spotlight about five years ago. Craig's talent for scrutinizing data was unparalleled. It made him a tech king. He's the reason 'data scientist' became a household term."

I'd never heard the term *data scientist* before this weekend, but I nodded anyway. The first time Craig had called himself one, I thought he was joking.

"Craig was brilliant," Ryan continued. "Everyone who's ever researched or interviewed him has agreed. All the way back to his childhood. His family and teachers say he just understood things, saw things that others didn't see."

"Pete wasn't the same?" I guessed, recalling what little I knew of him and what I'd seen online today.

"No." Ryan shook his head slowly. "Pete was a coed with above average technical skills and a deep desire for easy money. He had a little savings and saw Craig as the golden goose. They made a deal, and Pete became part owner by investing in the startup. Pete knows more than most about technology, but not enough to be useful to Craig, so he quickly fell into the role of management, finding work for them and promoting their company."

I plated the shrimp tacos, then added a light dressing to Judy's salad. "I've been wondering if Craig ever called Pete out on the fact Pete was making half the money for none of the work."

Ryan tapped his nose. "You and me both, Miss Swan."

I delivered Judy and Jasper's food and went to welcome and take orders from my newest arrivals, but my thoughts were stuck on Pete, wherever he was. Judy was the last person to call Craig's phone on the night he died, but I'd seen him take a call from Pete, and whatever the call was about, it wasn't something Craig was willing to stick around and discuss in front of Judy and me. He'd excused himself the moment he'd identified the caller as his partner, and we never saw him alive again. When I asked Pete about the conversation today, he denied making the call. That had to mean something.

The dinner crowd started pouring in, and I didn't even notice when Ryan left, but Judy and Jasper were still there a few hours later when I flipped the CLOSED sign and scrubbed down the café. Judy was working up the strength to pay Mrs. Miller a visit and stop by her family's home for dinner, since she'd put both off this morning. Her phone had rung a half dozen times before she'd finished her salad. She wouldn't be able to hide out much longer before her loved ones came looking for her. "I'm going out for a while," I told them. "Help yourself to anything you want, and be sure to lock up when you leave."

"We will," Judy promised. "Thank you. For everything."

"I'll be home tonight if you want to vent about how the family visits go."

She smiled. "I'll try not to fall asleep while we're talking again."

I hooked a bag filled with food from today's menu

over the crook of one arm, tucked a container of desserts under the other, and grabbed a jug of tea. I'd prepped a half gallon of Old-Fashioned Sweet Tea especially for my *tea*-totaler aunts, and a bunch of boozy grapes for me. I'd marinated the grapes in red wine from a local vineyard, frozen them, then rolled them in sugar and popped them back in the freezer. The process was slow but worth it, but now I was running a little behind.

I stopped on the wide wraparound porch when the distant rumble of a man's voice drew my attention, then eased around the corner for a better view of the beach, where Ryan and Pete stood toe to toe in the sand. I strained to hear what they were talking about, but their words were muddled by wind and waves. Their tones and postures, however, confirmed this was an argument.

Maggie leapt onto the railing beside me, and I nearly lost my tea.

"What are you doing?" I whispered, my heart hammering painfully. "A little warning next time?" I asked the cat.

She blinked luminous green eyes at me.

I adjusted the weight of my burdens, hoping to regain feeling in my hands where the bag and tea jug were fast cutting off my circulation. "Where have you been, anyway? You ran off the other night and never came back. I was worried."

Maggie took a seat beside a porch post and curled her tail around her feet.

When I looked back at the beach, Ryan and Pete were gone.

I waddled toward the carriage house, trying desperately not to drop anything. Normally, I would have pulled my little wagon into town and enjoyed the walk, but I wasn't interested in coming face-to-face with whoever had been following me, so I would take Blue, my golf cart, instead.

Blue was, like most things in my life, a bit of a fixer-upper. I'd gotten it secondhand off someone's front lawn. The sign on the windshield had promised it was "good for parts," so I'd traded the cash in my wallet for a vehicle in need of a little love and sprucing up. A few hundred dollars later, the cart ran like a ride half its age, and I'd painted it to match my wagon and thrift store bicycle. Light blue with little pink and white flower chains painted on the doors and a Sun, Sand, and Tea logo on the hood, it was cuter than a car and just as functional for running errands around the island.

My fitness watch beeped. **BE MORE ACTIVE.**

As if running around my café all day wasn't enough steps to satisfy it, not to mention the two trips I'd already made into town.

My phone rang a few steps later, and I freed it from my pocket with significant effort, miraculously managing not to drop anything in the process. Aunt Clara's number was centered in the screen. "Hello!" I chirped. "I'm running late, but I'm on my way now, I promise. I'm bringing dinner, and I'm driving over, so I'll be extra quick."

"Perfect," she cooed. "As long as you're well, we're happy. See you soon, then?"

"Absolutely. I'm just—" I stopped abruptly at the carriage-house door and stared at Blue.

"I'll keep watch by the door to help you carry everything in," Aunt Clara said in my ear. "Don't worry about rushing. We've got all night."

I inched closer to the driver's side of the golf cart, my stomach turning. "I'm going to be a little later than I thought," I whispered, terror sticking my tongue to the roof of my mouth. "I have to call Grady."

"Why?" she asked. "What's wrong? Has something happened? Why are you whispering?"

I blinked, but the reality in front of me didn't change.

"There's a bloody cake knife stabbed into my headrest."

CHAPTER

EIGHT

Pie filling," Grady said, touching the smear of goo on his gloved finger to his tongue.

"What? Gross." I crossed my arms and leaned away from him. "I can't believe you just tasted it. What if it was blood?"

"It's pie filling," he repeated, pushing his goo-coated fingertip in my direction. "Smell."

"No. Stop that." I swatted his hand away. Grady might be accustomed to seeing knives stabbed into golf cart headrests, but I wasn't, and as far as I was concerned the pie filling might as well have been real blood.

I stepped back, inhaling the dusty scent of my beloved carriage house, and attempted to recenter myself. The carriage house had always been one of my favorite aspects of the property. Painted gray and trimmed in white to match my home, it had one big bay door on the front and a small rectangular tower on top, complete with a weather vane powered by the near-constant ocean breeze. When it was built, it had been a place to house a carriage, horse, and all the necessary tack. Today, it was equivalent to a detached garage, but I felt as if I was transported to another time whenever I was inside—a proper lady of her day, wearing hoop skirts and corsets instead of cutoffs and flip-flops. Though I didn't have a horse or carriage, I parked my trusty steeds inside just the same. Blue, my wagon, and my bicycle deserved nothing but the finest.

I scanned the floor for a trail of dripping pie filling or muddy footprints or some other clue that could lead us to Blue's assailant, but found nothing—just the horse stall fully packed with aged wooden crates and musty boxes from owners and tenants who'd gone before me. The small living quarters in the back, where I imagined a caretaker had once stayed, was exactly the same, stuffed with the cast-off belongings of strangers, storage for ghosts. I sometimes imagined the profound pieces of history I might find in the older boxes when I opened them, but I'd yet to make the carriage house purge and clean a priority. I'd have to get to it on a day when my life was a little less *knife-in-the-headrest* exciting.

Grady straightened. "I'd think someone who spends as much time cooking and baking as you do would recognize cherry pie filling." He rolled the glove down, turning it inside out as he freed his hand. He'd already put the knife in an evidence bag. "Looks like a threat to me."

"You think?" I squeaked. "What am I supposed to do now? I was on my way to visit my aunts." I tapped my toe, thankful the knife hadn't been coated in blood, and focused on my new problem. "Any chance I can I wipe the cherries off the vinyl and take Blue to Blessed Bee as planned?"

Grady's brows gathered together. "I'm confused. Is Blue your golf cart?"

"Yeah," I said, feeling suddenly uncomfortable with the name choice, "because it's blue."

"Ah," Grady said, eyes sparkling. "Creative choice."

"Thanks." I evaluated his posture and expression, suspecting he was teasing me, but I was unwilling to ask. "So, I can take the cart into town?"

"No. This is a crime scene, and it's the second instance of vandalism on your property today. Less than twenty-four hours after a murder."

"That didn't happen on my property," I said. "That was property-adjacent."

Grady rubbed his forehead. The smell of his cologne and shampoo mixed with the more familiar scents of aged wood and a hearty Atlantic breeze as it swirled through the open door. "I need to go over the golf cart for prints and evidence before you can take it out again."

I sighed. I understood the importance of procedure. Most of my teas involved a careful process as well. Miss one step or rearrange them somehow, and the finished product lost its punch, resulting in wasted time, product, and effort—none of which I had to spare. I could only imagine how much more important it was to follow police procedure, especially at a time like this. "All right," I conceded. "How long will that take?"

Grady looked at the carriage house's cobweb-laden ceiling for a long moment, then back to me. He opened his arms and moved toward me, steering me outside. "I know you're in a hurry, so why don't I drive you to Blessed Bee tonight?"

I blinked as my eyes adjusted to the sun, temporarily blinded and somewhat confused. "You want to drive me to see my aunts?" I turned my attention to Grady's late-model black pickup. His ride was a lot better than mine. "Deal," I said, offering him my hand for a shake.

Grady slid his rough palm against mine and curled strong fingers over my suddenly electrified skin. It wasn't fair that his handshake could set my heart to sprint or that one of his broad, dimpled smiles could lower my IQ by ten points, but that seemed to be the hand I was dealt, so I lifted my chin and coped.

His eyes widened by the smallest of fraction as the spark between us threatened to knock me off my feet.

I inhaled long and slow, enjoying the rush of endorphins or whatever it was that inevitably came with his touch, then thanked my stars that we didn't make a habit of touching and I could therefore remain sane a little while longer. I wiggled from his grip and stuffed the tingling hand into my pocket. "I'll get my things."

Grady and I grabbed the food and iced tea from Blue's back seat and carried it to his truck. I texted Aunt Clara to let her know we were on the way the minute I buckled in.

The engine purred to life, and I ran a gentle hand

over the soft leather seat. The interior smelled like Grady's cologne and…bubblegum. I supposed the latter was a result of Grady's unreasonably adorable son, Denver. Grady also employed a beautiful blond au pair named Denise, but she had her own vehicle.

"How's Judy doing?" Grady asked, steering the truck across Oceanview and onto Middletown Road. "Any better?"

"I think so. Jasper's with her most of the time, acting as spokesperson and go-between for her family and Craig's." Grady had lost his wife. To cancer, not murder, but I imagined he could probably relate to Judy in ways I might never understand.

I patted my knees, needing a change of subject. "I saw Pete today. Any particular reason you asked him to stay in town?"

Grady turned to look at me. "Who told you I did?"

"Pete," I said, turning my face away.

The setting sun cast a warm amber and orange glow over the world outside my window. Most shops were closed, and the foot traffic had thinned to couples and families heading to and from dinner or the ice cream parlor.

Grady's gaze burned against my cheek. "Why would he tell you that?"

I lifted my hand and dropped it in my lap. "Because I asked."

The truck slowed. "When and where did you see him?"

I turned back at the sudden change in our speed

and the tone of Grady's voice. "I've seen him twice so far at my place, most recently right before I found the knife stuck in my headrest."

Grady straightened and bent his fingers, repositioning them on the wheel several times. "So, there's zero chance the knife in your headrest was meant for Judy."

"Probably not. Does that upset you?" I asked. Grady wasn't one to show a ton of emotion, but it looked to me as if smoke might start pouring from his ears.

"Yes," he barked, confusing me further. "Of course it upsets me."

I searched his expression for answers I didn't find. "Does it matter who the threat was for? There's still a criminal running loose."

Grady slid his eyes my way briefly before returning to the road. "Fine. The threat was pointed directly at you, so let's start with who else you've been talking to."

Tension rolled off him in waves tall enough to bowl me over, and I felt my blood pressure rise in response. "Everly." Grady spoke my name softly. "I need to know who you've spoken with so I can start looking for someone with motive to attack your golf cart."

I relaxed against the seat and did my best to name everyone I'd spoken to since breakfast, including customers I recognized and others I could only describe. As Grady pulled into a parking space outside Blessed Bee, I finished.

"Thanks," Grady said. "I'll see what I can figure out about Blue. If you want to go in and let your aunts know you're here, I'll bring your things."

The shop door swung open and my aunts appeared before I'd gotten a foot out of the truck's cab. Concern was etched across their brows. "Are you okay?" Aunt Clara asked as I climbed down.

"We've been worried sick," Fran complained.

"I'm fine," I said, going to meet them. I held the door for Grady carrying my things inside their store.

"What happened?" Aunt Fran asked.

I looked to Grady, unsure where to begin.

He frowned, probably imagining Blue's violated headrest. "Why don't you call me when you're ready to go home," he suggested.

I nodded. "Thanks."

I got comfortable at the counter and popped a boozy grape into my mouth, then another, before launching into a thorough recap of the afternoon. Many grapes later, I concluded with, "So, Blue is a crime scene, and Grady's my Uber for the night."

My aunts came at me in a group hug, professing their love and thanks that I was okay.

"I'm fine," I said, wiggling free from their grips and pressing kisses on their cheeks.

"And lucky," Aunt Clara whispered. "Detective Hays seems like he'd be an excellent driver."

I blushed, then smoothed the pages of their marked-up scripts on the counter. "I made some notes on your scripts," I said. "They need more work, but it's a good start."

Aunt Fran eagerly bent over the pages. Aunt Clara vanished into the stockroom and returned with an armload of clothing. "What do you think about these for the video?" she asked.

"That's a lot of clothes," I said, a little shocked by the size of the stack.

Clara smiled. "People in *the business* call this a wardrobe," she said proudly. "*The business* means people in Hollywood."

I did a slow blink. "You chose a wardrobe? For a three-minute video?"

She nodded. "Fran and I spoke after you left today, and we decided we need to make a video folks will remember. We'll start in period clothing and tape in black and white, like a peek back in time to when the bee population thrived along with crops and national flora. Then we'll update outfits and backdrops for each scene, and you can increase the speed that it plays, like a fast-forward through time. Maybe use a sepia filter after the black and white, then change to color as the population grows and the pollution worsens. Back to black and white as that climaxes with bees dying off as pollution and pesticides destroy their world. We can slow the tape way down at the end for impact."

My face must've expressed my shock because Fran clapped my shoulder, misreading my emotions.

"It's a hard truth to swallow," Fran said. "We know exactly how you feel."

Somehow, I doubted it.

Clara tilted her head, bottom lip protruding. "It's sad, but the apocalypse has already come for the American honeybee."

I pushed images of apocalyptic honeybees from my head. As if the fuzzy little killers weren't already scary enough. "I'm not sure we can cover all of that in a short video," I said. "What you're describing sounds more like a movie."

My aunts nodded.

"We don't have youthful faces and pop culture reference to wow the voters," Aunt Clara said, "but Swan women have been raising bees for hundreds of years. We just need to show them what we know in a way that elicits votes, and I think we can do it."

Fran nodded. "A short film about the heartbreaking annihilation of the American honeybee ought to be just what we need to get an edge on the competition. The overall genre we're going for is educational dystopian."

I nodded blankly. "A three-minute educational dystopian honeybee apocalypse movie."

Aunt Fran smiled. "Go big or go home."

I pressed a finger against the pulse beating in my temple. "Have you watched the other applicant videos yet?" I asked. "I saw some online."

"All of them," Aunt Clara said. "Lots of peppy young people who probably watched that bee movie from Pixar and decided to buy a hive. It's nice, but it's not the same as what we have to offer."

"Some of the applications have a lot of comments already," I said. A few applicants had chosen lovely outdoor settings with beehives in the background and sat in front of the camera with beekeeping masks on their laps. They'd spoken intelligently and factually for about a minute, then signed off. Those videos had gotten zero attention. Sadly, the hopefuls with over-the-top scripts, goofy costumes, and silly sound effects were leading the race in pre-poll buzz. The video with the most comments and discussion so far even included a three-second animation with a rocket ship. I wasn't even sure what it had to do with beekeeping.

Aunt Clara donned a yellow sun hat with pom-pom bees glued around the brim and a storm cloud of black fiberfill arranged on top. "The end is near," she said solemnly, "and the poor little bees don't even know it."

I served the food I had brought, and we worked on the script for another hour or two while we munched and traded ideas. Aunt Fran shared her sketches of ideal sets and backdrops that portrayed the passing of time, and Aunt Clara matched the wardrobe pieces to each era. She had a list of items she still needed to make or embellish, but she was confident she could finish them all by tomorrow night. Aunt Fran needed me to re-create the sketches as life-sized backdrops before filming. Eventually, I called Grady for a ride home.

"Who do you think stabbed Blue?" Aunt Fran asked as we waited for Grady to arrive.

I'd been thinking about the same thing. "I don't know. It could have been anyone. The carriage house doors were wide open, and I was inside the house." I scanned the dark street beyond the shop's window, and the creepy sensation of being watched slid over me once more. I rubbed my palms over my arms to brush off the chill. The fact that there wasn't an army of ants drowning in the pie filling says a lot too. I must've just missed seeing it happen." *The vandal might've even been there, watching as I called for help.* "What if whoever did it was there in the carriage house with me, and I didn't even know?"

Aunt Fran turned to face me, and I recognized the fear in her eyes. She looked as scared I felt.

Headlights flashed across the window, and my aunts and I jumped. Grady's truck pulled into an empty spot right outside.

I pressed a palm to my chest. "It's just Grady," I told them.

"Are you going to be okay?" Aunt Fran asked. "You can always come home with us tonight," she offered. "We'll make up your old bed, have some midnight pancakes."

I gave them each a hug. "Judy and Jasper are at my place. I need to go home and check on them, especially Judy."

The truck's driver's side door opened, and Grady climbed out. He leaned against the grille of his pickup and tapped his phone screen while he waited.

I tried not to notice his cowboy boots or how much I appreciated his nice-fitting jeans. "I guess standing there is his way of letting me know he's here without rushing me," I said, "in case I'd somehow missed his behemoth truck."

Aunt Fran laughed. She opened the door for me

and held it with one hip while she hugged me good-bye for a second time. "Call us if you need anything."

"Back at ya," I said.

I greeted Grady with a box of leftovers. "A little something for your kindness."

He tipped his hat and grinned. "What kind of gentleman would I be if I'd made you walk?" He opened my door, then grabbed the box before I set it on my lap. "I'll take my thank-you gift now."

By the time he'd made it to his side of the truck, there was a taco hanging partway out of his mouth. "This is really good."

"Thanks." I looked away to hide the heat rising in my cheeks. If I could just feed people and get compliments all day, I would be in heaven. That was my kind of magic.

We idled in front of Blessed Bee until the chicken wraps and shrimp tacos were gone. Then, he dusted his palms and smiled. "That was fantastic. I didn't realize how hungry I was. I must've forgotten to eat today."

"Forgotten to eat?" I guffawed. "What does that even mean?"

"I was busy." His gaze shifted to the phone buzzing in the cup holder.

"I've never been that busy," I said. "If you'd told me sooner, I could've packed you something to eat earlier."

He tucked the lid of his box in neatly but made no move to check the buzzing phone.

"I wish you would've come by for lunch today. I own a café, you know? I literally make food all day long."

"Busy," he repeated. The phone buzzed again, and Grady lifted it to peek at the screen. He dropped it back in the cup holder with a deep frown.

"You could've placed a carry-out order." I stared at the side of his head while he shifted into gear. "What were you doing all day?"

Grady's lips twitched. He pointed the truck toward my place and pressed the gas. "I processed your golf cart as evidence, so you can drive it again. At your own risk, as usual."

"Hey, Blue isn't new like your fancy truck, but she runs great," I said. I looped his words around in my head. "You finished? Does that mean Blue's not a crime scene anymore?"

"I collected what I could and dropped the evidence bags off at the lab. Now I don't want to see you walking around town for a few days until we get this cleared up. Agreed?"

"No walking alone at night. Got it."

"No walking alone," he corrected. "Any time."

I turned my wrist with the rubber fitness band back and forth under his nose. "I have to walk. You know the trouble this thing gives me if I don't."

He glanced at my arm. "Then find a friend and use the buddy system."

I frowned. "I'm not ten years old."

"No, but you are in danger, so think of it this way: someone's made a direct threat against you. If you're out walking alone and that person gets ahold of you, you might never take another step. Wouldn't your fitness band prefer you take a short break from walking rather than die?"

"I don't know. My fitness band is very demanding."

"You know what's even safer than walking with a buddy? Indoor jumping jacks or jogging up and down your steps, maybe one of those Zumba videos. No more walking alone until I arrest Craig's killer, and no more asking questions about him or the murder. That just gets you into trouble."

"Can I ask you a question?" I took his lack of response as a yes. "Were you busy chasing leads when you forgot to eat? Do you have any good ones? For example, who specifically should I avoid because they might be the killer?"

Grady's cheek plumped up with the lazy half smile I enjoyed. "I was busy doing my job, and I'd worry a lot less about you if you'd stick to doing yours."

"I'll try," I said. "First, I'd love to know if that was a new lead you got when your phone buzzed earlier."

"That was my mother-in-law," he said flatly. "She's planning another visit."

"Does she like iced tea?" I asked.

Grady snorted. "I'm pretty sure she hates everything except her grandson. Especially me."

I considered putting my hand on his as comfort but kept it to myself instead. "I'm sure you're wrong about that last part," I said. I couldn't imagine the complication of losing a spouse so young, then having to maintain lifelong relationships with the in-laws. Especially if my in-laws weren't my biggest fans in the first place. "What's not to like about you?"

Grady gave me a wry smile. "If you sincerely want to know, you can ask my mother-in-law. She's usually dying to tell anyone in a mood to listen, and some who aren't."

I gave him a profoundly disappointed expression. "Well, then she won't want to talk to me," I said. "I can't tolerate liars."

Grady's smile brightened as the truck rolled to a stop outside my carriage house. "I didn't have your keys to lock up after I left."

"I've got it." I grabbed my key ring from my purse and climbed out, eager to see Blue without a knife in her head.

Grady met me at the carriage house door and opened it for me. I flipped on the light, and my mouth fell open. Blue looked amazing. She was as clean and shiny as the day I'd painted her. "You washed her?"

He folded his arms and rocked back on his heels. "Yeah."

I circled her in awe. "She looks beautiful. Thank you. You really didn't have to do this."

"She was filthy, Swan. Someone had to. The wheels were caked in mud and sand. Dead bugs were layered so thick on the windshield and headlights I don't know how you saw to drive."

"I stuck my head out the side," I teased. I set a hand on the seat back, prepared to climb inside when something else caught my eye. The slit in the headrest where pie filling had oozed over the knife was now covered with a large silver star cut from duct tape. I turned to face Grady, my throat too full of emotion to swallow. "You covered the hole," I said, "with a star."

"Do you like it?" he asked, locking sincere gray eyes on me.

"Yes." The word was barely a whisper.

Detective Grady Hays had been a big-shot U.S. Marshal before he'd arrived in Charm looking for a new start. I could only imagine how much carrying that marshal star had meant to him, and seeing the one he'd made for me left me warm in uncomfortable ways. I reached for his hand without thinking and gave his sturdy fingers a squeeze. "I'm really glad to know you, Grady Hays. Anyone who can't see how wonderful you are must be mean, bitter, or blind."

A moment later, Grady squeezed back.

CHAPTER

❧

NINE

Grady's phone rang, effectively ruining the moment. He released my hand, then fished the device from his pocket and pressed it to his ear. "Detective Hays." His gaze darted to mine. "When?" He shook his head slowly. "Give me five minutes. I'm on my way."

"What happened?" I asked. "Who was that? Is someone else hurt?" *Or worse.*

Grady tucked the phone back inside his pocket and raked his fingers through his hair. "That was Mrs. Miller. Her rental was broken into while she and the rest of Craig's family went out to meet Judy for dinner. All of Craig's things are gone."

"Another break-in?" I asked, nearly unable to believe my ears. "That's two in one day."

"Don't forget what happened to your golf cart. I'll count it as three."

"What does it mean?" I asked, baffled. Craig was dead. What else could the maniac who killed him want?

Grady shifted his weight and looked through the

open carriage house doors. "I'd say whoever is doing this is either trying to create chaos to keep me and the rest of Charm's limited police force busy running in circles or they're smart enough to know time is of the essence and removing any evidence that links them to Craig's death."

"That was what I thought about Judy's room," I said. "I figured the burglar didn't take anything because they didn't find what they were looking for. Craig hadn't brought his luggage to my place yet. Now it's been stolen from his mother's rental. So Craig had something the killer wanted," I guessed. "That could be the motive for his murder." I chewed my lip, feeling a familiar buzz in my chest. "We have to get his things back."

Grady narrowed his eyes.

"Whatever the burglar is after will be the clue we need to know who killed him."

Grady lifted a palm. "How about you go inside and do whatever it is that you do every night to prepare for business tomorrow. I'll walk you to your door."

"Will you keep me posted?" I asked, locking Blue safely inside the carriage house.

"How about I promise to keep you in the loop on a need to know basis?" he suggested, stopping at my home's front door.

I sensed a small problem with his suggestion. "Who decides if I need to know?"

He smiled, and I immediately regretted asking.

I locked myself inside the house, giving him a sarcastic thumbs-up as he drove away.

The home was strangely still around me. I peered

through the dark foyer toward the café, where the wall of windows showcased endless black water and a velvet night's sky. The staircase that led to my living quarters was encased in shadows. Neither direction seemed inviting to my thoroughly shaken heart. "Hello?" I called, hoping Judy was home, but had forgotten to turn on a light.

The front door rattled before I could make a decision on which direction to go first, and my pulse thundered. I grabbed a beach umbrella from the stand by the door and raised it to my shoulder like a baseball bat, then peeked out.

Jasper and Judy stood inches apart on the porch, whispering and looking stricken.

I expelled a *whoosh* of relief and felt my shoulders droop in response.

The knob turned and the pair stepped inside. They started at the sight of me, and Judy pocketed her borrowed house key.

I forced a smile as I returned the big umbrella to its holder beside my always-packed beach bag and favorite flip-flops. "Hello," I said. "What's up?"

Jasper frowned. "How long have you been standing there?"

"Not long. How was dinner with the Millers?" Did they know about the break-in?

Jasper worked his jaw but didn't answer.

Instinct told me that any man who'd move in on a widow so soon was untrustworthy in general, but was he a killer? He had been at the reception, with access to Craig. He'd also been at my house with Judy when Blue was stabbed, and here when Judy's room was tossed. *But he couldn't have broken into Mrs. Miller's rental home while simultaneously having dinner with her.*

Judy groaned. "Dinner was okay. Mrs. Miller cried the whole time, which meant *I* cried the whole time, so no one ate anything, and I'm pretty sure everyone in the restaurant thought we were crazy."

"Lucky thing you had Jasper along," I said, secretly wondering if the Millers found it as strange and mildly concerning as I did to see him playing the role of supportive boyfriend right now.

"No," Judy said. "I didn't think the Millers would understand if I invited someone along, especially a man, so Jasper dropped me off and ran some errands, then picked me up afterward."

My gaze jumped back to Jasper. I took a step back and longed to pull Judy along with me.

"She needed time alone with the Millers, and I had things to get done," he said.

I unlocked the door to the second floor and held it for them to pass, climbing the steps slowly behind them, wondering if my guests were all as oblivious to the continued crime spree as they seemed to be. I headed for my kitchen and poured a glass of ice water. "Did you guys hear that Mrs. Miller's rental was broken into while you were at dinner?"

"What?" Judy asked. "Are you serious?"

"Yeah." I wet my lips, wondering how much I should say. "Someone also vandalized my golf cart tonight. Detective Hays was here with me when he got the call from Mrs. Miller."

Judy dropped into the nearest chair. "I don't understand."

"What did they take?" Jasper asked.

I lifted my gaze to Judy's. "All of Craig's things."

Judy tapped her phone screen. "I'm texting Mrs. Miller to see if there's anything I can do."

I pulled a chopping block and knife onto the counter before checking my fridge and cupboards for ingredients.

"I'm starving," Judy said. "Since I didn't eat dinner."

Jasper patted his stomach. "I haven't eaten since the tacos I had here this afternoon."

"I'm already on it," I said, chopping veggies and compiling a mental list of quick-fix dishes.

Fifteen minutes later, I'd washed a pile of zucchinis, split them into quarters lengthwise, drizzled the slices with olive oil, and covered them in parmesan, then popped them into the oven. I unlidded a container of sweet potato chips I'd baked Thursday night, then gave the dill dip in my refrigerator a stir before setting both on the kitchen island.

Judy leaned against the counter, her phone in hand. "Mrs. Miller wrote back. She said Detective Hays is there now, and there's nothing I can do. She'll see me tomorrow when she's calmer."

I squeezed her hand and went back to work, keeping my hands busy and my mouth shut.

Slowly, the house filled with the warm, buttery

scents of baking parmesan and zucchini. I kept going until the island was full of snacks and glasses filled with Old-Fashioned Sweet Tea.

Judy joined me at the counter and dragged an apple slice through the peanut butter and honey mixture, and Jasper went for another mouthful of dill dip using a slice of French loaf.

Once they seemed content at the island, I slipped into the master bathroom for a hot shower. I didn't realize how badly I needed it until I was under the water, steaming up the room and unknotting my bunched muscles.

Twenty minutes later, I'd dressed in a cotton shorts and camisole set and climbed into bed with my laptop to scan the *Town Charmer* blog for recent news and gossip I hadn't already heard—or experienced firsthand. None of it was useful, but one article was far more interesting than the others: an exclusive interview with Cynthia Preston, Craig's girlfriend on the side. According to Cynthia, she and Craig had been college sweethearts, but his fast rise to fame and single-minded dedication to work had eventually pulled them apart. She stuck around after the breakup, attending events as his plus-one and traveling to his house when he needed a friend. It wasn't until he met Judy that Craig began to distance himself from Cynthia.

I scrolled through the photos of Cynthia and Craig that were included in the article, then opened a new window to look at her social media accounts. They had an undeniable amount of history, and surely a stronger than average connection to stay close after a breakup, but he'd made his choice, and it wasn't Cynthia. *At least not full time, the cheater.*

She had no criminal record, and her social media content centered on her work as an international publicist. It was mostly photos of food, fancy events, sunsets, and her face in front of a thousand perfect backdrops: Australian beaches. Venice canals. Mumbai skyscrapers. I moved her lower on my list of potential killers. Additionally, Cynthia hadn't reached the beach for nearly an hour after the police had arrived. Hard to be the killer when she wasn't even in town at the time Craig died.

I clicked the weather link in the *Town Charmer*'s sidebar. Thinking of Craig's untimely death had reminded me of the vigil tomorrow night. A hurricane passing the southern coast of Florida was throwing a lot of wind our way. Charm was in for a round of high winds and potentially a storm. Hopefully both would hold off for Mrs. Miller.

Restless energy soon whirled in my heart and head, erasing the calm and fatigue I'd felt in the shower. I set my computer aside and went in search of a way to burn off steam without leaving home. The kitchen was empty when I left my bedroom, and so were the trays of food I'd set out before my shower. I could hear the low murmur of voices in Judy's room as she ran down a list of concerns about handling Craig's funeral and memorial details once his body was released to go home. Jasper seemed to be doing his best to encourage her.

I crept downstairs. The darkened café seemed less intimidating with people upstairs than it had when I'd arrived home earlier. I passed through Sun, Sand, and Tea, dragging my fingertips over the long service counter and smiling. *I own a seaside café and iced tea shop in Charm. I get to make my family's recipes and share them with people all day while wearing flip-flops and messy ponytails. I own the big Victorian house on the cliff that I've admired all my life, and I get to see my aunts any time I want.* The word *blessed* came to mind, and now that my heart was calm and my head was clear once more, I grabbed a notepad and pen from behind the counter and made notes for my aunts' over-the-top video. I had no idea what I was doing behind the camera or otherwise, but I had the internet and a head on my shoulders. For Aunt Clara and Aunt Fran, I would figure it out.

I wove through the tables and crossed beneath the archway into my home's former ballroom, the site of my future café expansion. I lit a small lamp and admired the cavernous space. Beyond the series of tall, narrow windows, continuous white rolling waves crashed against the darkness of the beach. It was the perfect indoor spot to tape some of their footage, especially with the storms headed our way.

I cracked open one window, just enough to enjoy the rhythmic whoosh of the ocean as I worked, then grabbed a spot on the floor across from the windows and rested my notepad on my thighs. The steady back and forth of the tide was soothing and predictable, quieting the remaining noise in my scrambled mind.

I'd been through so much in the past twenty-four hours, spoken with so many people and experienced so many things. There was a killer loose in Charm, and I may have already spoke to him. *I might be housing him.* I imagined Pete stabbing his partner, then I swapped Pete's face for Jasper's in my mind. I even tried Ryan the reporter, then Judy. None of them fit.

A sudden flash outside the glass snapped me back to the moment. I stilled my pen on the paper and waited for a second strike of heat lightning or the rolling sound of thunder that never came. Pushing to my feet, I forced my lungs to keep working as I approached the window in search of a cause for the flash.

Shadows stretched and waved over the sand as dark clouds raced across the moon. I imagined killers hiding around the dark garden corners, maybe even on the veranda just beyond the glass. I shut and locked the window as quickly as my bumbling fingers could manage, then hightailed it back upstairs where I wasn't alone and no one outside could reach me.

I fell asleep hoping no one inside would want to.

CHAPTER

TEN

I shot upright in my bed several hours later, coated in a sticky sheen of sweat and mentally clutching the slick remains of my nightmare. I'd been outside, somewhere dark and damp, in danger, hunted. I shivered head to toe with lingering unease. *Just a dream*, I told myself. *Not real*.

Beside me, Maggie swung her long white tail over the bed's edge and rotated her ears like little feline satellite dishes, tuning in to things I couldn't begin to know.

Wind whistled around the window frames and rattled the glass. There were dozens of windows in my home, all old and in need of replacement. The combined sounds registered somewhere between a band of wailing banshees and a demolition crew, no doubt contributing to the nightmare.

I squinted at the glow of small green numbers on my alarm clock: 6:15 a.m. I turned off the buzzer that was set to wake me in fifteen minutes and went to check the dreary overcast sky outside. "Thanks for sharing, Florida," I mumbled.

The house was silent, aside from the maniacal winds trying to dismantle it. My guests were somehow sleeping through the racket, and I was eternally thankful for a moment of solitude in a weekend of chaos. I shuffled into the kitchen to start a pot of coffee, then took my full mug out to the deck where I could enjoy the balmy morning temperature and thirty-mile-per-hour winds.

Maggie appeared at my feet and wound around them a few times before I scooped her onto my lap. "Hello, darling," I said, sinking my face into her fluffy white fur. "Are you following me?"

She arched and purred as I stroked her soft fur, kneading her claws on my thighs.

"Hey." I put her back down. "Those are my bare legs, lady, not a pair of scratching posts."

She trotted to the edge of the deck and watched sandpipers race the waves.

I propped my feet against the railing and formulated a plan for the day. I didn't always open Sun, Sand, and Tea on Sundays, because business was usually slow to the point of costing more to keep the lights on than I made all day. It didn't make sense to open today, especially when there was so much prep work to do for my aunts' video, and I had a great idea for making Aunt Fran's backdrop sketches come to life. On top of all that, I really wanted to attend Summer Splash. I'd never missed the event when I'd lived in Charm before, and this was my first summer back home, so it felt particularly important that I get there.

I ran through my tasks as the caffeine kicked in, then went to change for my morning walk. Halfway to the front door, I remembered I wasn't supposed to walk alone for a while, per Grady's orders. My fitness bracelet had already told me twice to **BE MORE ACTIVE**. Luckily, it thought I was walking while I brushed my teeth and counted the strokes as steps.

I took my time weaving through Sun, Sand, and Tea for some indoor exercise, imagining what it would be like to finally trade in the mismatched thrift shop seating for cohesive, good quality pieces. In a clear space between tables I turned to face the deck, stretching my arms overhead, enjoying the ocean view. Grady had suggested I exercise indoors, but stretching was the best I could do for now. Jumping jacks and high-knees were out of the question until I bought a sports bra. I lunged. I reached for my toes. I windmilled my arms.

I missed the beach.

The wind had stopped abusing my windows, but a thick layer of fog had moved in. When I'd gone through all the stretches I knew, I moved closer to the glass for a better view of the vast apparition now reaching over the earth and sea. The flash I'd seen the night before edged into my mind. What had I seen, exactly?

I went outside to water the roses, which was not the same as walking alone because I wasn't leaving my property. While I was out there, I checked the space outside the ballroom windows for footprints and found plenty. Unfortunately, anyone could have walked through the gardens and along the back side of my home. Locals, tourists, policemen, wedding guests. I should've examined the perimeter yesterday morning so I would be aware if something had changed.

Ten minutes later, I'd loaded a couple of full tea dispensers into Blue's back seat, dropped a shopping bag of plastic cups and business cards inside, and was on my way to town. My aunts had agreed to give away tea samples from their booth today, and Amelia had me covered tomorrow. My heart swelled with appreciation as I took in the fresh ocean air.

The ride through town was peppered with early risers and artists setting up their booths for the Summer Splash kickoff extravaganza. According to signs posted everywhere, the local childcare center and dance studio would have a Tiny Tot parade at eleven, the Wild Bunch Rodeo Team would show off their roping skills at one, and local bands would be performing throughout the day. The entire week was always filled with nonstop fun, and I was more than a little disappointed not to be able to set up shop on Main Street for a few days.

I nabbed a front-row parking spot outside Molly's Market, Charm's general store, and ducked inside for a few things. Molly's was one of the first shops to open every morning, and I stopped by most days after my morning walk, usually for a Popsicle. Mr. Waters, the owner, had named the place after his daughter, Molly, who had once been my babysitter and now had a brood of her own.

"Hey, Everly," Mr. Waters called from the register. Five decades of chain-smoking had whittled his voice into a windy rasp, and a lifetime in the sun had weathered his skin to the perfect shade for a leather tote bag. He'd been the cautionary tale my grandma had used to enforce my use of sunblock and avoidance of nicotine.

"Hello." I stopped at the counter with a smile. "Are you ready for Summer Splash?"

Mr. Waters waggled his bushy salt-and-pepper brows and smoothed his matching mop of hair. "I was born ready. How about you? Where will your booth be this week? You know I've always got room for you at my side if you haven't reserved a spot yet."

"Thanks, Mr. Waters," I said. "You're very kind, but Amelia and my aunts will be distributing my tea samples for me. I have some folks staying at my place now, so I won't be able to keep a booth this year. I feel obligated to be home as much as I can."

"Southern hospitality." He groaned. "Well, I certainly understand that. What else can you do?"

Mr. Waters rubbed the skin beneath his glasses. "My wife and I were sorry to hear about what happened to that man. Judy always seemed like such a sweet kid. I never knew her well, but she always had a smile when she stopped in here, and she always used her manners. Kids with manners aren't nearly as common as they should be. How's she holding up?" he asked, a look of parental concern in his eyes. "I don't know what Molly would have done in a situation like that. It's just awful. Unthinkable, really."

"Judy's doing okay, considering what she's been through," I said. "I think she's kind of in shock right now. It will be a process, but she'll get through this."

"Good." He nodded. "Well, I hope you can at least get away long enough to enjoy some of the shows and demonstrations. I know how you love your cowboys."

I laughed. "I did not know you knew that."

"Honey, there are no secrets in this town," he said with a wink.

I really hoped that wasn't true. Then again, no one seemed to know whoever was on a crime spree this weekend, so apparently someone was able to keep a few things to themselves.

"Is there anything I can help you find?" Mr. Waters asked.

"Nope. Thank you."

The phone beside his cash register rang and I took my leave, heading straight to my most frequented section of the store: home improvements. I picked up an armload of white drop cloths, then filled a shopping bag with battery-operated candles, a few photo mats and frames, Sharpie markers, and fabric paints.

Mr. Waters welcomed me back to the register a few minutes later. "That was my wife," he said, tipping his head toward the old-fashioned phone. "She said Craig's mom had her rental home broken into last night. Can you believe that? What's happening to this town?"

I lined up my items on the checkout counter. "I

bet you hear all sorts of things working here," I said. "The whole town probably comes through at least once a week."

"I try to stay on top of what's important."

"Have you heard anything else?" I asked. "Have people been sharing stories or speculating about who could have killed Craig Miller?"

"No, nothing like that," he said, "but the new real estate agent was in here around closing time last night and said Judy's looking to move home to Charm permanently."

"Really?" She hadn't mentioned that to me, but I could certainly understand wanting to come home after a trauma. After all, what was left for her in Massachusetts?

"Apparently she's thinking of buying her family a nice home closer to town. Plus something for herself on the bay. Can you believe that? She's not even thirty and talking about buying multiple homes." He scanned my items with his wand. "Judy belongs in Charm. You do. I do." With a shrug, he added, "Locals can't explain it, and tourists don't understand it, but Charmers belong in Charm. It calls to us."

He wasn't wrong, but I supposed everyone felt that way about their hometown.

I paid for my items and said goodbye, then headed back to my cart with a new idea on my mind. Could someone in Judy's family have gotten rid of Craig as a means of motivating Judy to move back on the island? Jasper was the first name that came to mind, but I didn't know all the people from Judy's family or her past. There could be others. Maybe I hadn't even thought of the person who'd done all this yet.

Maggie sat on the passenger seat of my golf cart, waiting.

"Well, hello," I cooed. "You followed me into town?" I dropped my packages onto the passenger-side floorboards, then climbed behind the steering wheel. "I don't want to accuse you of being a harbinger or anything, but the last time you were following me this closely, bad things started happening."

She stared at me, her green eyes luminous.

"Well, you're welcome to visit my aunts with me," I told her. "You know they adore you."

I dug a hair tie from my bag and squinted down the street. The heavy morning breeze had returned, thinning the fog and working its voodoo on my already unruly hair. I wrangled the mess into a ponytail before starting Blue's engine. This was going to be a day of obstacles, I could feel it.

Maggie meowed, drawing my attention back to her bright green eyes.

"No, you're right," I said. "I shouldn't have called you a harbinger. Bad things are already happening to me whether you're around or not, and you are a cat, not an omen."

When I was confident she'd accepted my apology, I motored onto the mostly empty street and headed for Blessed Bee. I slowed at the sight of a woman with an overstuffed handbag and a weird fedora who was hurrying down the sidewalk.

She stopped at the corner and turned her head, preparing to cross the street, when we made eye contact. *Cynthia?* The only time I'd seen her, she had been wearing a rumpled red sundress, fresh off an airplane. Now she was in black capri pants and a matching sleeveless black blouse, looking neat as a pin except for the pin-striped shirtsleeve hanging out of her handbag and the man's fedora.

Cynthia turned away and picked up the pace, apparently having changed her mind about crossing the street. I couldn't help wondering why.

I pressed the gas pedal and followed along at her side, passing Blessed Bee. I waved at the aunts, who were setting up a Summer Splash display on the sidewalk, as I motored by.

"Cynthia," I called. "I'm Everly Swan. I own Sun, Sand, and Tea. We met Friday night. Do you remember?"

She kept moving, pretending not to notice me hollering across the seat of my bright blue golf cart.

"I'm so sorry about your loss," I said, desperate to stop her. I nearly gagged on the sentiment. *Her loss.* I loathed cheaters and the partners who knowingly engaged in relationships with unavailable men and women. Much as I tried not to judge a situation I'd never been in, I was certain I'd never tolerate a man who wanted to add me on as a secondary love interest. I'd rather eat my weight in chocolate and cry over a broken heart.

Cynthia stopped walking.

"Can we talk?" I asked. "Please? I read the article

about you on our local blog, and I realized you must have known Craig better than anyone. I hoped you could help me figure some things out."

"I'm sorry," she said. "I'm busy. I have somewhere to be." She took notice of the sleeve hanging out of her bag, and her cheeks flushed red. She quickly pushed the material out of view.

The designer leather hobo didn't seem like a reasonable place to keep clothing, but I didn't ask. Who knew how long she'd entertain my questions. "Do you have any idea who would've wanted to hurt Craig?"

She glared. "You mean besides Judy?"

I lifted my shoulders and bit my tongue.

"Her fiancé was cheating on her," she said, "and she knew it. Of course Judy wanted to kill him. She probably wanted to kill me too. It doesn't hurt that she's probably entitled to half his net worth now. Tomorrow's headline should be: *Townie gets away with murder and a billion-dollar bonus.*"

I was speechless. Was I being naive by not considering that Judy might have been mad enough to hurt him? Would she be motivated by revenge? By money?

"You're probably not willing to think your sweet friend could do such a thing. Right?"

"Right," I said, feeling the weight of truth in the word. I might not have been as close to Judy as I had been to some of my other childhood friends, and I hadn't kept in touch with her over the years, but I had seen plenty of her in the last few days, and she wasn't a murderer. She was a confused, shocked, and grieving woman. "I don't think she did this, but I really want to find out who did. I promised her I would."

Cynthia's gaze dropped to her shoes for a long beat, then bounced back up to meet my eyes. "Do you really think you can?"

"I hope so." Sincerity flooded the words, and I watched as Cynthia's expression softened. "I could use some help, since I didn't know him or anything about his life."

"Okay," she said, speaking without hostility for the first time. "Have you talked to Pete about their work?"

"No." We'd talked about Maui and Judy, but not his job.

"Do you know Pete?" Cynthia asked.

"Not really, but I'd like to."

"Maybe you should ask him about the companies he and Craig were working with," she suggested. "It was Craig's job to dig through all the files on a company's computer server and look for patterns in the data. Sometimes he found ways to save companies millions by cross-promoting items that are frequently purchased by the same households. Sometimes he found evidence of fraud, theft, or embezzlement. Maybe someone didn't want to be found out."

Mr. Granger's round face popped into my head. "Thanks," I said. "I'll do that."

She heaved a sigh. "Whatever. I have to go."

I leaned across the seat, stretching an arm in her direction, my business card pinched between two fingertips. "If you think of anything else, please call me."

She stared at the little paper rectangle. "Fine." Cynthia reached for the card, and as her sleeve rode up her arm, I spotted a braided hemp bracelet on her wrist—exactly like the one Craig had worn the night he'd died.

"Where'd you get that bracelet?" I asked, my tone sharp and accusatory.

"It's mine." She jerked her arm back hard, snatching the business card and frightening Maggie out of the golf cart.

"That's Craig's bracelet," I accused, fumbling to free my phone from my pocket.

"It's mine," she snarled.

"No." My phone fell from my pocket and bounced on the floor at my feet. "I saw that bracelet on him before he died. How'd you get it?"

"It's mine!" she shouted, drawing the attention of a small group passing on the street. "Craig and I each bought one in Cancun on spring break the year we met. That was the night I fell in love with him, and he loves me too, so we never take them off!"

"What about the hat?" I asked. "And the shirt in your bag?" I furrowed my brows.

She didn't answer.

"I'm calling Detective Hays." I dialed Grady on speaker.

Cynthia turned tail and ran.

"Detective Hays," he answered.

"Hey!" I called after her, slamming my foot against the gas pedal until it hit the floorboards. "Stop!"

"Everly?" Grady barked. "What's going on?"

Cynthia darted down an alley and cut through a restricted loading area behind the shops on the next block.

I jammed my foot on the brake. "Darn! She got away," I groaned. I wanted to blame Grady for insisting I take my ancient golf cart everywhere, but the truth was I couldn't have outrun her on foot either. She was like a big blond ninja. "I think Cynthia Preston is the one who broke into Mrs. Miller's rental."

A gust of breath came over the phone speaker, and I could practically see Grady pinching the bridge of his nose. "Why are you harassing folks at eight thirty on a Sunday morning?"

My mouth fell open.

"I just disconnected my second call from a concerned tourist saying that a woman in a bright blue golf cart was terrorizing, or possibly trying to abduct, another woman on the street."

I gasped. "That's not what was happening."

"Were you in your vehicle harassing her while she screamed?"

My cheeks heated in embarrassment. "I didn't mean to cause a scene. I just wanted to know where she got the bracelet she was wearing. I saw it on Craig's wrist at the reception. Judy and the photographer saw it too. I think Cynthia broke into Judy's room and Mrs. Miller's rental looking for it. She said it was special to her."

"If he had it on at the reception, then it's probably

still on him," Grady said. "At the very least, it's with his body. The bracelet wouldn't have made it back to his luggage."

"Maybe," I conceded, "but can you please just talk to her?"

"Everly? I like you," he said.

Aww. My chest warmed. "I like you too."

"Thank you." His voice was low and eerily calm. "And because I like you, I don't want to have to arrest you for obstruction in my murder investigation, so I'm asking you kindly and for the last time to knock it off."

I hiked my shoulders up to my ears. This was not where I thought the conversation was going. "I didn't do anything."

"Swan?" Grady said. "I need a confirmation on your immediate disinvolvement in this matter."

"Will you at least go after Cynthia?"

"I will agree talk to her about your public altercation."

"Fine."

"Fine," he agreed. "Still waiting on the confirmation from you."

"I won't bother Cynthia again," I said, making a wide U-turn on Main Street and heading back toward Blessed Bee. "If I see her on the street, I will go the other way."

"That's a start," he said. "I'll take what I can get. Where are you going now?"

"I'm delivering tea to my aunts."

"Good. Stay busy, then go home and stay there if

you can. I have a lead to run down, but I'll check on you later. Until then, remember your promise."

I rolled my eyes and disconnected our call. Cynthia was unhinged, but she'd made a good point about Craig's business. What if he had uncovered something criminal?

As soon as I found Pete, I was going to make him something utterly delicious and hope his lips could be loosened with enough butter.

CHAPTER

ELEVEN

I swung Blue into a parking space outside Blessed Bee. My great-aunts were setting up their Buzz about Bees display on the sidewalk outside their shop, including a table of beekeeping paraphernalia that made my skin crawl. Thankfully, they didn't bring any bees this year. I'd lost more than one snow cone to those little devils as a child. They'd chase me relentlessly until I threw the treat away, or worse. Upending one particularly delicious cherry snow cone on my lap at fifteen had left lasting emotional scars.

"There you are," Aunt Fran said, sounding mildly exasperated.

I was shamefully thankful for her irritation. Maybe her problem could take my mind off the things that were bothering me: Grady Hays, Cynthia Preston, Craig's killer, and whoever was following me. "Here I am," I said. "I brought two full tea dispensers and some cups for samples. I thought you could fill your cooler with ice around lunchtime and start handing them out to anyone who looks thirsty."

Aunt Clara kissed my forehead, then went to collect one of the tea dispensers. "Perfect. It's set to be a steamer today if we don't get rained on. I'm already sweating in my bobby socks."

Aunt Fran stared at her sister's feet. "I don't know why you wear bobby socks. We live at the beach. Wear sandals."

"I can't ride my bicycle in sandals," Aunt Clara said, "and I hate that *flip flip flip* sound sandals make when they smack my heels."

I delivered the second dispenser to the table and positioned it beside the first. Yep. Fran was in a mood.

Aunt Fran stared at the mass of shopping bags on Blue's back seat. Her long-sleeved silk blouse puffed and beat in the wind. It must be nice, I supposed, to be rail-thin and of a certain age. She was perpetually cold, even in the stifling summer heat. "Is all the rest of that for us too? What'd you buy? Tablecloths?"

I beamed proudly. "Those are drop cloths. I did a little research last night on budget theater groups and learned that painted drop cloths can be hung from a clothes line that moves in a circle between posts with the help of pulleys. I bought Sharpies to draw outlines of the scenes you sketched yesterday, and I think I can sew the finished pieces together to create a visual passage of time."

Aunt Clara's eyes went wide as she attempted to hold her messy silver and blond bun in place despite the breeze's hearty attempts to blow it down. "That's so smart. Isn't it smart, Fran?"

Fran nodded, but she didn't look half as impressed as her sister. "Clara and I were up all night finalizing a script we can both believe in."

"And our wardrobes," Aunt Clara added.

"Great!" I clapped my palms together. "I'll work on the backdrops, and we'll be ready to start filming."

Aunt Clara pressed her lips into a flat line and leaned her head toward her shoulder. "As soon as we get the props," she said.

I paused. "What props?"

"And actors," she added.

I felt my eyebrows reaching for my hairline. I looked at Aunt Fran for signs her sister was joking, but she just looked dejected. "It's a three-minute video," I said to Aunt Clara. "There isn't time for actors."

Aunt Clara waved her hand dismissively, as if to clear up the confusion. "Well, no. I guess they aren't actors. They won't have speaking roles. They'll be more like extras." She waited a beat. When I didn't respond, she added, "*Extras* are what people *in the business* call the background folks that the actors don't talk to, and even if they do talk to them, the extras are irrelevant to the plot."

I tilted my face to the sky and counted silently for a few seconds. I'd thought we'd be ready to film as soon as I painted the drop cloths. "The deadline for application submissions is next week. Where are you going to find extras that fast?"

"Amelia stopped by this morning," Aunt Clara said. "We'd completely forgotten about all those plays she was involved in during high school, but she volunteered to lend her expertise and help however she can. She's going to run the auditions for us, and she even volunteered her dad to help paint props." Aunt Clara wagged her narrow silver brows. "If I was twenty years younger…" she said suggestively.

"Oh my." I laughed. "Well, I'm glad they can help." Amelia loved the theater. She was a wealth of knowledge in that area, and her father was an excellent painter, so whatever he was helping with was sure to shine.

Aunt Clara nodded. "We'll start taping as soon as that one climbs out of her mood." She pointed at her sister.

Aunt Fran harrumphed and plopped into a folding chair.

"What's wrong?" I asked Fran. "Did something happen? Is there anything I can do?"

"She's mad at Mayor Dunfree," Aunt Clara explained.

Aunt Fran scowled. "That's because I tried to talk sensibly to the man, but he doesn't understand basic human compassion. Not only did Mayor Dummy refuse to budge on Mrs. Miller's paper lantern request, he's also decided not to retire this fall. That means he'll remain seated until next year's election."

"Well, thanks for trying," I said. "Wait a minute." I replayed her commentary on the mayor and frowned. "So, Mayor Dunfree is planning to relinquish his office during the election next November? Or do you mean he intends to continue on as mayor, but you think he'll lose the election?"

Aunt Fran inched her chin up. "I think he's decided to rule the roost until he dies, and I've resolved not to allow it. He's dragging our town down. We used to be built on mutual support and community values. Now it's all about the rules." Her scowl deepened on the final word. "Unless I come to my senses before then, I'll be running for mayor in fifteen months." She slapped one palm against the tabletop. "I should probably get a campaign strategy together. I won't be the only one running for Dummy's spot. That little Bracie Gracie is still planning to take over."

Clara swatted her sister's shoulder. "Don't call people names. It's not nice, and you're about sixty years too old for it."

I chuckled. Bracie Gracie's given name was Mary Grace Chatsworth, and she was the worst. She'd been in my Outdoor Girls troop when we were children, and she'd told everyone I didn't have a mother because my mother had run off to be a circus clown. In truth, my mother had died, and most people had the common courtesy not to bring it up, but Gracie used Mom's absence as a means of humiliating me. I wasn't completely over that. "I'll help you," I said. "You can beat them both, if that's what you want. This town loves you, and they should because you're amazing. Right now, I need to go home and get busy on these drop-cloth backdrops." I leaned in to give Aunt

Clara a kiss on her soft cheek. The bell sleeves of her cream-colored dress snapped in the wind as she gave me a quick squeeze.

A gust swept down the street, wreaking havoc on banners and signs. Those that didn't blow away would need to be re-anchored as soon as possible. A woman in knee-length shorts and a cat shirt stood dumbly as her sun hat was wrenched off her head and tossed half a block down the street.

I was instantly thankful Mr. Waters had kept so many battery-operated candles on hand. Real candles would never stay lit in this weather, and to reschedule would be heartbreaking. Hopefully my whip-thin aunts didn't blow away before they got to my place.

A fiddler came around the corner, sawing away on a hearty rendition of "Devil Went Down to Georgia," apparently unaffected by the aggressive wind. A group of men in chaps clapped along behind him. Boys in dark jeans and cowboy hats swung their fists overhead and hooted. Two little cowgirls in pink boots and white hats stretched a sign between them announcing the arrival of a line-dance troupe. Their ruffled gingham tops and thick, layered petticoats fluttered.

I smiled brightly at the tiny dancers and excellent fiddling. I tried not to stare too long or hard at the full-grown cowboys among them, but their enthusiasm was contagious. Before I had time to think better of it, I tossed my head back and gave a whoop along with them.

"Maybe we can get a few of those strapping cowboys

to appear in the video," Aunt Clara said. Her grin spread ear to ear as the group danced slowly forward.

"I'd better get going before I start picking them out myself," I said, returning her grin. I waved goodbye and climbed back behind the wheel.

"We'll see you tonight," Clara promised. "Let us know if there's anything you need before then."

A rusted green pickup came to a stop at the intersection when the fiddler and his crew cleared the way. The words *Wild Bunch Rodeo Team* were painted on the door, and I smiled at their chosen name, one they shared with Butch Cassidy's infamous gang. The driver adjusted his black Stetson, glancing briefly in my direction.

My stomach sank. I stared as the truck rolled into the distance, slowly being blocked from view by the crowd following the fiddler.

I performed a three-point turn at my first opportunity and went in the other direction, trying to ignore the fact that the driver of the pickup looked nerve-rackingly similar to my ex. Wyatt wouldn't dare come to Charm, and he couldn't belong to any rodeo team. The doctors had told him he'd never ride again. I'd heard it myself.

I stepped on the gas pedal and shook off the itchy thoughts. My newly healed heart couldn't afford to rehash my time with Wyatt or any of the pain his rejection had caused me. I had enough on my plate already.

By eight o'clock, I'd finished two of Aunt Fran's period backdrops, and Jasper had transformed Sun,

Sand, and Tea into Miller Memorial Headquarters as a personal favor to Judy, who'd barely left her room all day. While I'd waited for the paint to dry on my drop cloths, I'd prepared comfort foods in bulk and printed photos of Craig from the internet. Jasper framed the pictures, then hung them on walls and stood them on tables. When the food was finished, I installed one hundred AAA batteries, two by two, into fifty battery-operated candles.

Just as I was considering collapsing from exhaustion, Aunt Clara and Aunt Fran showed up with a picnic basket of sustenance from the vendor trucks at Summer Splash. Cheese sticks. Steak kabobs. Vinegar fries. I didn't feel one bit guilty indulging while they ate fruit salads and drank water.

Jasper hung one unpainted drop cloth to be used as a makeshift movie screen, and I pointed a borrowed projector toward it. Judy had convinced Pete to help too, and thanks to the world's love of social media, he'd been able to create a photographic account of Craig's life from images shared by his friends and family over the years. The resulting slideshow would be projected onto the drop cloth during the vigil. Pete had also promised to arrive early and help set up, but so far no one had seen him.

When she arrived at Sun, Sand, and Tea, Mrs. Miller stared open-mouthed at the café's transformation. Scents of the most comforting foods I could think of filled the space: buttery homemade mashed potatoes, salty garlic bread, and tangy baked ziti. No special recipes or personal twists, just lots of love and compassion baked into each meatball, deviled egg, and bite of pasta salad.

"Come in," I encouraged. "Take your time. Have something to eat or drink. We're on your clock now."

A pair of women with the same hair and eye color as Mrs. Miller's rubbed her back. "She's right," one woman said. "We're all here for you."

Mrs. Miller buried her face against the curve of her neck, and the trio huddled in a group hug. "No one could ever ask for better sisters," she told them. "Thank you so much for being here." They pulled themselves together as another gust of wind rattled the windows.

Aunt Clara and Aunt Fran were handing out battery-operated candles to the guests pouring in the door. Aunt Clara widened her eyes when she saw me. "Looks like a storm is coming," she said. "You'd better get moving if you want to have a nice moment on the beach without getting soaked."

I helped with the candle distribution while one of Craig's aunts told warm stories about him, then initiated a moment of silence, broken only by a few stifled sobs. When everyone had collected themselves, I took the crowd along my wraparound porch to the path that led to the beach.

The winds ebbed and flowed as we walked. Candles were occasionally blown from people's hands, forcing mourners to chase them into the surf. Jasper and Judy walked side by side behind Mrs. Miller and her sisters, followed by family members on both sides, then friends and lookie-loos. I puttered along at the back, keeping stragglers moving and answering quiet questions about the town or my recipes.

Finally, we stopped at a humongous piece of driftwood and waited while Mrs. Miller pulled herself together.

I turned away from the group as a too-familiar sensation licked up my spine. Someone was nearby, lurking, watching. A shadow moved along the beach behind us, the figure slowly coming into focus.

The thick dark clouds that had been racing across the sky parted, shining a beam of moonlight down on the shadow.

Ryan, the reporter, lifted a hand hip-high. "Fancy meeting you here."

I slumped. "Oh. It's you."

"It's nice to see you too," he said. He'd abandoned the local T-shirt and cargo shorts in favor of black dress pants, a white shirt, and black tie. "Did I miss anything so far?"

"No." I checked to be sure the wind hadn't thrown the skirt of my dress into peep-show territory. "Craig's mother needs a minute. What are you doing out here walking around in the dark?"

He lowered his gaze. "I'm here for the memorial. Craig meant a great deal to me. He held a special place in my heart."

"Oh, stop."

Ryan smiled. "Right. I forgot who I was talking to.

You and I are here for the same reason, I believe. You want to know what really happened, and you think one of these truly sad people might have something useful to share. I hope you're serving alcohol tonight. It helps loosen tongues, if you know what I mean."

"I most certainly am not," I said. "What is wrong with you?"

"What?" He wrinkled his brow. "You think I'm crazy for asking about liquor at a memorial service? How else are people going to forget their pain?"

I stepped away from him. "I'm not talking to you anymore. I want to hear what Mrs. Miller has to say."

"She hasn't said anything."

"She will," I hissed. "Now shush." I counted heads to be sure we hadn't lost anyone in the dark.

Everyone seemed to be accounted for, except Pete, who still hadn't shown his face. Suspicious? "What were you arguing with Pete about on the beach earlier?" I asked Ryan.

"I don't know what you mean." Ryan shoved his hands deep into his pockets and stared out at the sea.

"Yes, you do," I challenged. "The two of you were standing toe to toe earlier and using your deep man-voices. Ring a bell?" I could recall the scene perfectly.

"No." Ryan shook his head. "I don't know what you mean. Why? Did Pete say we were fighting?"

"I haven't had a chance to ask him about it," I admitted. "He was supposed to be here by now, but he never showed."

Mrs. Miller started to talk, and I pressed a finger

to my lips. Her emotions were getting the best of her, and I could barely understand the words coming out of her mouth.

The winds increased, tossing hair into my eyes and moving clouds back across the moon. Another plastic candlestick went rolling into the water. I couldn't help wondering how much worse these battery-operated candles were for the ocean than the paper lanterns Mrs. Miller had really wanted.

I rubbed gooseflesh off my arms and the back of my neck as a sickening shiver slid down my spine. I turned around to scan the darkness behind me. Maybe Pete was finally headed our way.

"What are you looking at?" Ryan asked. "Mrs. Miller is over there. Not that we can hear her over the wind."

I smoothed the hair back down on my arms. "Do you feel as if someone's watching us?"

"No. Why? Do you?" He glanced around nervously. "I don't see anyone. I think you're probably paranoid, given recent events. Now turn around and stop talking. She's sounding more coherent up there. I think this could be useful to our cause."

The next gust of wind blew Mrs. Miller's candle from her hands and tossed it several yards away. She covered her mouth with both hands and wailed.

"I've got it," I said, jogging past the crowd and behind the huge piece of driftwood. Hopefully, she hadn't been imagining that the light represented her son.

The little lightbulb flickered as the candle came to

an abrupt halt, its tiny light dimming. I froze, hands outstretched, as Pete's slack face came into view beside it on the sand.

The scream that nearly shattered my eardrums was my own.

CHAPTER
❧

TWELVE

I pressed shaking fingers to Pete's cold throat, praying the temperature of his skin had more to do with the lapping water and wind than the absence of a heartbeat. His body was near the water's edge, pants rolled above his ankles, as if he might've been enjoying a moment alone at the edge of the ocean. The rhythmic rush of water licked his side and swept his hair, sneaking under his neck and around his limbs before racing back out. Any footprints that might have been in the sand had already been washed away.

Judy hovered behind me, Jasper at her side. "Why is this happening?" she whispered breathlessly. "I don't…I can't understand why—" Her knees buckled and she collapsed in a faint.

Anxiety tightened my throat as I swung an arm out to break her fall, but she slipped out of my grasp.

Jasper caught her before she the ground. "I've got her."

"Thanks," I choked. For once, I really was thankful for his constant presence.

He scooped Judy easily into his arms and carried her away from the water.

I turned back to Pete, my fingers still searching for signs of life. I closed my eyes and tuned everything else out, pushing away the sounds of raging wind and my thrumming heart until all that was left was Pete.

A thin pulse registered beneath his skin. "He's alive!" I gripped his jaw in my hands and leaned over his face, listening for breath I couldn't hear or feel in the current conditions. "Pete?" I cried. "Someone get help!"

Ryan stepped into view, a phone pressed to his ear. "Police and paramedics are on the way," he told me as the other vigil participants gathered around. "I'm on the line with them now."

A rush of relief set me back in the sand, face in my palms, knees to my chest.

"He's alive," Ryan explained to whoever was on the other end of the line. "Unconscious. Nonresponsive but breathing."

Mrs. Miller moved to my side. "He's okay?" she asked.

I looked up and nodded, feeling the weight of her emotions as she moved her weary gaze from Pete to me. Simultaneous relief and heartbreak had dampened her eyes and tugged her mouth into an expression of profound sadness. The scene was too reminiscent of the way she'd last seen her son, and it was far too soon to witness something like this again. *Ever*, I imagined, would be too soon. "He has a pulse," I told her. "That's something, and Ryan says emergency responders are en route."

Ryan paced across the sand, pointing a pocket flashlight at the ground. "I hate the beach," he said. "No footprints. Just mounds of loose sand up there." He flicked the beam of light toward the dry sand, then swung the light toward his feet. "And water washing everything away down here."

He'd described the most complicated and lovely thing about life at the ocean. The steady, predictable tides never failed to change everything in their paths. No sandcastle, moat, or message ever persevered on a beach where the sea never changed.

I stepped back as paramedics arrived and Ryan came to stand with me, looping a steadying arm around my shoulder. "You okay?"

"No." I leaned against him, unsure my legs were worthy of my trust. "Thanks for the support."

"Don't mention it," he said, drumming his fingers at my waist. "Hey, be frank with me for a minute. Are you seeing that detective romantically?"

"No. Why?" I pulled back to get a look at his face. Was he looking for another scoop? An island romance scandal? My limbs went rigid. Or was Ryan about to ask me out? Whatever he was up to, we were in the middle of an enormous trauma. It wasn't even close to time to discuss my romantic life. I chose my words carefully in case they wound up in a misconceived news article. "I'm not dating anyone now, nor do I have plans to date anyone anytime soon. Why do you ask?"

"Well," he began, clearing his throat, "because the good detective is headed this way, and he's not a small man. I didn't think being caught with my arm around his girlfriend was in my face's best interest."

"Your face?" I asked.

"He looks like a puncher," he said.

I snorted. I'd only known Grady for four months, but I'd never seen him lose his cool. "I don't think he's a puncher," I said. It was actually scarier when he went stone-faced and clenched his jaw. His voice got eerie cold when he did that, and a little vein throbbed above his left eye. I shivered just thinking about it.

I'd seen that look a lot.

Ryan dropped his arm and stepped away from me anyway. "How about I don't test your theory." The *Pink Panther* theme song started playing from his pocket, and Ryan grabbed his phone with a quick smile. "I have to take this." He stepped aside as Grady's boots hit the sand.

I held still as Grady arrived on his signature wave of authority and cool confidence. "Swan," he said, looking me over from head to toe, "you okay?"

"Yeah. Just shaken." I rubbed my palms up and down my thighs, fighting a whole-body tremble. "I think Pete's going to be all right," I said. "He's breathing, and there are no signs of a cake knife anywhere."

Grady's lips twitched as he turned to Ryan. "Reporter," he said, his voice a little deeper than it had been when he'd addressed me. "You have anything to do with this?"

Ryan pushed the phone back into his pocket. "Of course not. I was only here to talk to the attendees afterward."

Grady seemed to accept that answer. He swept his gaze over the scene, stopping to study Judy and Jasper, seated side by side in the sand, knees bent. Judy had tipped forward to rest her face between her knees while Jasper rubbed her back.

"She passed out when she saw Pete," I said.

He dipped his chin once in stiff acknowledgment. "I want to talk to you before I go."

I nodded, unsure how to answer correctly with Ryan's curious gaze on me. Grady went to speak with the EMTs loading Pete on a gurney.

"He still hasn't opened his eyes," I told Ryan, "and I noticed blood on the back of his head when they were lifting him."

Ryan winced. "I saw that too."

We stood in stunned silence on the busy beach.

"Are you ready to partner up on this thing yet?" Ryan asked, his attention roaming over the emergency responders. "I really think that together we could crack it."

"I'm getting there," I admitted, mostly because I wasn't getting anywhere on my own, and I couldn't bear to see anyone else hurt by this lunatic, whoever they were.

As I watched, Grady scanned the shoreline, and I wondered if he was thinking the same thing I had: driftwood would make a great attack weapon.

Readily available in various weights, shapes, and sizes, it wouldn't stand out once it had been used and discarded, so there was no need to hide it afterward. A total time-saver for the hurried criminal, and if the wood was left in the surf, the tide would not only wash it clean, it would eventually deliver it to the other side of the world.

"Detective." A first responder flagged Grady down. He had an evidence bag in hand.

"What could that be?" Ryan asked, stepping forward.

Grady turned the plastic bag over.

I followed Ryan past the invisible good manners and respectable distance line and into the rude and obviously rubbernecking area. "What is it?" Ryan whispered.

I craned my neck for a better look but couldn't make out the shape. "I can't tell," I whispered back. "It's too dark."

Grady cast us a warning look. "You two think I can't hear you?"

Ryan and I exchanged an impish look. "Yes," we admitted in unison.

Grady's mouth turned down. "There are the contents of Pete's pockets. Wallet. Loose change. Breath mints. Cell phone. My business card. A card for Granger Industries, and a disposable wedding camera."

"There was a bin of those cameras available at the dessert station," I said. "Judy wanted to see some truly candid shots, not just the perfect cropped and filtered ones. Very few guests remembered to return them after things went sideways that night."

Grady chewed on that a minute. "Can you think of any reason Pete would have it with him now?"

"Not when he has a cell phone," I said. "Do you think there's evidence on there? Maybe someone got a picture of the killer?"

"We'll know soon enough," he said.

My hair flapped relentlessly against my face, sticking on my lip gloss and stinging my eyes like a thousand skinny whips. I grabbed it in my fist and tried to wrangle it back. "Were you able to catch up with Cynthia earlier?"

Grady glanced at Ryan, then back at me. "Yes. She says she found the missing suitcase in an alleyway, recognized it as Craig's, then took a few mementos, but didn't break into Mrs. Miller's rental. She claimed not to know about the break-in."

"Do you believe her?" I asked.

Again, he shifted his attention to Ryan. "I believe in what can be proven."

He'd told me something similar on the night we first met. Grady assumed everyone was lying about something, or at the very least, they were capable of lying about something, so he didn't take anyone at their word during an investigation. This was only my second experience with a killer on the loose, but I was beginning to understand where he was coming from, even if I didn't fully agree with him.

"Any chance either of you saw or heard something out here before you found Pete?" Grady asked. "Something unusual on the beach or maybe a vehicle on the road, headlights, a jogger? Any activity aside from the vigil?"

I shook my head. "No."

"Well, wait," Ryan said. "What if it felt as if some-one was watching us?"

Grady crossed his arms. "You felt like someone was watching you? Tonight?"

Ryan pointed at me.

Grady turned his eyes to mine, staring silently until I explained.

"It was the same sensation I had in the garden Friday night. It's happened a lot since then, actually," I admitted. "Tonight, I was sure we were being watched or followed more than once during the vigil, but I never saw anyone or anything unusual, and all I can hear out here is the blessed wind. Can we please go back to my place and talk? There's plenty of seats, and my aunts are there with food and drinks."

"No alcohol, though," Ryan said.

Grady rolled his eyes, sweeping a hand toward my home. "After you."

I led the group, plus a handful of policemen and Grady, back to Sun, Sand, and Tea, where my aunts stood at the ready. Jasper waited with Judy until a paramedic could look her over. I didn't blame him for wanting to know if her collapse was stress induced and nothing more serious.

Aunt Clara blanched at the appearance of my uni-formed guests. "What happened?"

I explained the situation while helping pour two dozen glasses of iced tea.

"Goodness," Aunt Clara said.

Aunt Fran pressed her lips into a thin white line. "Someone's clearly gone round the bend," she said sourly. "Did any of these folks slip away while you were out? Could one of them be the killer posing as a mourner?"

"No. I kept a head count while we were out. They were always accounted for."

A zing of excitement snapped on my skin. *I'd kept a head count.* That meant I could take everyone present off my potential killer list, including Jasper. *Assuming all the crimes this weekend were committed by one criminal.* My gut said that they were, and my gut was usually pretty clever.

Ryan, on the other hand, had come up from behind us late. He'd never been part of my head count. I watched him pretend to console strangers near the patio doors, all while searching for a good story to improve his career. Was he capable of something worse than being a fake? Was he a wolf in sheep's clothing? Could he have hurt Pete, then circled around to arrive from the other direction, thereby creating an alibi? I supposed that would depend on when Pete was attacked and how long he'd lain there before I found him.

"Everly?" Grady's voice broke through my pointed thoughts. "Do you have a minute?"

"Sure." I moved into a quiet corner across the café and stood before a window, overlooking the sea.

I stroked my tangled hair self-consciously, trying in vain to pull my fingers through the mess without ripping any loose in the process. Given the shape of my silhouette in the glass at my side, the wind-battered knot probably looked like something birds would want to lay their eggs in.

Grady stood close to me, his cool gray eyes searching.

My body tensed in anticipation of whatever he might say next. "You okay?" I asked.

He tucked long fingers into the front pockets of his blue jeans and rolled his shoulders forward. "I think you should consider staying with your aunts for a bit."

Tension drained from my muscles, and I smiled. "Oh, good. I thought I was in trouble again."

"You are in trouble," he said. "Trouble has literally been circling you for the last forty-eight hours. I'm especially concerned with the fact that all the crimes, except for Mrs. Miller's break-in, seem to be happening to you here. It's as if your property has become the hub for this nut's violence and instability."

"I can't leave," I said. "I have houseguests, and I don't want to leave Judy right now."

Grady frowned.

"Maybe my aunts can stay here with us," I suggested.

He rolled his head around on his shoulders. "The idea isn't that they can protect you," he said, "the idea is to relocate you somewhere crimes aren't happening three or four times a day." He leveled a pleading stare at me and raised his thick brows. "Whoever is taunting and threatening you is only doing it here: On the beach outside. Your golf cart in the carriage house. Maybe relocating you will slow things down. Throw the stalker off-center. Especially if the person doing this is from out of town. You can leave a note as a distraction to say you're going to stay at a friend's in Kitty Hawk, then I'll drive you to your aunts' place and make sure no one follows us."

I scanned his face in search of what he wasn't saying. "You think the person who's doing this is from out of town. Anyone local would be able to guess that I would be staying with my aunts, and just go look for me there."

He released a small breath and worked his jaw. "I'm working on something like that. Yes."

"Is it horrible that I feel relieved to know it wasn't someone from Charm?" I asked.

Grady offered a small smile. "No. You love these people, and I admire that, but don't go thinking the case is closed just yet. I've still got work to do before I know anything for certain. Which is one more reason I'll feel a lot better if you leave home for a night or two."

I looked to my aunts. They stared back from across the room.

"Can they read lips?" he asked.

"Maybe." Truth was, my aunts were old and odd, and I had no idea what they were capable of, but I could see his point about them not being able to physically protect me. Together they barely weighed as much as Grady. More importantly, my great-aunts were all the family I had left, and there was no way I'd risk leading trouble to their doorstep if I could help it.

"I feel safe here," I told Grady. "I appreciate you

worrying about me, but I'm not alone, and I'm going to be okay."

A man in a blue windbreaker appeared in the café doorway, stopping whatever rebuttal I could see forming on Grady's lips. "Detective?"

Grady's brows went up. "Everything okay?"

"Just wanted to go over what we have," the man said. "Then I'm ready to head back to the lab unless you need me here for anything else."

"Give me two minutes," Grady told him.

I turned away from the chatting guests, intensely aware of the number of curious eyes on us—Ryan's included. He seemed nice enough, but that was his schtick, wasn't it? I hadn't been able to stop wondering if he'd had time to hurt Pete, then double back to join the vigil late. "Before you go…" I said.

Grady took immediate interest, refocusing on me, arms crossed, eyes intent. "Yeah."

"I saw Pete on the beach yesterday with Ryan. It sounded like they were arguing, but when I asked Ryan about it, he said that they weren't fighting. Still, it seemed to me like it was something. Then Ryan showed up late on the beach tonight. He was coming from the opposite direction of where we found Pete, so it's probably nothing, but I thought I should mention it."

Grady turned his face toward the guests.

I followed suit and found Ryan watching.

"Noted," Grady said. "I'm going out to talk with the crime scene investigators, then I'll be back. Until then, why don't you concentrate on never going any-where alone again."

"Okay."

He didn't look convinced, so I drew an *X* over my heart. He shook his head and left.

My aunts had their hands full cleaning up messes throughout the room: abandoned plates and cups, spilled food, dropped napkins. I jumped into action, checking on guests and helping put the café back in order.

The crowd thinned slowly as policemen finished taking reports. Judy, Mrs. Miller, and her sisters remained on my wicker furniture near the deck doors and bookshelves. Mrs. Miller didn't look fit to go anywhere just yet; Judy didn't look much better.

I delivered a heaping tray of desserts to the coffee table. "Take your time," I told them. "I'll be here all night, and you're welcome to stay as long as you need."

Ryan was at the counter when I returned. "I heard you and the detective talking about me earlier. What was that about?"

I'd assumed this conversation was coming, so I'd prepared a fib for the occasion and hoped I could pull it off. "You told me you were an investigative reporter at heart, and I know you're looking into Craig's death."

"True," he said.

"And you know more about Craig's life and his guests than we do."

"Also true."

"So I thought you might have uncovered something

about the case that you'd like to share. Something that can speed up the process of finding Craig's killer."

Ryan smiled. "You want to know what I know?"

I tipped my head sideways and smiled back. "Yes, please."

Ryan barked a laugh, obviously pleased with himself. "Well, I don't believe that was what you were really saying, but I do appreciate your attempt to fool me." He rubbed his chin and pondered a moment. "Huh," he said, bright eyes flashing. "You tried to fool me because you're hiding something."

"No, I'm not," I lied. Poorly.

"What don't you want me to know?" he asked.

I frowned. "I wasn't lying. I do want to know if you're holding back on something you've uncovered." I suspected he wouldn't mind interfering in a murder investigation if it got him a big byline. "I told Detective Hays about the argument you had with Pete on the beach yesterday."

Ryan straightened with a snap. "Why would you do that?"

"Why wouldn't I?" I asked. "You were coy when I asked you about it. Now he's unconscious, and you showed up late to the vigil. It seemed like it was relevant."

"That's my crime? Being late?" he asked. "Be serious. And for the record, just because someone doesn't want to discuss a private conversation with you doesn't mean the exchange was sinister. Now you've turned your detective on to me for no good reason, which will only slow me down while I work." He slumped onto a stool at the counter. "Thanks for nothing."

I gasped. "Rude."

He narrowed his eyes on me. "Before you go putting me at the top of your detective friend's suspect list, you should know I asked Pete for an exclusive interview about Craig, and it made him mad. That's what you saw. I wanted something full of cherished memories and private anecdotes from his partner. A personal piece like that would be marketable to a dozen papers and magazines across the country."

"He said no?" I guessed. "And you got mad."

"Pete refused. He said he didn't have anything nice to say about Craig, and he wouldn't make something up just to make Craig seem like a nicer guy. In fact, he stated emphatically that Craig was not a nice guy. Then he stormed off."

I evaluated Ryan's tone and posture, wishing I was a better judge of body language. My problem was that I could empathize with everyone, and I believed most people were good at the core. Sadly, someone on my island was not so good, and I wasn't sure if that was Ryan. "So you don't have any information that will help the case," I concluded, letting his argument with Pete go. At least I'd told Grady about it. Maybe he would know the right thing to ask and be able to tell if Ryan was being honest.

Ryan's eyes went cold. His shoulders squared, and his expression hardened. "Just because I don't have anything concrete to share about Craig's killer two days after the murder doesn't mean I won't soon. I'm looking under every rock for something to break this case. I've already spoken with half the town, and I've learned plenty. I just have to figure out how the pieces all go together."

"What pieces?" I asked. "What have you learned?"

"Plenty about you." Ryan turned his smug gaze my way. It was then that I realized investigative reporting could mean digging up dirt on people for shock value rather than actually uncovering facts that could improve the world somehow. And just when my week couldn't get more complicated, I had my very own investigative reporter digging up dirt on me.

"Me?" I squeaked, glancing at Aunt Clara and Aunt Fran, who were working steadily behind the counter.

They looked as surprised as I felt.

"What about me?" I asked.

Ryan smiled, delighting in the attention. "Apparently it's a widely known fact on this island that your entire family is cursed, along with any man who dares to love you." He waited, looking carefully at me, before continuing. "That's rough, huh?"

"Please," I scoffed. "Be serious."

Who had he been talking to? How many people in this town thought these things? Had they always? Did I need to hold a press conference or an intervention?

"I am," he said. "The man I spoke to knew all the details. He said he could personally vouch for the curse's validity. I believe his name was Wyatt something or other."

My heart clenched and my lungs ached.

Ryan inhaled, savoring the impact of the arrow he'd shot directly into my heart. "So you do know him," Ryan went on. "To be honest, I'd assumed he was pulling my leg. His story was a bit extreme. He said he's a bull rider who was told he'd never ride again after several years of injuries and losses on the rodeo circuit. Then the two of you had a falling-out last year. You moved home, and he healed up. It's so strange, really, because he looked great when I saw him—a bit brooding, but healthy. Apparently, he hasn't had a single injury since you left."

I willed my frame not to double over with the gut-wrenching hit.

The cowboy I'd seen in the green pickup this morning really had been Wyatt.

He was in town, and he thought it was my curse that had nearly killed him last year.

Just knowing he believed I'd cursed him somehow hurt worse than any physical injury I'd ever experienced.

CHAPTER

THIRTEEN

I excused myself and went to my room to breathe.

I splashed cold water on my face, then stared at my heartbroken expression in the bathroom mirror. "Pull it together, Swan," I said, using my best Grady Hays impression. I'd let Ryan get under my skin. Rude reporter: one, delightful iced-tea-shop owner: zero. I wouldn't let it happen again. Who cared if Wyatt was in town? Not me. Who cared if he did or didn't think I was cursed? Not me. I couldn't feel responsible for the things that went on in his head. He was a grown man. Who'd clearly taken one too many blows to the noggin. I grabbed a hairbrush and worked through my tangles, then reapplied lip gloss and mascara. Once I felt a little more like myself, I changed into soft blue jeans and a long-sleeved white T-shirt, then grabbed my laptop from the nightstand.

Muddled voices carried through the vents from downstairs, along with soft classical music from my café radio. A lazy rotation of red and white flashers swept across my window from the remaining police cruisers below. I leaned closer and peered behind the curtain. Two uniformed officers accompanied Grady on the sand, roaming the beach in search of clues. I dropped the curtain back into place before Grady saw me watching, and I climbed onto my bed.

I opened my laptop and brought up the *Town Charmer* blog. I couldn't go back downstairs until I knew more about the Wild Bunch Rodeo Team and memorized their schedule for the week so I could actively avoid them. I scanned for recent articles, but found nothing. No reference to any cowboys, the Wild Bunch, or our wild horses. The *Town Charmer* was too busy following up on Craig's murder to waste time covering festival acts.

When I couldn't find a website for the Wild Bunch either, I put that frustration aside and refocused on an equally infuriating man: Ryan O'Malley.

I'd already seen his social media profiles, but I hadn't taken the time to read any of his articles or trace the course of his career. I typed his name into the search bar and examined the results. Ryan's name appeared on dozens of wedding-themed pieces over the last four years. Before that, there was a gap of time where Ryan seemed to be silent. Going back further, his name appeared regularly again, this time in articles related to technology. He was a busy guy back then. Online articles. Magazine articles. Guest blog posts. Exposés and investigative stories.

One particular headline caught my eye: TECH

DYNAMO CRAIG MILLER FACES OFF WITH UNDERCOVER
REPORTER. I skimmed the article in a state of shock:
Ryan had done more than simply follow Craig's career,
as he'd said. He'd *known* him. The year Craig and
Pete's company was breaking into the news, Ryan was
already working there, posing as an intern.

"I knew it," I whispered to the screen as I scrolled.
Ryan had spent time at Craig and Pete's company,
pretending to be a low-level tech support staffer when
in fact he was spying on the fast-growing firm, hoping
to score a big story for the local-interest paper.

Adrenaline rushed in my veins as I gobbled every
word. Ryan's complete exposé portrayed Craig's new
data science services as glorified internal espionage,
and he claimed they'd created a new method for the
age-old practice of spying on employees and consum-
ers alike.

The article had gone viral, causing enough
upheaval in the tech community that Pete was forced
to speak out in a press conference to try to save the
company. There was a link to the video!

I swung my legs off the bed and hovered my finger
over the little white triangle as I twisted with energy.

Pete began a charming speech, explaining what
data science truly was and how it benefitted everyone,
increasing sales for companies and creating promo-
tional discount opportunities for customers. He had
flow charts and infographics. It was very nicely done,
well planned, easy to understand, and informative—
until Craig strode red-faced onto the stage and took

the mic. Craig re-explained data science in terms that confounded everyone as Pete stood back, looking rightfully furious for being bulldozed when he'd had things under control. Craig went on to publicly out Ryan as a wolf in sheep's clothing, having intentionally lied about who he was for the sake of his article, taking advantage of those with less technical understanding by manipulating the truth with irresponsible journalism. Craig unloaded for more than five minutes, pleading with the public to see that his company was the victim of a reporter in need of a story and nothing more. He even shared stories of the heart-to-heart conversations he'd had with Ryan, believing he was truly just an intern looking for a mentor.

In the end, Craig and Pete's business boomed from the exposure, and Ryan got the ax, both as Craig's fake intern and as an investigative reporter. It seemed as if the press conference had worked. Craig and Pete's company stock soared, and judging by the comments and follow-up articles, the public believed Ryan was an opportunistic liar, manipulator, and irresponsible journalist. He might even have been blacklisted to some degree, because it was another ten months before his first puff pieces started appearing in smaller papers and another three years before he appeared on the wedding circuit at the *New York Times*.

I closed my laptop and set it on my nightstand, my stomach knotting. Craig Miller had busted Ryan publicly for his unscrupulous ways and put him out of work for nearly a year. When he found work again, it was covering weddings. That smelled like motive for a confrontation to me. Maybe even murder.

I took the steps back to my café at double time. Ryan was nowhere to be seen when I got there.

My great-aunts were cleaning up. Aunt Fran stooped, hands full, in front of the dishwasher. Clara made large wet circles on my counter with a polka-dotted dishrag.

"Where is Ryan?" I asked.

They exchanged a look. "He left right after you did," Aunt Fran said.

"We assumed he went after you to apologize," Aunt Clara added.

I was incredibly thankful he hadn't gone after me for nefarious reasons, since no one had thought to follow him or warn me he was coming. "He didn't," I said, "but I want to talk to Grady about him. Everything okay in here?"

"Yes," Aunt Clara said softly. Only Mrs. Miller, her sisters, Judy, and Jasper remained.

"They're okay," Aunt Clara said, "and we've nearly got it all cleaned up. Don't worry about us."

"Okay," I agreed. "I won't be long this time. I'm going outside to catch Grady before he takes off too."

I hurried out the front door and along the wrap-around porch to the back, then dashed into the gardens and down the beach access path to where Grady stood. He was staring into the distance with a flashlight.

"Hey!" I called.

Grady swung the light around, illuminating my middle. His free hand rested on the butt of his gun.

I pulled my palms up. "Don't shoot," I said. "It's just me." The intoxicating scent of the sea put me instantly at ease. Grady's presence didn't hurt either.

He relaxed his stance and dropped both hands to his sides, extinguishing the beam on his flashlight. "What on earth are you doing out here? You just agreed not to go anywhere alone, but here you are."

I stopped to catch my breath as he closed the distance between us on the dark beach. "I needed to talk to you."

He lifted his cell phone and wiggled it in the air. "Ever seen one of these?"

"You're right outside, and I didn't want to call. Someone could overhear me."

He moved closer and lowered his voice. "Listen. I meant what I said. You need to use the buddy system or stay inside. Understand?"

"What buddy system?" I panted. "Who should be my buddy for a dark night's walk? My aunts are busy. There's a killer on the loose. I don't know who it is. What if I accidently asked the killer to keep me company and he kills me?"

Grady gripped the back of his neck and looked at the sky for a long beat. "What brings you out here, Swan?"

I told him about the articles I'd found and the video I'd watched. Ryan had known Craig much better and in darker ways than he'd let on, and now he was missing.

"All right," Grady said, "I'll find Ryan and see what he has to say about it."

"Say about what?" a familiar voice asked. Ryan moved through the shadows and into view. Wind whipped through his shaggy hair, pointing it in every direction. His shoes were caked with sand, and his previously pressed suit was rumpled, as if he'd been hiding in the bushes somewhere.

I gaped. "Are you following me?"

"No." He puffed air and tried to look offended. His cautious gaze moved from me to Grady.

"I'm serious," I said. "Are you the one who's been following me?"

"No," he repeated. "Why would I do that?"

I looked to Grady for a little help. How could I possibly talk to someone so determined to give me the runaround? "For starters, you told me you would be sticking to me the night we met."

Ryan shrugged.

The hint of betrayal in his eyes confused me, and I took a beat to consider what it meant. Was Ryan a good guy who'd made past mistakes and hoped to prove himself by attending the wedding of his enemy? Had he stayed to find justice for Craig when the reception went awry? Or was Ryan the weasel I'd been quick to assume he was, carrying a grudge for years and following Craig all the way to North Carolina to claim his revenge?

"What are you doing?" Grady asked Ryan. "Why are you lurking around?"

"I'm just listening," he said. "Observing. Hoping to catch wind of something to break the case or at least make an excellent article."

I pointed at him. "See."

Ryan frowned. "What are you going on about? Still upset because your ex-boyfriend's in town?"

My traitorous gaze jumped to Grady, and my heart thundered. "We're talking about you," I said, pulling my focus back to Ryan, but it was too late.

"Everly!" Amelia's voice rang through the night. She jogged into view a moment later, looking unharmed, but a little wild around the eyes. "Oh my goodness," she said, throwing herself against me for a hug. "I saw the lights and thought something had happened to you. I stopped inside, and your aunts said you were out here. They told me about Pete. Are you okay?"

"I'm okay," I said. "Pete will be too." I hoped.

"Good," she said, backing up. "That was terrifying." She ran a shaky hand through her windblown hair. "I was restocking the Little Libraries and saw the cruisers' lights. Once I realized they were right outside your place…" She paused. "I'm just so glad you're okay."

"I'm okay," I promised.

Ryan smiled politely at Amelia and bowed his head slowly in greeting. "Amelia. Nice to see you again."

She gave him a coy smile and color rose to her cheeks. "You too."

I narrowed my eyes at Ryan, not liking where that exchange was going.

"Detective." A man in a blue windbreaker waved one arm overhead from outside a white panel van down the beach. The van's blue letters matched the white ones on his coat: CSI.

Grady looked at me, and I nodded.

"I'm okay," I repeated.

He turned to Ryan. "Don't go far. I want to talk to you."

Ryan's smile widened, broad and annoying. "I wasn't planning on it."

I couldn't help wondering why. Was he really hanging around to catch a story? Or was his trying to cover his crimes?

CHAPTER

FOURTEEN

I trudged downstairs the next morning, feeling the lack of sleep in my bones. I'd lain awake most of the night trying to fit together the puzzle pieces that were already in play and make a guess at what was missing. I tried imagining a scenario where the person committing the break-ins wasn't the same one who'd killed Craig, but I couldn't. I tried convincing myself that Pete's attack had been random, but I couldn't. Yes, life was sometimes wacky and things weren't always what they seemed, but I didn't believe in coincidence, and a sudden spree of different crimes committed by multiple criminals seemed much less likely than one killer trying to cover their tracks while attempting to keep me off the case.

I flipped on all the lights in the café and brewed a pot of coffee. Normally, I liked to clean while I processed a landslide of thoughts, but my aunts had already scrubbed the place spotless. They were getting double hugs the next time I saw them.

I filled a soup mug with coffee and paced through the immaculate space, haunted by memories of the weekend. Judy with a bloody knife. Craig's mom begging for a vigil. Pete unconscious on the sand. I paused beside the archway to the former ballroom and future café expansion. I'd seen a flash outside the window the night before last. I'd assumed it was heat lightning, but could it have been a camera's flash? What was on the wedding camera in Pete's pocket? The line between paranoia and reality had become thoroughly blurred these past few days, and nothing seemed black or white.

Maggie trotted into view, weaving a path between tables and chairs, purring softly and watching me as she went.

"Good morning," I said, sipping my coffee and wondering uselessly where she'd come from. "Big plans today?" I asked.

She turned for the patio doors with a long meow.

"Always in such a hurry to leave," I said. "Trapped inside all night, away from the relentless, beating wind. It's tough. I know."

She paced in front of the patio doors, meowing continuously.

"I was on my way out to say good morning to Lou, anyway," I said, "so don't think I'm obeying your commands or anything. Lou only wishes he had a ticket to get inside like you do, and here you are, always on your way out." I flipped the lock on the patio doors and slid them apart.

A gush of salty air rushed in as Maggie trotted out. She hurried to the deck railing and leapt onto the edge, tail switching as she surveyed her world. Lou squawked at the sight of us, busy preening and prepared to protect his corner turf. Maggie gave a disinterested glare before turning her attention to the beach below and arched with a hiss.

Chills ran down my spine at the sight of her. She'd recently made that same sound and movement in my presence, the night of Craig's death. "Maggie?" I asked, hoping she wouldn't go tearing off the deck railing and over the hill the way she had on Friday night. The drop from my first-floor deck was significantly steeper than the drop from my garden, thanks to the angle of the cliff, and I wasn't emotionally prepared for her to get hurt or disappear again. Even for a little while. In fact, after finding Pete on the sand, I'd been battling the urge to collect all my loved ones and hold them hostage in one place until whatever was going on in Charm had ended.

Lou stretched tall and spread his wings as if he might take flight. His stout body elongated and bobbed as wind rushed around his outstretched wings.

I ignored the glaciers of ice sliding across my skin and forced my feet forward, stopping between my animal protectors at the deck rail. "Oh." I set my coffee aside and stared at the drawing on the beach below. A crude crime scene–style outline of a body was etched into the sand, legs bent at unnatural angles, arms wide. A big rock interrupted the curve of the drawing's head. Large straight letters rose above the drawing in a simple three-word command.

DON'T BE NEXT

I patted blindly at my pockets, afraid to take my eyes off the horrid drawing, lest it come to life and attack me or disappear. With my cell phone, I took a dozen pictures as the tide reached closer to the words with each new wave. I texted the photos to Grady before the threat was erased by the sea and made me sound insane when I claimed it had been there but it wasn't.

Suddenly, I wondered if I was being gaslighted. I'd assumed whoever was following me was keeping an eye on my progress in finding Craig's killer, but now I couldn't help wondering if this was personal. An attempt to make me bonkers. The person who made the drawing must have known that I would see this before the tide washed it away. Otherwise what would be the point? The artist must have known I sat on this deck every morning as the sun rose.

Was that person watching me now? Enjoying my response? Did they want me to be afraid? To scream? Cry? Something else? What? I scanned the beach for signs of a sicko, watching, waiting.

There were a handful of people in the distance, collecting shells or stretching or running. No one in a trench coat and dark glasses, if that was what I'd expected.

My phone buzzed with a response from Grady.

Go inside. Lock up. On my way.

I stumbled back at that. Knowing he was on the way instantly stripped away my bravery. "Come on, Maggie," I cooed. "Let's go inside and get some breakfast." I clucked my tongue and collected my coffee before stepping back through the open doorway. I straightened and curled my fingers. "Come on."

Lou cocked his head and opened his beak, but didn't say anything.

"I can't bring you," I said. "If I could, I would, but I'm pretty sure bringing Maggie in here is already violating about a dozen health codes."

Maggie slunk off the railing, ears up, tail high as she reluctantly came inside.

I shut the door and locked it, but she sat steadfast, nose to the glass, watching Lou and the world outside.

My phone rang, and Grady's face filled the screen. "Hello?" I croaked.

"Are you inside?" he asked.

"I'm in the café," I said. From my vantage just inside the doors, I could still see the tops of the letters etched above the drawing's head. "Are you still on your way?"

"Yeah, but I wanted to make sure you weren't running around out there trying to figure out what's going on."

"I'm not. Did you get a chance to talk to Ryan again last night?" Ryan was moving to the top of my suspects list faster than anyone else. He was the only person I consistently talked to about this case. Last night Amelia had coerced me to come inside and settle down instead of waiting to eavesdrop on Ryan's conversation with Grady. She'd put on a kettle and made hot tea, then plied me with lemon cake until I felt more like myself.

The steady tick of a turn signal came through the receiver. "We talked," Grady said. "Not sure I got anywhere. That guy's slick. It's like interviewing a politician."

That sounded about right. "Do you think Ryan could be the one who's been following me? I mean, he told me he was going to stick close, and someone definitely has."

"I'm three minutes out," Grady said. "Let's talk when I get there. I just wanted to be sure you were inside."

"Okay." I disconnected with gritted teeth. Ryan had tried to shame me into letting him stay at my place. And it had almost worked! I tucked the phone into my pocket and spun on my toes.

"Hello," Ryan said, standing just a few feet away.

"Ah!" I clutched my chest, then covered my mouth to stifle the scream. My eyes widened painfully, and my knees threatened to dump me on the floor. "What are you doing?" I gasped. "Are you trying to kill me?" The last two words came more softly off my tongue than the others. Suddenly, the trivial expression had far too much meaning. "How did you get in here?"

Ryan stepped aside and pointed behind him. "Door."

"You broke in?" I hoped Jasper and Judy had heard me scream and were on their way to save me. I backed away slowly.

Ryan wrinkled his nose. "I didn't break in. The door was unlocked."

"No, it wasn't," I said.

Was it? I hadn't checked the front door when I'd come down for coffee, but I'd double-checked every window and door before bed. Had someone unlocked it during the night?

Too many scary thoughts circled my head, and black dots formed in my vision. A panic attack was coming. Maybe that was good: I'd be even heavier to carry off as dead weight.

Ryan bypassed me on his way to the rear deck doors. I went rigid as he passed.

"What's that bird doing?" he asked.

I craned my neck to look around him.

Lou was pretending to fly again, stretched high on his stumpy legs, wings aloft in the ocean breeze, being pulled and weaved from side to side without leaving his roost.

Ryan unlocked the doors and went out. "What's this?" he asked, palms on my railing. "Is that meant for you?" He glanced back at me while pointing toward the giant outline below. "Is that what has you all out of sorts?"

"Did you draw it?" I asked, keeping my distance.

"Me?" He spun around, looking utterly baffled by my accusatory question. "Why would I do something like that?"

"Why do criminals do anything?" I asked. "Why are your shoes caked in sand? Where were you before you came here?" I wondered where Grady was.

"I was on the beach," Ryan said, "down by last night's crime scene. I wanted to be sure nothing was missed in the dark." His shocked expression morphed smoothly into a smile. "You still think I'm behind all this somehow." He rocked obnoxiously with laughter. "That's adorable. I hope you won't take this the wrong way, but please don't quit your day job to become a detective."

Fear leaked from my system, and my blood began to boil. Ryan was a bully. He'd scared me. Taunted me. Manipulated me. "I know you had a public fallout with Craig five years ago," I said. "I know he's the reason you lost your investigative reporter job and cover weddings now. I know it's not because the wedding gig pays better." I crossed my arms. Who was the hack investigator now?

"It really does pay better," he said.

I dropped my arms back to my sides. "Why are you enjoying this?" I asked. "You want me to believe you're innocent, but bad things are happening everywhere and you're smiling."

"I like smiling," he said. "Some people find it charming, you know, not proof that I'm a criminal." His grin widened. "Besides, I'm not happy there are crimes, I'm happy that I made the choice to come to this wedding. If I hadn't, I'd be missing the opportunity to score the story of a lifetime, now, wouldn't I?" He tapped a fingertip to his temple and took a step towards me.

"Detective Hays is on the way," I warned.

"Shocker," he said, not looking in the least bit

shocked. "I guess I don't have time to waste, then." He pulled out his phone and turned to snap photos of the beach.

"What did you do with your disposable wedding camera?" I asked.

He lowered his phone. "The one like they found on Pete? I didn't get one of those. I wasn't even invited to the wedding."

My jaw went slack. "What?"

He stared. "Surely you've figured that out by now. Why would Craig Miller invite me to his wedding? We have a terrible history." He shook his head, then scrolled through the photos.

He'd crashed the wedding. "Jeez. I'm going to be honest with you right now," I said. "You're a mess."

"I'm a mess?"

The front door opened, and I went toward it. "We're in here," I called. "Ryan's here too." I stopped halfway into the foyer.

Jasper pushed the door shut behind him with one foot, balancing a steaming cup from the local coffee shop in each hand. "Did I wake you?"

I blinked. When had he gone out? "Where were you? You left the door unlocked."

He grimaced. "Sorry. You never gave me a key, and everyone was asleep when I went out for a run." A halo of sand had fallen around his shoes on my floor. "I brought Judy a double mocha coconut latte. I didn't know if you drank anything besides tea."

"You've seen me drink coffee." I narrowed my eyes

on him. He was dressed for a run, but that didn't mean he hadn't also drawn a threat in the sand.

I'd discounted Jasper as a suspect after Pete's attack, but I couldn't deny the fact that this wasn't the first time Jasper had gone out and left my door unlocked intentionally, and trouble had conveniently found its way in.

He gave an apologetic smile. "Would you like mine?" He pushed a coffee in my direction.

"No." I stared into his eyes, willing the truth from him. "You went for a run on the beach?"

"Yeah. Sorry about the door. I didn't think it would be a problem to leave it unlocked for a little while. I've barely been gone an hour."

Grady's truck appeared outside the front window. "Thank goodness." I angled past Jasper, then dashed onto the porch. It took all my remaining willpower not to hug Grady. "The drawing is out back. I'll show you," I said, leading him around the side of my home at full speed.

He easily matched my pace. "Slow down. When did Ryan get here?"

"I don't know," I stage-whispered. "Jasper went out this morning and left the door unlocked. Ryan was just standing behind me in the café when I hung up with you. I have no idea how long he'd been standing there." I slowed to look him in the eye. "Both of those guys had sand on their shoes."

"It is an island," Grady said. "Most folks have sand somewhere. I think it's in the dang air."

I stopped at the beach. The awful drawing was even creepier up close. The tops of a few letters had been wiped clean, but the message was still painfully clear. "What do you think?" I asked.

The rigidity in Grady's stance put me on edge. He gave the drawing a long look before turning to face me, deep concern pooling in his clear gray eyes. "I think this is serious," he said.

The chill in his tone slid smoothly beneath my flimsy mask of bravery, and my bottom lip began to quiver. "I'll meet you inside," I said, feeling the panic build in my blood. "I should check on Judy." I hadn't seen her yet this morning, and I also wanted to check on the men I'd left inside my café. What were they up to now? What were they talking about?

I hurried around the side of my house, stopping just out of sight to catch my breath and gather my marbles. I closed my eyes and pulled in deep lungfuls of air. Every fiber of my being screamed *It's too much!* The murder. The attack. The break-ins. The fact that I liked being alone but hadn't been alone in days. The fact that I was missing Summer Splash. All the big and little things had mounted into one unbearable heap, and I longed to scream.

My fitness band beeped, and I considered slinging it into the surf.

BE MORE ACTIVE.

I pinched the Dismiss button until my fingers hurt. "I cannot be more active," I told it. "I'm not allowed to go anywhere alone right now. I'm being stalked and threatened." I hung my head. This was my life now: standing alone in the garden, forbidden from leaving home unattended, and talking to a bracelet. "At least things can't get any worse," I murmured.

"Everly?" A deep, heart-thumpingly familiar voice raised my head.

My greatest heartbreak moved along the path at the edge of my garden, cowboy hat in hand, his steel-blue eyes searching me with a sincere mix of interest and caution.

I forced my chin up and went to meet him before the tears could start to fall. "Hello, Wyatt."

CHAPTER

FIFTEEN

I crossed my arms instinctually in Wyatt's presence, protecting my heart. "I guess you really are in town."

"I guess so," Wyatt said. His fitted white T-shirt emphasized a hard-earned tan, and a lifetime of horse training had molded his body into something inspiring. Everything about him was just as I'd remembered, from the jeans and boots to the straw cowboy hat and easy smile.

And he thought you cursed him, I reminded myself. *Don't forget that.*

"Wow," he said, a shaft of soft, apricot sunlight shining down on his face. "I'd convinced myself you couldn't be as beautiful as I remembered. Clearly I was wrong."

My heart fluttered. "Thank you." I cringed at the involuntary response.

Wyatt chuckled. He dragged his gaze from me to the gardens around us, then took his time admiring my house. "I can't believe you really bought this place. You always wanted to see inside. Now it's yours."

"True," I said, forcing myself not to fidget and trying not to say more than I had to. I'd had a thousand conversations with myself in the shower, rehearsing all the things I'd say to Wyatt if I ever had the chance. Now that he was here, none of it seemed appropriate. I was truly glad he looked so well, and that he was riding again. It was important to him, and everyone deserved to be happy.

"No one in town can stop talking about your big return," he said, "or the iced tea shop where you make your family recipes." He turned proud blue eyes back on me. "You did good, E. So much better than some dumb office job and culinary school. You never needed any of that."

I managed to hold my composure and refrain from asking tartly why he thought he knew anything about what I needed. "What are you doing here, Wyatt? I haven't heard from you in eight months. Now you show up at my house, telling me I've done good? Why?"

His cheerful smile softened, and he dropped his chin to his chest, looking humble and insanely sweet. He peered up at me from beneath thick dark lashes. "I came to apologize for the way things ended between us."

"It's fine," I said. I hadn't considered what he might want, but an apology seemed a bit surreal. "We weren't meant to be, I guess."

"Do you forgive me?"

"Of course," I said. Sure, my heart was still a little bruised around the edges, and seeing him felt like I'd put it in a vise, but if he hadn't dumped me, I'd still be on the road with him, chasing his dreams instead of living mine.

He lifted his head, a small, sad smile on his too-familiar lips. "I swear I never meant to hurt you. I just got scared. You wanted me to stay in Kentucky while you finished learning how to bake cookies, but I needed to heal, train, and get back on a bronco. Rodeo's in my soul, E. It's the only thing that's been consistent throughout my entire life, and it's the only thing I've ever—" His eyes widened, and his lips snapped shut.

"Only thing you've ever loved?" I asked, choosing to start there instead of telling him what I thought about his suggestion that my years at culinary school had merely taught me "to bake cookies." My aching heart was suddenly on the mend. I squared my shoulders and pushed away from the gazebo. How had I never noticed how selfish he was?

"There's that fire," he said, coming back to himself. He stretched to his full height and grinned. "Man, I missed that. We used to be good together, didn't we?"

"Not really," I said.

Wyatt barked a laugh. "You know, I'm in town all week. Maybe we can meet on the beach later, for old time's sake. You remember our spot, right?" He stepped closer. The toes of his boots nudged my flip-flops. His palms found the curve of my waist.

My traitorous heart skipped. "I don't think so." I gently removed his hands from my body. "I'm sorry, Wyatt. I have to go. I was in the middle of something

when you showed up, and I need to get back to it."
As I took a step away, his arm snaked out to stop me.

"Wait." His long fingers encircled my wrist. It was
something he'd done a hundred times in our past, but
it had never felt so much like handcuffs.

I shook him off. "Go home, Wyatt."

"Everything okay up here?" Grady's protective
voice rose on the morning breeze.

A blush senselessly burned a path across my cheeks.

Wyatt's eyes narrowed at mine as Grady
approached. "Well, now. Who's this, visiting you so
early in the morning?"

Grady stopped at my side, facing Wyatt.

My stupid heart went bonkers, sounding alarms
and inciting me to run. I opened and shut my mouth,
envisioning the lights of a runaway train headed right
for me. I didn't want Grady to meet my ex-heartbreak,
and I didn't want Wyatt to meet my...well, I wasn't sure
what Grady was to me, but it felt like something, even if
nothing had come of it. Either way, I braced for a train
wreck as the two men eyed one another up and down.
"Grady, this is Wyatt," I said. "Wyatt, meet Grady."

. Grady's eyes lit with recognition, and his blessed
dimple sunk in. I'd told once him about the mistake
that had taken me away from home, and now he got
to see him in the flesh.

Wyatt bobbed his head in a series of tiny nods,
evaluating the detective. "Nice to meet you. So, how
long have you known E?"

"I met Everly in April," Grady answered,

pronouncing my name carefully, his voice a strange mix of assertion and challenge. "How about you?"

Wyatt smirked. "She ran away with me once."

Grady extended a hand. "Well then, I think I speak for the whole town when I say I'm glad you two didn't work out."

A sharp laugh burst from my throat. "Sorry," I said, waving a hand. What was Grady doing?

Wyatt dragged his gaze back and forth from Grady to me. He motioned between us. "What's the situation with the two of you? Are you her new man?"

Grady turned a puzzled look in my direction. "Do you need a man?"

"Not particularly," I said, loving the truth of the words. "No."

Grady smiled proudly at me and nodded. "Darn right." He turned back to Wyatt with a less congenial expression. "Everly's become very important to me," he said. "I'd hate to see her upset." He set his hands over his hips, in his favorite cop stance, pushing back the sides of his unzipped windbreaker and drawing attention to the shiny badge on his belt.

My heart inflated with hope and pride. "Would you like to join us for breakfast?" I asked Wyatt. "We were just headed inside from the beach when you popped in."

Wyatt's brows furrowed in apparent confusion and disappointed. "I think I'll just let you guys get back to it." He shook Grady's hand, tipped his hat at me, then headed for the boardwalk.

I turned to Grady, a surge of victory pumping in my veins. "Thank you." I threw my arms around his middle and squeezed before bouncing away. "That was amazing. He was making me feel like I should have fallen all over him just because he showed up."

"I heard."

He'd heard? "How much did you hear?"

Grady looked at the sky. "All of it."

I groaned.

He adjusted his hat, setting it slightly askew to block the sun and shade his eyes. "It wasn't my place to interrupt, and you didn't ask for help or need rescuing," he said, looking mightily guilty. "Guys like that get under my skin. That's all."

"It's fine," I said. "It was kind of nice to feel wanted by someone other than Wyatt, even if it was made up and only lasted a minute." My dumb heart panged with regret, wishing ridiculously that Grady had come to my rescue as more than a good cop and friend.

Grady rubbed a palm over one stubble-covered cheek, a small smile blooming on his lips.

"What?"

"Nothing. I'm just glad you're not mad at me for butting in."

"Not at all. Do you want breakfast?" I asked. "I was serious about that."

"Always." He followed along at my side on the way to the door. His gaze warming me. "You really have a thing for cowboys?"

"Yep." I pulled my gaze from his boots and tried to

look as unaffected as possible. I was a grown woman who was allowed to have a preference in things. There was no reason to be ashamed about it. "There's something about a man and his horse, the boots, the blue jeans, a pickup truck, cowboy hat, or any combination of the above to make my head and heart go a little bonkers," I said, trying not to stare at his boots, jeans, or cowboy hat in the process. I lifted and dropped a palm. Cowboys were loyal and true. They appreciated hard work and natural beauty. They were patriots and animal lovers. What wasn't to love? "The rodeo part I could live without," I admitted. "It's not about the performance. I've just always loved what cowboys stand for, if that makes any sense."

Grady gave an accepting nod. "I think it does."

"Good." I'd felt that way since I was in high school and had spent a good portion of my time wondering what sort of man I'd fall in love with one day. I'd never pictured anything else. "Now, let's never talk about this again." Grady had already seen my extensive collection of romance novels with cowboys on the front, and now he knew the full extent of my obsession. *So embarrassing*.

Grady's phone rang as we reached the counter inside my café. "Detective Hays," he answered.

Ryan returned from the deck and climbed onto a stool. "Took you long enough."

I got out the eggs, cheese, veggies, and a thick slice of ham while Grady listened to whoever was on the other end of his line.

"Breakfast?" I asked Ryan, assuming he planned to stay and wear out his welcome.

He put a finger to his lips, indicating I should pipe down so he could eavesdrop. I had half a mind to leave a piece of shell in his omelet.

"Send them over," Grady said. He disconnected and rubbed his shoulders. A series of buzzes sent Grady's thumb across the screen, and he released a sigh. "I'm going to need a rain check on breakfast."

"What? Why?" I asked.

Ryan shifted on his stool. "What about me? Are we still going to talk?"

"Yeah, I'll take your statement at the station," he said. "I'm headed there now. Do you want a lift?"

Ryan hopped off his stool.

"What happened?" I repeated. "Is someone else hurt? Did Pete wake up?"

Grady pulled keys from his pocket and fixed Ryan with a pointed stare. "Why don't you meet me at the truck?"

Reluctantly, Ryan headed out.

"What is it?" I pressed. "Did Pete get worse?" I prayed he wasn't dead.

Grady turned his phone over in his palm and faced it toward me. My face was centered on the screen. "There weren't any fingerprints found on the camera in Pete's pocket, but there were twenty-seven clean exposures," he said. "Every one of them was of you."

CHAPTER
SIXTEEN

Amelia arrived at closing time with a bag full of books and an apologetic smile. "Thank goodness you're still open," she said. "I'm in desperate need of an Iced Chai Latte and the latest scoop on your life. I know things are bananas over here, but I've been so busy with the festival and your aunts' video application, I'm basically the world's worst friend."

I ushered her inside, then flipped the sign on the door behind her from OPEN to CLOSED. "I'm always open for you," I said. "I'm the one who should be apologizing. That application video has been consuming all my free time too. I just finished the last drop cloth for their spin through history, and Aunt Clara texted me an hour ago to ask if I would review her playlist for the movie's score. Then she sent a follow-up message to be sure I understood what she meant by *score*."

Amelia smiled. "I think it's sweet that they're so into this."

I didn't disagree, but even for my aunts, things had gotten a little over-the-top. "They aren't even calling it an application or a video anymore. They're calling it a three-minute journey through the historic plight of the American honeybee." *An apocalyptic, dystopian film.* A bout of laughter bubbled through me.

Amelia laughed along with me. "It's kooky, but it's cool. Your aunts are so much fun. I mean, who gets involved in stuff like this?"

I wiped my tears and settled myself. "Us?"

"Us," she said, looking quite pleased.

"How's it going with the hunt for extras?" I asked.

Amelia's smile went soft and wistful. "I've been interviewing cowboys and artists all day. Fun, but time consuming." She deposited a giant bag of books on my freshly scrubbed counter top. "I've been so busy, I completely forgot to restock my Little Libraries, so I'm going to do that next. It's like my brain can't keep up with the to-do list."

"You were smart to come here," I told her. "Tea fixes everything."

She turned her gaze upward, checking the big chalkboard behind the counter. "Do you have Iced Chai today?"

"I keep it on tap for you," I said. "If we're going to do some catching up, I think we need something sweet to go with the tea. And I'm dying to hear all about these cowboy interviews." I looked at my closed refrigerator doors, trying not to think of my own recent run-in with a cowboy, and seeking the perfect dessert to match with an Iced Chai Latte. "I made hazelnut and almond truffles this afternoon."

"You're a goddess," she said, sliding onto a bar stool at the counter and dropping her chin into waiting palms. "I love truffles."

"Tell me about the interviews," I said.

"Your aunts wanted a couple of guys to wear costumes and mime various actions in front of the backdrops, or fill in as stage hands when needed. The gig pays one basket of honey products and a gift certificate to your café."

It sounded like a solid trade to me. "Have any trouble finding volunteers?" I asked.

"Nope." Amelia grinned. "I marched right up to a group of cowboys, told them what I needed, and got two instant volunteers. They agree to wear costumes and do whatever we wanted for a few hours this week."

"Wow." I guessed it was true: cowboys would try anything.

"They said it sounded like fun. I knew they were the right group to ask as soon as I saw their trailer. It had *Wild Bunch* painted right down the side. I figured those guys would be game for anything, and I was right."

My tongue stuck to the roof of my mouth. She got a couple guys from the Wild Bunch? "Did you recognize any of them?"

"No, but they're going to be hard to forget," Amelia said. "Dad finished the set and wooden props while I rounded up the extras. He's going to set it all up in your aunts' garden. I think they have a real chance at winning," she said. "Those two have enough personality to merit their own documentary on about ten different topics, and the way they play off one another is fantastic. Absolutely hilarious."

I smiled. I suspected my aunts had no idea they were funny, and I'd never had the nerve to tell them. I slid a jar of Iced Chai in her direction. "We're going to start filming here tomorrow morning."

"That's going to be fun," Amelia said. "I'll try to be here if I can." She took a long pull on the straw in her drink, then exhaled. "How was your day?"

"All right," I said, piling truffles onto a small plate. "Someone drew an image on the sand in front of my house. Grady had to come over and take a look."

"An image?" Amelia bit into a truffle and let her eyelids flutter. "I'm guessing the drawing wasn't very nice if it summonsed the sexy detective."

"It wasn't, but that's not even the worst thing that happened before breakfast."

Her narrow brows rose. "Go on."

"Well, while I was in the gardens, trying to pull myself together, Wyatt showed up looking like a million bucks. I, however, was in my jammies."

"Wyatt?" Amelia raised the half-eaten truffle and gaped at me. "He's back?"

I nodded, selecting a truffle. "Yes. With the Wild Bunch."

"Shut. Up," she said, clearly aghast.

"Dead serious," I said. "I was excited by the hunky

distraction until he invited me to take a roll in the sand with him later, like we were square. Like my heart wasn't a bloodied mess from the breakup that feels like five minutes ago instead of eight months."

"And you were in your jammies?" she asked with utter heartbreak.

"Yep." I sank my teeth into a truffle. "My hair was uncombed and battered by the wind. I'd just woken up, so no makeup. I wasn't even in good jammies. I was wearing the ones with little suns on the legs and a big pair of sunglasses across the chest." I mimed the sunglass placement.

Amelia bonked her head with one palm.

"Exactly. Then Grady came up from the beach, saw my distress, and tried to help by implying he and I are an item without saying it directly."

Amelia sipped her drink. "Interesting. How'd that go?"

"Extremely awkwardly." I had another truffle. "This hasn't been my favorite day." Sadly, despite everything that had gone wrong, it wasn't nearly my worst, either.

Amelia groaned. "I swear I had no idea he was with that rodeo group." She made a disgusted sound and wiped her mouth with a napkin. "Bad as that must've been for you," she said, "at least you were never afraid, and you weren't in danger. Considering the last few days you've had, that's what really matters."

"Well"—I rocked my head side to side—"I also learned the crime lab developed the photos on the camera found in Pete's pocket, and they were all of me."

"Good grief," she whispered. "Are you okay?"

"I'm torn," I said. "On the one hand, it was definitely an unsettling turn of events. On the other hand, I'm a little thankful I'm not crazy. I've been feeling watched for days. I started to wonder if the stress was making me paranoid. At least now I know I was right. My instinct is intact."

Amelia stuffed a truffle into her mouth. "So, Pete was stalking you?"

"I don't think so. There were no prints on the camera, and it seems counterproductive to wipe the prints from something he kept in his pocket. I think it was another threat. Whoever knocked him out wanted me to know they're watching."

Amelia shivered. "Creepy."

"Add finishing the drop-cloth paintings, and that's my day in a nutshell," I said. "Luckily the café was busy most of the time. It kept my mind off things." I finished my third truffle, then dusted my palms and pressed a napkin to the corner of my mouth. "Enough about me. How's Summer Splash going? Is it as busy as usual? Is it as much fun as I remember?"

"Summer Splash is always fun, which is another reason I'm here," she said. "I asked Dad to cover for me so I could see if you want to join me at the festival tonight." She smiled around the little pink-and-white-striped straw in her tea.

"Absolutely," I said. Grady would be thrilled to know I was working the buddy system. "What else is new with you?" I asked, repacking the leftover truffles.

"Not much." She pumped her straw in and out of her tea. "That handsome reporter interviewed me last night."

It took me a minute to realize she'd meant the colossal thorn in my side. "Ryan?"

She blushed. "He's really charming. Don't you think?"

Not even a little. "I think he's a fake," I said. "He only wants one thing. And it's not even a fun thing. He just wants to advance his career."

"I know," she said, "but his determination is admirable, and I get that he'll be leaving the island soon. But he is kind of cute, right?"

I bopped my head noncommittally and refilled her glass with tea. Ryan was a little cute, but he knew it, so that made it less fun to admit.

"I'm meeting him for coffee later."

I stared, unsure what to say—and unwilling to say anything that might make her unhappy. "Be careful," was all I could manage.

Thankfully, she changed the subject. "How's Judy doing?"

"She and Jasper have been with her family all day. I haven't seen them since this morning."

A sneaky grin slid over her lips. "So, you're alone and the shop is closed for the day?"

I untied my apron with extreme enthusiasm. I knew exactly where she was going with this.

"Do you want to leave now? We can drop these books off at the Little Libraries on our way, then fill up on fried foods and talk about the criminal in our midst."

I hit the light switch behind the counter. "You had me at 'fried foods.'"

⁓

Forty minutes later, we'd restocked Amelia's Little Libraries and were following the delectable scents of Summer Splash vendors along the boardwalk toward town like Fred and Barney after a whiff of brontosaurus stew.

Music, laughter, and voices rose from the festival on a warm evening breeze. Strings of white bistro lights swooped in arcs from telephone pole to telephone pole, outlining designated blocks and reaching in crisscross patterns above the pedestrian-only portions of the street. Barricades stood sentinel at either end of the festival, protecting pedestrians from motorists. Neon signs flashed over vendor carts. A jug band played on the corner, and older couples danced in the street.

I hoped I wouldn't run into Wyatt.

We hurried over the wide, weathered planks of the boardwalk, getting closer to the fun with every step.

"I hate this part," Amelia said, slowing before a short section of boardwalk where the lush summer overgrowth blocked our view on both sides. "I usually run through it when I'm alone at night."

We stepped into the deep shadows together, and the world fell away. Main Street became little more than a soft, distant glow, the lights and sounds of music eerily muffled. The sea disappeared.

I tuned in to the steady beat of our feet across the

boards, counting a nonsensical rhythm to busy my darkening thoughts.

Something snapped behind us, and my steps faltered. Instinct prickled over my skin. My muscles tensed to spring.

I turned to examine the emptiness. Nothing but stretching shadows and the shrinking silhouette of my home hundreds of yards away.

"What was that?" Amelia asked, frozen in place, head cocked in the direction of the sound. Fear stretched her blue eyes wide and drained the color from her skin.

A stick underfoot? A kicked pebble? A nearby animal?

"I'm not sure," I said, "but let's not hang around and find out."

"Deal," Amelia agreed. "Except I can't move. What if I turn my back and something jumps out and gets me?"

The sound came again, louder this time, closer.

The fine hairs on my arms and neck rose to attention. "It's better than standing here until something gets us," I said. I grabbed Amelia's wrist and ran, dragging her forward until she found her pace beside me. We ran until the boardwalk arched closest to the road, and my throat and lungs burned with fatigue.

"Here," I said, pulling Amelia across a thin portion of marshy land where a tree had fallen in the spring. We scrambled over the log, taking a natural shortcut away from the boardwalk and directly into a crowd of happy locals on their way to the festival, clueless to our racing hearts and terror-filled minds.

I rubbed my aching chest and stared back at the boardwalk from a place of safety beneath a lemonade vendor's sign.

Amelia bent forward at the waist, gasping for air. "I don't see anyone back there. Do you see anyone?"

"No." I blew away the panic and winced at the painful stitch in my side. "I'm so sorry. I'm spreading my paranoia to you."

Amelia straightened and turned around, away from the shadows that had chased us, and moved to the end of the lemonade line. "I need a drink."

"Make mine a double," I teased, still warily checking the boardwalk behind us. Had we really run away from nothing, or was the person who'd taken twenty-seven photos of me nearby even now?

A portly man in a tan suit walked into line at the funnel cake station next door, effectively disrupting my view of nothing on the boardwalk.

He was the local businessman who'd worked briefly with Craig before his death. I combed my brain for his name, then waved an arm overhead. "Mr. Granger," I called.

He looked around before landing his gaze on me. "Oh, hello."

I gave Amelia some cash and placed a request for strawberry lemonade, then slipped across the vacant space between vendor trucks. "It's nice to see you," I told him. "You're back in Charm? Or maybe you haven't left?"

"I never miss Summer Splash," he said. "I drive

over from Corolla every year to enjoy the arts. I wish our town would put on a show like this for crafty locals. My polka band can really rev up a crowd."

I immediately imagined him in striped suspenders and short pants.

He shuffled forward with the line.

My gaze darted back to the distant boardwalk. Silent. Deserted.

"Are you feeling well?" he asked.

"Yes. Thank you." I shook off the idea we'd been chased, and let the experience be what it was—a fear, trauma, and paranoia cocktail. Nothing more.

Mr. Granger cringed. "And how is Judy Miller?"

"It's been a tough few days," I said. The line ahead of us grew shorter by the second. I needed to ask what I wanted to before he took his funnel cake and said goodbye. I cleared my throat of the residual thickness and fear that had followed me through the marsh. I couldn't do anything about who was or wasn't on the boardwalk. I could, however, ask Mr. Granger about Craig. "So, Craig Miller worked for your company?"

"Briefly, yes. He was very good." Mr. Granger seemed unfazed by the sudden shift in topic.

"How so?" I asked. "Did Craig find anything useful to your company?" *Maybe something detrimental that you didn't want anyone to know?*

"I'm not sure," he said, bushy brows furrowed. "I just wish we'd been able to talk about it." Mr. Granger's polite expression went distant for a long moment. "It's a real shame about what happened to him."

"Next!" a man in a white apron and matching paper hat called across the counter.

Mr. Granger ordered two funnel cakes and two elephant ears. One of each for now, the others in to-go bags.

Amelia arrived at my side with two large lemonades and eyeballed Granger at the counter.

I took the ice-cold strawberry lemonade from her hand and sucked down several life-changing gulps. "Thank you for this."

"Sure," she said. "I kept your change. Handler's fee."

I laughed.

Mr. Granger paid the man, then smiled at Amelia. "Well, hello," he said. "When did you get here?"

"Just now," she said. "I'm Everly's friend, Amelia. It's nice to meet you."

They exchanged pleasantries while I watched the men working inside the truck, frying sheets of dough and piping lines of batter into a bubbly golden vat. My mouth watered at the sight of the giant cinnamon sugar shaker.

I forced my attention away from the dough and sugar before I bought an elephant ear for myself. "Did you hear about Craig's partner, Pete?" I asked Granger as the man in the paper hat presented his order.

"Of course." Mr. Granger stacked two plates of deep-fried dough on one hand, funnel cake on top, elephant ear on the bottom, then slid the handle of his to-go bag around the opposite wrist. "Your whole town's talking about it."

Amelia pulled a few napkins from the dispenser and offered them to him. "What's everyone saying?" she asked.

"The company was cursed," he said, ripping portions of the sweets with his fingertips and stuffing them into his mouth. "Doomed. They burned too bright. Flew too close to the sun."

I tried not to get hung up on the word *cursed*, but memories of Wyatt's endless trips to the hospital flashed in my mind's eye. I'd seen him concussed, in casts, in traction, and heading to and from surgery a dozen times while we were together. Today, after eight months without me, he looked as perfect and healthy as the day we'd met. As far as I was concerned, the guy was finally learning how to ride. "Curses aren't real," I said.

Mr. Granger sucked powdered sugar off his finger and tucked the suddenly empty funnel cake plate beneath his elephant ear. "Regardless," he said, "I think whoever hurt those men has made his point, and now this whole thing can be put to bed."

"Maybe," I said, "but what was the point?"

The local ice cream man strode into view, distracting Mr. Granger. "Milkshakes!" the man called. He was dressed head to toe in white and had lined up a load of prefilled disposable cups on a tray hanging from his neck like a vintage cigarette vendor. "Vanilla! Chocolate! Strawberry!"

Mr. Granger gave a guttural moan and hurried away to stop the ice cream man.

Amelia shook her lemonade cup, rattling the ice inside. "I wish he would've stuck around to tell us the point," she said.

"Me too. Do you think he meant anything by when he said the killer was done now, or was it the sugar and cholesterol talking?" I asked.

"Hard to say."

I sucked on my straw again, enjoying the sharp tang of freshly made lemonade and savoring the exact right amount of added strawberries. "Did you hear him say Craig found something in the company server data that he wanted to talk to him about?"

"Yeah."

"What if Craig found evidence of something illegal going on at Granger's company?" I theorized. "Embezzlement. Theft. Maybe a personnel scandal, like an interoffice affair."

"An affair with Granger?" she asked, eyes wide. "Who?"

"I don't know who," I said. "There's someone for everyone, and maybe it was harassment or some other thing he'd be desperate to cover up. It'd make sense to attack Pete if he thought Craig told Pete what he'd found out." Another idea came to mind. "If he thought Craig had the information with him, it would give Granger a reason to search for his laptop or a thumb drive, something like that. That would explain the break-ins."

Amelia scrunched her nose while I spoke.

"What?"

"You're creeping me out," she said, pushing a swath of hair behind her ear. "You had that same look on your face in April when you were after Mr. Paine's killer, and you remember how that turned out. I think you'd better leave this alone. I can't go through all that again."

"Too late," I said. "It's not like I can pretend I'm not involved. Someone's been following me since Friday night, and Grady has photographic proof. Someone drew a threat on the beach outside my house. Someone stabbed Blue," I said. "I'm already in this. Deep. Finding the truth before I wind up hurt or worse seems like the smartest thing I can do right now. Don't you think?"

"I think you should leave this alone," she repeated.

I pushed my straw between my lips before I could say anything to start a debate. We'd come to Summer Splash to have a little fun and forget about the scary stuff, not rehash every ugly detail from April. Amelia and I would have to agree to disagree.

I was absolutely going to find the killer before the killer found me.

CHAPTER

SEVENTEEN

Amelia's dad had drawn a crowd to the face-painting booth outside her bookstore, painting dazzling fairy wings on some children's faces and turning others into a variety of heroes and villains. Amelia jumped in to help a pair of ladies waiting to pay for their book selections when we were close enough to see the line there.

I whistled at Mr. Butters as I approached. "Looking good," I told him. "I really appreciate all the help you're giving my aunts with their video application."

"It's no trouble," he said, smiling as he worked. "You know I love to paint and create. I'm looking forward to seeing it all come together tomorrow morning." He turned my way with a wink. "Eight a.m. at your place?"

"Absolutely." I hadn't realized Mr. Butters would be there, but I loved knowing he would. I'd known Mr. Butters all my life, and it wasn't long ago that I'd sat in his tall chair and been transformed by his paintbrush into anything I could imagine. Amelia's dad was a former art teacher, lifelong artist, and true inspiration for creative expression. He'd never tired of my requests to see him paint something more when we were young, and he'd encouraged me to learn the art of cake decorating before I was tall enough to reach the counter properly. I'd always loved creating delicious things, and Mr. Butters helped me make them look pretty too.

I recognized the little boy climbing down from the face painting seat as a pigtailed princess scrambled up. Grady's son looked just like him, from the big gray eyes and signature dimple, to the confident strut of someone who knew his daddy had his back no matter what. It made me smile every time he looked my way.

"Hi, Denver," I said, admiring Mr. Butters' work. "I almost didn't recognize you. When did you grow a beard?"

Denver beamed. "I grew this beard when I became a pirate." He gave a menacing growl and raised a plastic sword.

"Oh my," I said. "You are quite the pirate." I folded my arms and nodded in approval. Amelia's dad had painted thick black eyebrows over Denver's narrow brown ones and dotted in a solid three-day stubble. The look paired perfectly with his plastic eye patch and red bandanna.

"Dad let me rip my jeans," he said, holding my hand for balance and sticking one foot into the air so

I could check out the shredded pant legs. "They were too short because I got taller, so he said it was okay if I used them to play pirates and the Hulk."

"Nice." I nodded appreciatively. "I think the pants make the whole thing work."

"Me too," he said. "It's not like the time I used my scissors on my hair. I didn't ask first that time."

"Gotcha," I said. "Is your dad here now?" I scanned the area for Denver's six-foot doppelgänger and came up empty.

"Yeah," he said. "With Denise."

The willowy blond au pair waved from the opposite side of a table piled high with books. A few months ago, I'd mistaken her for Grady's wife and made a number of insensitive assumptions. Denise turned out to be the epitome of amazing, and unbelievably good for both Denver and Grady. She probably didn't weigh a hundred pounds soaking wet, but she seemed to keep both Hays men in line, on schedule, and out of trouble. I loved her.

"Hey, you," she said when she arrived at our side, looking runway ready as usual in a plaid sundress and matching red flats. "It's so nice to see you again, Everly." She scanned the crowd around us with an exaggerated frown. "Have you seen Denver, because I've been looking all over for him."

"Here I am!" Denver said, bouncing on his toes.

"No," she said, "I'm sorry. I'm actually looking for a little boy. You're a very tough pirate, and my Denver is a tiny cuddle bug."

"Arrrgh!" he said, waving his sword once more. "I will help ye look for me, then."

She nodded. "I accept the offer. May I pay you in cotton candy and grape soda?"

Denver jumped up and down at my side, dropping my hand in favor of clapping. "Ice cream! Ice cream!"

Denise laughed. "All right then, ice cream. Boy, you drive a hard bargain, Mr. Pirate." She scooped Denver onto one hip and kissed his nose.

"Are you enjoying Summer Splash?" I asked her.

"Absolutely. This whole town is great. It's just what Grady and Denver needed, if you ask me, though no one ever does." She rolled her eyes. "I was trying to get Grady to buy a painting of the wild ponies for Denver's room, but Grady thinks everything is too expensive, so that was a big no. Nixed painting aside, we're all having a blast."

"Is Grady still here?" I asked, still not seeing him in the crowd.

"He went for cotton candy and grape soda," she said. "I guess when he gets back, we'll also get some ice cream." She tickled Denver's tummy and he squealed.

Grady's determined face appeared on the corner, bobbing several inches above most of the rest of the crowd. He threaded his way through the throng, cowboy hat pulled low and a large canvas pressed to his side beneath one bent arm. Clear plastic bags of cotton candy and cans of soda hung from his hands.

"Whoa," I said, rushing to meet him. "Let me help."

"Thanks." Grady let me work the bags from his

death grip, then he flexed his fingers until color returned to the tips. "I was losing feeling in that hand."

I laughed. "I don't suppose there are ponies on that canvas?"

He heaved a sigh. "Yeah. I guess you already heard about what a mean guy I am. Saying no to a kid and his au pair."

"No." I smiled. "It wasn't like that at all."

Denise's smile was ear to ear when we approached. "You bought the painting." She pressed a palm to her heart, kissed Denver's head, then lifted her gaze to mine. "He's one of the good ones."

"The ponies!" Denver yelled. "Thanks, Daddy! That's awesome! Can I have ice cream?"

"What about the cotton candy and soda?"

"Ice cream!"

Grady smiled. "Yeah. Have some ice cream." He turned his happy face to Denise. "I'll meet you guys there. I'm going to take this stuff to the truck. I can't carry it around all night."

"Ice cream!" Denver yelled.

Grady turned tired eyes on me. "Ice cream," he said.

"What can I say?" I shrugged. "Ice cream is way better than grape soda. You've got a smart kid."

Grady rubbed his brow.

"Are you enjoying Summer Splash?" I asked as we headed in a new direction.

"If you mean am I hemorrhaging money, then yes." He groaned. "Sorry. That's not true. It's a bad habit."

"Complaining about money?" That was my life.

Grady glanced my way, readjusting the painting beneath his arm. "I've worried about money my entire adult life. From the moment I left home, I was determined to make it on my own, and I did. I pinched pennies. Made tough financial choices. But I made it."

"And now you don't have to worry as much, but old habits die hard?" I guessed. I felt exactly the same, though my current spending dilemma wasn't over a painting. I was coaxing my tight financial grip to loosen up for all-new café seating.

He beeped the doors to his truck open and slid the canvas inside. "You could say that."

I put the bags beside the painting. "I like your hat," I said, enjoying the moonlight on his Stetson. He was wearing it more often these days.

Grady raised his hand to the brim, as if he'd forgotten it was there. A slick grin slid over his face. "Cowboys." He shut the door, then leaned against it, clearly in no hurry to get back to the festival. "What about you? Are you having a good time tonight?"

"I am now," I said, feeling heat rise in my cheeks.

Grady's smile grew until it reached his eyes and his blessed dimple sunk in.

I looked away.

"Has the cowboy from your garden been back to try to charm you?"

"No," I said, sending Grady a wry smile. "I still can't believe he's in town, even for a few days."

"For what it's worth, I can see why you left him,"

Grady said. "He was presumptuous this morning and borderline rude. You want to talk about that?"

"Not really," I said. "I'm glad things worked out the way they did. It's like you said, losing him brought me back here, and I'm really happy right where I am." I cast a bashful gaze at Grady. I meant the last statement literally, and the look in his eyes told me he knew it. "He dumped me, though, I didn't leave him. Which made the way you stuck up for me all the sweeter."

Grady studied me a long moment. "That's what friends are for, right?"

I nodded, a weird mix of emotions pressing on my lungs.

"If you're ever ready to date again," Grady said, a crooked smile on his lips, "let me know."

My heart seized, and my mouth fell open.

Grady's smile widened. "I'll run a full background check on your prospect and teach you some self-defense moves in case the new beau gets handsy."

I laughed on a huge exhale of breath. "Why, Detective Hays," I drawled, "how do you know I don't like 'em handsy?"

Grady snorted. "Now I'm definitely running those background checks." He offered his arm and I slid my hand over the bend of his elbow.

We moved back toward the crowd with our steps in sync.

"What happened?" he asked. "With you and the cowboy."

"It's complicated," I said. "Short version: He's a bulls and blood guy. I'm a sand and the seashore girl."

Grady stared down at me as we walked. "That's it?"

"That, and I just learned from Ryan that Wyatt thought the reason he was hurt all the time when we were together was because of my family curse." My cheeks warmed again, this time with humiliation and a pinch of embarrassment. "He looked good today, but when we were together, he spent more time in the emergency room than he did on any bronco."

"Maybe he finally learned to ride," Grady said.

A wide smile split my face. "That was exactly what I'd thought!"

"How's your aunts' video thing going?" he asked.

I gaped at him. "How did you know about that?"

He tapped his temple. "I know things."

I tugged his arm tighter in mine. "Yes, you do," I said. "They're ready to tape. We're starting first thing tomorrow at my place."

"Let me know if you need anything. I'm not sure what I could do to help shoot a video application for a honeybee documentary, but the Swan women are just about my favorite part of this island, so I want you to keep me in mind."

A touch of pride lifted my chest. "I will," I said. "And for the record, it's an educational three-minute honeybee apocalypse movie."

His loud laugh rumbled all the way from his core. "Well, that sounds about right."

Denise and Denver were in the street tossing ropes

at a wooden steer when we made it back into the mix. We stopped to cheer them on from behind.

"Hey," I said to Grady, clapping as Denver threw his rope three feet wide of the steer. "Has Pete woken up yet?"

"Not yet. He took a good whack on the head. The way I understand it, he's lucky to be alive."

"That's too bad," I said. "I'm dying for him to open his eyes and tell you everything he can remember from that night."

Mr. Granger moseyed into view, sipping on a straw that was stuck in one of my sample cups.

Grady's gaze locked on the drink. "Is that your tea?"

"My aunts are giving out samples since I don't have a booth this year," I said. "Life's too cuckoo for me to do anything remotely normal this week."

Grady's gaze trailed after Granger. "I think you need something normal right now. Why not close Sun, Sand, and Tea for a day or two and sit out here instead? Clear your head. Breathe."

"I try to clear my head," I said, "but you have no idea what it's like in here." I pointed to my forehead. "I have a curious mind and a thirst for justice."

"You'd better let me dish out the justice."

"I want you to," I said, "and I have plenty of other things that keep me up at night. Heck, I still have questions from April. It's awful."

"April?" he asked. "Do you mean Mr. Paine's murder? I can probably answer those questions for you. That investigation is about as over as it can get."

I chewed my lip. I hadn't meant the murder. "Do you realize we haven't really talked since the close of that investigation?" I'd seen him around, often with his son, but we never exchanged more than a bunch of pointless niceties, and I didn't like it. "In fact," I said, "the last time we had a conversation, a parade of black SUVs and a limousine showed up at Sun, Sand, and Tea and it took you away." It had been the strangest thing: I thought Grady and I were having a moment, and I was going to introduce Denver to Lou, but before I could get the deck door open, an intimidating string of vehicles pulled up to the café. Denise took Denver from my hip and marched solemnly toward the limo with him as if it had called to her. Grady followed, and that was that. "Seems like you could've called in the last four months to let me know what that was about."

Grady's attention moved back to Denver, now seated atop the wooden steer and waving one fist in the air. "Probably," he admitted.

"Now also works," I suggested with a nudge and a smile. "I believe the woman in the limo was your mother-in-law."

Grady sucked his teeth. "I believe you're right."

"Why the entourage? Kind of a big show for a friendly family visit."

Grady had told me once that his mother-in-law had insisted on an au pair and handpicked Denise. I'd wondered on more than one occasion, after seeing the mysterious cavalcade, if Denise was a spy reporting back to them and if she was military trained to protect their grandbaby at any cost.

"She worries," he said. "My mother-in-law hates that we left DC. She lost her daughter to cancer. It seemed like she was losing Denver too, but we're only a few hours away. I had to make a change, and she knew it."

"Was she able to see how well you're both doing here?"

"Yeah." Grady looked at me, lines forming on his forehead. "She liked it here too. A little too much."

I raised my brows. He'd dodged a call from her while we were together recently, and he'd said she was returning for a visit. "So, she's coming back?"

Grady shifted his weight, then fixed me with his soulful gray stare. "My mother-in-law is Senator Olivia Denver, and her husband worked at Langley before he went missing. She always travels with a protective detail. Somehow those facts didn't seem as weird in DC as they do here."

My jaw dropped. "Your mother-in-law is a senator?" My mind raced back to the limo and the caravan, then to something else I'd learned this spring. "Denver told me he was named after his grandma. You used your wife's maiden name."

Grady ducked his chin. "She's determined to finish her term with grace and dignity, but afterward, she's looking for a change too. I get that. It's been hard on her, maintaining a public face, keeping up the façade of normal when nothing is normal anymore." Grady rubbed a heavy hand over his lips. "I felt that way too. For a long time. Like I'd lost myself when I lost Amy."

My heart broke for him whenever I thought of all he'd been through these past couple of years. "How about now?" I asked, crossing my arms to stop myself from reaching for him. "Are you feeling more like yourself now?"

Denver squealed, and we both jumped.

A slow smile spread over Grady's face as he watched Denver take a bow for the cheering crowd. "More than I have in a very long time."

Denver ran full speed past Denise and leapt into Grady's arms, a length of rope in his dimpled grip. "Did you see me, Daddy? Did you see?"

"Yes, sir, I did." Grady covered his son in love and squeezes, then hoisted him onto his shoulders. The rope draped over the brim of Grady's Stetson.

"Can I keep the rope, Daddy?" Denver asked. "That cowboy said it's okay with him, if you say I can have it."

"I suppose so," Grady said. "Let me thank him before we go." Grady stepped forward, and I froze in place.

The cowboy was Wyatt. Of course it was. He tipped his hat in my direction, a look of regret in his eyes.

Grady shook his hand and spoke to him briefly before turning back in my direction.

Denise met them with a smile and reached for Denver. "How about that ice cream now?"

"Yeah!" Denver hollered.

Grady kissed his son's cheek as he passed him off to the au pair. "I'll catch up with you two at the ice cream stand," he promised.

I waved goodbye, hoping not to look as freaked out as I was by Wyatt's interaction with Denver and Grady. My past and present were colliding, but my brain was struggling to reconcile it.

Grady placed a palm on the small of my back and lowered his face to my ear. "Don't look now, but your ex is watching you awful closely."

My gaze jumped to Wyatt. Grady was right. He was staring, jaw locked. "I don't know why," I admitted. Wyatt had cut me loose and never looked back, as far as I could tell. So what was his problem now, after the better part of a year had passed?

"He told me to take care of you," Grady said. "You know what that means."

"Not at all," I admitted, fighting the ridiculous sting of unbidden tears.

"It means he knows what he lost."

"What did you say?" I asked, half afraid to know, and heavily distracted by the gentle weight of his palm on my back.

Grady's fingers curled protectively against the curve of my waist. "I told him he could count on it."

My gaze jumped to meet his. Electricity spun and snapped between us.

"Can I interest you in some ice cream?" he asked, his voice a little deeper than usual.

I blew out a steadying breath. "I walked here with

Amelia," I said, scanning the area for signs of her. She was bending before a little brunette outside her shop, painting butterfly wings on the child's face. "I should probably wait on her."

Grady didn't take his eyes off of me. "Amelia lives right above her shop, and you live down a deserted boardwalk. How about I drive you home so you aren't tempted to walk by yourself later? You can text Amelia and let her know."

I gave Amelia another long look. She was laughing and joking with the line of kids awaiting their turns in her seat. She'd understand, and Grady had a point. I would have eventually grown bored and headed home on my own rather than interrupt her for a ride back. "Okay," I agreed. "Thank you." I was emotionally spent, and it was time I put some distance between myself and my problems. Plus, how could I turn down a ride home from my new favorite cowboy?

CHAPTER

❧

EIGHTEEN

The following morning was off to a great start when my aunts arrived. No new break-ins, no attacks on people I knew or golf carts I owned, and no new threats etched in the sand. Maybe Mr. Granger was right, and whoever had been behind the crime spree was finally finished. Of course, if Mr. Granger was right, how could he have known, unless he was the killer? Or a psychic. Or knew the killer personally. I pressed a finger to my twitching eyelid.

Aunt Clara bustled around Amelia's dad, helping as he set up the wire and pulleys contraption that dragged my newly finished backgrounds across the wall of my former ballroom. I'd painted the scenes Aunt Fran had sketched on an eight-foot scale, then sewn them end to end for a continuous loop of passing time. Mr. Butters would steadily pull the painted scenes in his direction until they were out of frame and the next painting arrived center screen. The first painting depicted a lush, green forest with an abundance of local flora and fauna cohabiting peacefully with the bees. The next illustrated early settlements in the area, log cabins and farms. Next, a landscape impacted by a growing population and advanced industry. Then, a drop cloth painted to represent Main Street today, and finally the darkness that was coming. I'd added a layer of gray to the top of all the paintings after the first one that grew darker and moved lower over each progressing canvas. The presence of bees grew thinner and thinner in each painting as well. The final canvas was done wholly in shades of gray, with honeybees littered over the ground of a scene packed with people, houses, businesses, cars, and robust genetically modified plants. I'd felt half-depressed while painting it.

I opened the curtains to invite in the sunlight and positioned a few borrowed floodlights to further illuminate the drop cloths.

Aunt Fran set up a boom box in the corner and popped in a mix tape, a.k.a. *the score.* "What do you think?" she asked, adjusting the volume. "Is it too much?"

A series of classical pieces grew slower and darker from one song to the next and ended with thirty seconds of low whale cries before complete silence. *Too much?* "I thought it was quite fitting," I said. "The score moves nicely with the backgrounds you designed."

"I thought so too," she said, adjusting her brown and white early settler costume. "Is my bonnet straight?"

I wasn't used to seeing her or Aunt Clara with their hair wound up in a knot, and the hats hid their waist-length locks completely. Looking just at her face, I could see my grandma in her eyes, cheekbones, and the sturdy set of her lips. "You look perfect," I said, fighting a sudden rush of emotion. I shook it off and set the cue cards on easels in each corner facing the backdrop. I'd broken the finalized script into chunks and made two copies of it that covered twelve poster boards each so that my aunts wouldn't have to rely on their memories, and if we were all lucky, the indoor filming could be done in a day.

Judy appeared in the archway between Sun, Sand, and Tea and the ballroom. "What's all this?" Her small smile said she was amused but not upset, as I'd worried might be the case when I'd agreed to such an early start. Judy had barely slept in the four days since the wedding, and if she happened to be resting this morning, I didn't want the commotions of a bee-pocalypse to disturb her.

"Sorry," I said. "Did we wake you?"

"Yeah." She leaned against the jamb and crossed her arms. "But this is the best thing I've seen in days. Are you making a pilgrim movie?"

"It's a bee-pocalypse," I told her. "My aunts are educating America on the plight of the American honeybee."

Judy smiled. "Of course they are."

"Can I get you something before we start?" I asked, heading in her direction. "We're still waiting for the extras to arrive."

Judy took a seat at the counter and folded her hands in front of her. "Coffee and toast sounds good.

My stomach never seems to settle these days, but I'm definitely hungry."

I flipped a mug up and filled it with black coffee, delivering it with an encouraging smile. "Toast will help."

Judy sipped her coffee and dragged my tattered copy of *Beach House* magazine across the space to her cup, then flipped through the folded pages. "Cute," she said. "Are you thinking of redecorating?"

"I like the furniture," I said, dropping some bread into my toaster and setting little pots of my aunts' organic honey and preserves on the counter for Judy. "I'd love to upgrade my seating here, but I hate to spend the money when these seats work fine."

She shook her head. "Investing in your business is never wasted money. You want current guests to see improvements being made and new guests to be impressed with a clean, professional atmosphere. The thrift store stuff is okay to get you going, but you have to keep plugging ahead." She sipped her coffee, looking from the magazine to the space around her. "You can write it off at tax time, you know."

I hadn't thought of that. "Maybe I'll revisit it," I said. I liked the idea of getting a deduction on my taxes for doing something good for my business. "I really do like the pieces."

Judy folded the magazine in half, leaving the photo of my dream furniture in full view. They composed a perfect seaside palette of pale blue, white, and tan. Everything about the collection screamed blue skies, warm waves, and soft sand. The wicker pieces were fun plays on the home's Victorian charm, and the more streamlined designs gave a nod to the Adirondack chairs on every beach in the country. Judy tapped a fingertip to the page. "I think you have to have it. All of it."

I smiled. "We'll see."

The toast popped up, and I delivered it to Judy.

The doorbell rang, and my aunts squealed from the next room. "The extras!" they shouted. My elderly aunts, dressed as early settlers, skidded around the corner and made a run for my front door.

I poured myself some coffee and wandered into the ballroom, eyeing the backdrops critically. My aunts' excited voices dropped into silence, and I lifted my eyes to find Mr. Butters looking over my shoulder, eyes narrowed. Aunt Clara hurried to my side with a strange expression. She seemed caught somewhere between fright and panic. "Everly," she began.

I looked past her, out toward the café. "What?"

Two cowboys stood with Aunt Fran in the archway between the café and our makeshift movie studio. One of them was Wyatt.

"Morning, E," he said with an easy smile.

"What are you doing here?"

He took a step forward. "I heard you could use some strong hands and a little muscle."

Aunt Fran glared up at him. "What do you want me to do with him?" she asked, and for the briefest of moments, I wondered if there was any limit to what she would do to protect me. Aunt Clara ushered the other cowboy away to make introductions as Wyatt sauntered closer.

Aunt Fran followed. "Everly?"

I released a long breath. "I'm fine," I said. My aunts needed two extras. Amelia had chosen two extras—but she definitely wouldn't have selected Wyatt. There was no reason for my previously broken heart to put a kink in the whole project just because my ex showed up uninvited. Again. My pride still stung a bit at the sight of him, but I didn't love him anymore. Didn't long for him. "Give us a minute?" I asked her, then turned my gaze on Wyatt and nodded my head in the direction he'd come.

We strode into the café, which was empty aside from Judy, still munching her toast.

Wyatt smiled. "Nice to see you."

"Amelia didn't hire you," I said. "What happened to the guy she picked?"

"I volunteered for Chip's job," he said. "When I heard where he and Franco were headed this morning, I encouraged him to let me take his place."

Obnoxious. Rude. Presumptuous. My stomach knotted with nervous energy and the urge to throw him over the cliff outside my deck doors. Then something he'd said circled back to mind. "Did you say you're here to be the muscle for our project?"

He crossed his arms and widened his stance. "That's right. Just point me to whatever needs done and I'll get it done."

A small smile budded on my lips. "I like that go-getter attitude," I said. "I guess you can stay."

Aunt Clara poked her head around the corner. "Sweetie?" she called. "How's it going out there? Should we reschedule for another day?"

"Nope." I smiled. "We're ready."

Judy chewed her toast purposefully and ping-ponged her gaze between Aunt Clara and me as Wyatt and I headed back through the café, probably thankful to not be the center of drama for the first time this week. I tossed a warm smile at Judy as we passed, and I could practically feel Wyatt's misplaced sense of victory streaming behind me as I reentered the ballroom.

Aunt Fran led Wyatt behind the wire-and-pulley apparatus Mr. Butters had constructed. "When the music changes," she said, "you hold these over the canvases, but keep your hands out of the shot."

I stifled a laugh imagining Wyatt's expression as she handed him the four-foot dowel rods with four dozen pom-pom honeybees tied to each by transparent fishing lines.

My aunts moved to the front, nearest the camera, and prepared to read the cue cards while Wyatt dangled pom-pom bees in front of the slowly turning canvases. Franco would strike some bees down during each of his vivid but silent portrayals in front of the backdrops, first as an early settler, then an Industrial Revolution millworker, a railroad conductor, a GMO scientist, and finally the Grim Reaper. If it made Wyatt feel any better, his job really did take muscle. Those dowel rods of fake bees got pretty heavy.

"How about a dry run before I start filming?" I suggested. "Let's make sure everyone knows their parts."

Aunt Fran clapped her hands. "Excellent idea. Everyone in place," she called.

Mr. Butters checked his watch. "Amelia should be here any time," he said.

Franco donned his costume and took his place just off to the side. My aunts moved to stand on the blue Xs I'd made with painters tape on my floor. Two sets of bees flipped over the canvas and dangled against a blue sky and lush green forest.

Mr. Butters manned Aunt Clara's cue cards.

Judy nabbed Aunt Fran's. "Can I flip these for you?" she asked, truly interested in what we were up to.

My aunts gave their hearty approval.

Someone passed by the window, and I turned toward the glass for a closer look.

I didn't see any stalkers, but I was certain someone had been out there. Hopefully, Amelia. "I'll be right back," I told our little crew. "Go ahead with your dry run, but don't cut the bees down, Franco," I warned. "Not until I'm filming."

I circled through the garden in search of whoever had passed the ballroom window. I found no one, and I reminded myself to breathe. Maybe the crime spree really was over.

Ryan was seated on the railing of my porch when I returned to my front steps, swinging his feet and smiling. "Good morning," he said, touching the brim of his newsboy cap with two fingers.

"Were you just in the garden?" I asked. "I thought I saw someone when I was still inside."

"Nope." He hopped off the railing, opened my door, and motioned me inside.

"Hello, Ryan," Aunt Clara said as we entered. She carried a tray full of tea jars toward the ballroom. "Can I get you some tea?"

I rolled my eyes. That's all I needed, for someone to make Ryan feel more at home than he already did.

Ryan got comfortable at the counter as usual. "I hear there's going to be a big video shoot going on here this morning."

"Yes," she cooed, offering him a jar. "Can you stay? It's going to be a hoot."

Ryan sipped and smiled. "I can't make any promises. I'm waiting for a very important phone call." He shot me a smug look as he overenunciated the final four words.

"Who told you about the videotaping?" I asked. Maybe he was the one stalking me. Had he been listening from outside, then hurried around to sit on my porch when I went looking in the garden?

"I listen," he said. "Plus, I saw sweet Amelia talking to those cowboys, so I asked them what it was about." He leaned in my direction. "You don't think Amelia's interested in any of them, do you? She and I had coffee this morning, and I thought it went rather well."

"Why do you keep bothering her?" I asked. "Do you think she's an easy mark? The weak link to information you need or something? She's not. She's one of the smartest people I know, an excellent judge of character, and my best friend."

Ryan smiled. "It's so cliché, isn't it? Don't hurt my best friend or I'll hurt you." He made a mock angry face. "I'd tease you about it if I wasn't so glad you feel that way. I like Amelia, and I like knowing she's got real friends who have her back."

"You can't like Amelia," I said. "You don't even know her."

"I know enough," he said. "I think she's sweet and kind. She's accepting and funny and all sorts of things that most people aren't these days. I might have to make a habit of coming here so she won't forget me."

I rolled my eyes and held my tongue. I doubted anyone who met Ryan forgot him very quickly. I tried to imagine what Amelia saw in him but couldn't. Maybe the difference was that I'd had more time to get to know him. "What's the important phone call you're waiting for?" I asked.

"Oh, nothing," he said, not even trying to hide the lie.

I narrowed my eyes. "Spill it."

"Okay," he said. "You got me." He sipped his tea, long and slow, shredding my nerves. "I'm on to something big. And while you were apparently the local hero-slash-amateur gumshoe this spring, I'll be the one collecting the byline and glory for cracking this case soon. Don't be too jealous. I offered you a partnership. You refused."

"What are you talking about?"

Ryan dropped his smug act and leaned in my direction. "I'm about to blow the lid off the Case of Who Killed the Brilliant Billionaire," he said, swinging one hand in a dramatic overhead arc. "I like that headline. I think I'll keep it."

I moved into his personal space, angling my back to the buzzing cafe behind us and lowering my voice. I didn't want anyone to see me knocking a New York City reporter off his chair. "Tell me what you know."

"Ah, ah, ah," he sang. "This is my victory, not yours."

"Is it Granger?" I asked. "He said the crime spree was over when I talked to him last night, and nothing else has gone wrong since then. How could he know that unless he's the killer? Right? Is it him?"

The *Pink Panther* theme rose from Ryan's phone, and he gloated. He spun away to take the call. "This is Ryan," he said, already on his feet and striding out the door while I gaped after him.

"Hey, E," Wyatt called from behind me. "You okay? We're about ready to film."

I released a frustrated breath and turned back toward the ballroom, stopping abruptly at the sight of him. "Where is your shirt?"

Wyatt leaned against the doorjamb, showing off his tanned torso, giant bee poles in hand. The crisp white T-shirt he'd worn before was now draped over his shoulder like a dish towel.

He grabbed the shirt off his shoulder, patting it dramatically on the back of his neck, stretching his elbow skyward to expose his triceps like a calendar model. "This pole gets heavy," he said with an evil grin.

I imagined throwing some ice water on him, then pushing him off the balcony. That last part was a reoccurring urge I should probably talk to someone about. "Knock it off."

I marched past him, wondering about the mystery phone call Ryan had taken, and how long I could maintain my calm and sanity under my current conditions.

"Your home's beautiful," Wyatt said, following me back to the set. "But don't you ever get lonely? I've still got all three roommates in an apartment that could fit into this room." He arched his back for an appreciative look at the ornate ceiling, but I couldn't tell if he was truly admiring the historic details or trying to make me look at his washboard stomach.

"I'm rarely lonely," I said. "I've got a cat and a seagull to talk to, plus books, the seaside, and plenty of work to keep me busy."

"You always were a bookworm." Wyatt smiled, straightening to his full height. "I screwed up with you, E. You should know I aim to make that right."

Maybe I could just throw myself off the balcony.

CHAPTER
∽
NINETEEN

The filming of the indoor portion of my aunts' movie went off without a hitch on the fifty-first take, which was fine because, according to Aunt Clara, everyone knows the first fifty takes are just warm-ups. Wyatt had done his best to charm me between scenes, asking about my life now and reminding me of private jokes we'd once shared, but I could tell it was about him, not me. He'd thought I might fall in love with him all over again when he got here, and when that hadn't happened, it had hurt him somehow. I wanted to care, but I had bigger problems.

Ryan's smug face stuck in my head all day. Amelia had arrived a few minutes after he left, but she didn't have any idea what he'd meant about blowing the lid off Craig's murder case. The question had lingered in my mind. Why wouldn't he tell me? Did he know who the killer was, or did he just have a new lead? Was I wrong for not partnering with him like he'd suggested? By five o'clock I was wound tight and overdue for some fresh air.

I closed up Sun, Sand, and Tea, got dressed for an evening in town, packed Blue with tea samples and marketing paraphernalia, then went to keep Amelia company at Summer Splash. If I happened to run into Ryan and managed to avoid Wyatt, I'd call it a win.

Amelia waved as I approached with a cooler and a half dozen shopping bags. "Saved you a seat," she said, patting the empty table beside hers. "You made my day when you texted to tell me you were coming."

I smiled, admiring the excellent location just outside her store. "If I hadn't taken the night off to do something fun, my head would've exploded." I set up my dispenser and poured her a cup, then lowered myself into the foldout chair she'd saved for me. "You get the first sample. Old-Fashioned Sweet Tea." I set a stack of informational flyers about my café beside the cups. "People-watching with you is just what I needed," I said. "Plus, since I don't have a booth to tend, I'm free to run for snacks any time we want."

Amelia sipped the tea with a wide Cheshire Cat grin.

"What?" I asked. She'd had the tea a hundred times over the years, first from my grandma's kitchen, more recently from mine.

"You look nice," she said, dragging the compliment into something weird and singsongy. "You did your hair, put on makeup, and those sandals have heels." She set the cup aside and dropped her chin into her palms. "What are you up to?"

"Nothing," I said, wrinkling my brow. "I always look like this."

"You are always pretty," she agreed, kicking back in her seat. "Very effortless, girl-next-door pretty. Tonight, you look bombshell amazing, so what's up?"

I shrugged, hyperfocused on the arrangement of my iced tea propaganda.

"With the exception of Craig and Judy's wedding, I haven't seen you in anything fancier than logoed T-shirts and cutoff shorts for weeks," she continued. "Now you show up in a powder-blue sundress and matching heels to sit at a noisy street festival for a few hours. You traded your ever-present ponytail for perfect va-va-voom curls, and your lips are so shiny I want to know where you got that lip gloss."

"It's Vaseline," I said, "and you know my hair is naturally curly."

"Uh-huh." She smiled. "Should I guess who you got all dolled up for or are you going to tell me?"

I looked away from her. "Can't a woman want to look her best without doing it for someone else's benefit?"

"Sure," Amelia said. "I do, but you normally couldn't care less, so I'm trying to figure out what's changed."

"Nothing has changed."

"Does this have anything to do with your ex being in town? Or the fact you spent half the day in close proximity to him and he refused to keep his shirt on?"

"No." *Okay, maybe a little.* Wyatt had popped up twice, unfairly and without warning. He'd looked amazing both times, while I had been in my pajamas.

This morning I'd at least worn yoga pants and a T-shirt, but honestly, I slept in them sometimes too, so they still qualified as pajamas. I needed to recoup some of the pride points I'd lost in those encounters.

Square dancers do-si-doed past us, followed by a man on a tractor chanting directions into a microphone. Amelia tapped her pen against an empty notebook. "How's the novel coming along?" I asked. "Have you decided to give it a try after all?"

"I want to, but I can't decide how to begin." She looked at the blank paper and sighed. "What do you think about 'It was a dark and stormy night' for the opening line?"

"Worked for Snoopy," I said.

Amelia laughed. "Oh my goodness, I knew it sounded familiar. I'm plagiarizing a cartoon beagle." She shoved the pen and notepad in my direction. "Please take these from me before I ruin the industry."

I accepted the offer, then doodled *You can do this. I believe in you* across the paper before pushing it back to her.

By nine thirty, my tea dispenser was empty, and Amelia was on the last stack of art books she'd marked down for the event. I hadn't seen any sign of Ryan or Wyatt, so I was thankful for half of my dream coming true.

Amelia snagged the final prepoured, lidded cup of tea from my table and handed it to a woman who'd just purchased a book. "Try some Old-Fashioned Sweet Tea," she said. "The recipe has been going strong for generations, and it's some of the best I've ever had. You can get more at Sun, Sand, and Tea on the boardwalk."

"Thank you." The lady smiled, then picked up a flyer about my café. "Enjoy the night," she said, sipping tea as she merged into the crowd.

I smiled at Amelia, already helping another customer choose a book.

Ryan appeared across the street, talking on his cell phone.

He pivoted away from the festivities and picked up his pace as he headed down Main Street toward Middletown, looking over his shoulder as he crossed the next street before breaking into a jog toward a poorly lit alley.

"Did you see that?" I asked Amelia.

She handed a woman some change and a paper bag with her store's name. "You're gonna love it," she promised. "The photographs are phenomenal."

She turned her bright smile on me as the woman walked away. "What did I miss?"

I looked back toward the alley, but Ryan had disappeared. A figure in dark clothes and a hoodie went into the alley next. "Look!" I pointed at the figure. "Do you see the black hoodie over there? Across Middletown. Look between the vinegar fries and steak-on-a-stick stands."

"No," she said. "I must've missed it. Who was it?"

"I don't know, but I just saw Ryan go down that same alley, and he told me earlier that he had a major lead on whoever killed Craig. What if this is a clan-destine meeting?"

"What if whoever is in that hoodie is on his way to hurt Ryan?" she asked, a glimmer of fear in her eye and panic in her tone.

"Maybe I should follow them," I said.

"No!" She grabbed my wrist. "Don't follow them. You could get hurt. Call Detective Hays instead."

I looked back in time to see the figure climb into the driver's side of an SUV, previously hidden in the shadows of the alley. "Maybe I was hasty," I said. "The hoodie just got in that SUV."

"Oh, I see it." She released my wrist with a sigh. "Thank goodness."

Once again I'd assumed the worst, as if two men couldn't use the same alley a few seconds apart. Considering the fact that most of the island was gathered in one place at the moment, it made perfect sense that I'd see more than one person at the same time anywhere I looked.

"He was smart to park there," Amelia said. "The alley's close to the action, and no other cars are crowding him."

The SUV's headlights blazed and it peeled down the alley like a NASCAR vehicle. A moment later, there was a loud squealing of brakes.

"Whoa," Amelia said. "What just happened?"

I stood on shaky legs. "Do you think that SUV just hit Ryan?" I didn't want to ignore that Ryan might be injured or dying, but I also didn't want to find another body or be caught snooping by someone in a position to run me over.

I forced my way through the crowded street with 911 on my phone screen, and my thumb hovered over the Send button. I picked up speed with each step, the seriousness of what I might've witnessed propelling me forward. What if Ryan really needed my help?

I skidded to a stop at the mouth of the alley and peered cowardly into the darkness.

"Hello?" I called, shining my phone's flashlight in the direction the SUV had gone. A wave of goose bumps flowed over my flesh as I swept the light beam around the empty space.

There was no answer. No Ryan. No SUV. No driver in a black hoodie.

Just me and the prickling sensation I should have stayed at my booth.

CHAPTER

TWENTY

I paced my room until nearly ten, unable to relax since first seeing Ryan at Summer Splash. My tea samples had all been distributed by the time I'd returned to Amelia, and I left Grady a rambling message about what might have happened, though I didn't actually see anything and Ryan wasn't lying in the alley. Maybe he'd just been running to meet a friend, and the person in the hoodie was also in a hurry for some other reason, and they'd never crossed paths.

If it was any other week, I might've let it go. I might not have thought anything about it to begin with, but given the set of terrible events lately, I couldn't get the alley out of my head.

Shutting my bedroom door so my voice wouldn't wake Judy if she'd managed to fall asleep, I dialed Grady again.

"Swan?" he answered on the first ring. "Everything okay?"

"I'm still thinking about Ryan," I said. "Did I wake you?"

"No, and you're not the only one thinking about Ryan tonight."

"What do you mean?" I climbed onto my bed and pulled a pillow into my lap.

"Tell me again what you saw tonight."

I rubbed the aching muscle at the base of my neck as I retold the story. A low murmur of voices carried through the phone line.

"Where are you?" I asked.

"I'm in the alley," he said. "I came to check out what you reported, then calls started coming in at the station and other officers showed up."

"I wasn't the only call?" Immense relief washed over me. I hadn't gone completely bananas.

"Nope. We've had seven reports with similar statements. A dark vehicle flew down an alley that a man had recently gone into. The brakes squealed, and when the vehicle emerged from the alley, a man was in the passenger seat. One witness believed the man's eyes were closed and his head tilted oddly, possibly unconscious."

My stomach churned. "Unconscious?" If I had been cooperating with Ryan, he wouldn't have gone into that alley alone. Now he was gone, and I needed to find him before he wound up like Pete—or worse, Craig. "The vehicle was an SUV. The driver was in head to toe black with a hood pulled up to shield his face."

A soft click against glass drew my attention to the window. I tugged the curtain back and peered carefully around the blinds. Nothing, just darkness.

"Anything else?" Grady asked.

The click came again, and I raised the curtain more boldly. My garden was empty, but the soft notes of a familiar tune rose to my ear. "Hang on," I said, unlatching the window lock and sliding the frame upward. "I think I hear music outside, but I don't see anyone." The theme from *The Pink Panther* registered between gusts of warm night wind. Ryan's special ringtone. My heart leapt, and suddenly I wasn't sure if I wanted to hug Ryan or smack him for scaring me. "He's here," I said, shutting and locking the window. I wasn't sure what he was up to, but Grady would be able to listen to the whole conversation if I kept our call going when I confronted Ryan.

"Who?" Grady's tone was instantly hard.

"Ryan. I can hear his dumb cell phone outside." I hurried down the steps to my front door and checked the window before opening it. "Stay on the line with me," I said. "I'll bring him inside and get him talking while you head our way."

"Go back inside," he said. An engine roared to life across the line. "I'll be there in less than five minutes, and I'll bring him inside."

I walked onto my porch. "That seems silly. I'm already here. He's going to knock before you get here, anyway." I walked the length of the porch toward my garden. I felt safe with Grady on the phone, but the music had stopped, and I didn't hear Ryan talking to anyone. The only thing visible in the moonlight was shadows. "I really need to get some motion lights out here," I said.

"I'm almost there. You need to go back inside."

The music started again, and I exhaled. "Wait. I hear it again." I covered the receiver with one palm and called into the night. "Ryan?"

A small thud drew my attention to the ground near my gazebo, where the faint glow of a cell phone screen caught my eye. "Oh no."

"What?" Grady growled. "Whatever it is had better be prefaced with, 'I just went back inside.'"

"I think Ryan's phone is on the ground," I said, taking a step back in the direction of my front door, away from the darkness. If Ryan's phone was on the ground and he wasn't answering when I called his name, chances were that he was also on the ground.

Craig, Pete, Ryan... All the men being taken out were much bigger than I was. What could I do to save myself that they hadn't?

"Everly." Grady sounded mad enough to reach through the line and shake me. "Go. Inside."

The porch light blinked out, and I was thrown into darkness.

A little swear popped from my mouth as I spun around to make a run for my door.

A piece of driftwood collided with my face and tiny stars shot through my vision. I flipped tail over teakettle onto the porch, the scents of earth, bark, and sand in my nose. Three blurry figures weaved in the air above me, my brain struggling to mash them back into one. My limbs were temporarily disembodied as fear pinned me to the ground. The driftwood went up again, and I braced for impact.

Bright light washed over us as Grady's big truck roared into my front lawn. I squeezed my lids shut, blinded with pain.

"Freeze!" Grady's voice echoed in my ears under the slamming of his truck door.

Heavy footfalls bounced the porch floorboards beneath me as my assailant tore into the night.

I rolled onto my side and curled into a ball, tears already falling.

Grady scooped me off the floor and carried me inside while barking orders into his cell phone. "Be right back," he promised, leaving me to pull myself together on the wicker love seat.

"What's going on?" Judy whispered.

"Everly's been hurt," Grady answered. "An EMT is on the way. Let him in when he gets here and keep an eye on her. I'm going to check the property."

"Everly?" Judy rushed to my side. "Goodness, what's happened to you?" She didn't wait for an answer. "Hold on."

I listened as my refrigerator door opened and closed. Ice rattled.

"Your face is red and bruised. Were you attacked? I can't understand what is going on in this crazy town," she said, releasing a growl of frustration. "It's like the earth tilted, and I slid into some alternate reality where

Craig is gone and I'm in limbo. Not a wife. Not single. I'm not even sure where I live now. His home is my home, I guess, legally, but all I can think about doing is running back here, and it's so stupid because I literally counted the days until I could leave this place." She sniffled loudly as she moved through the room. Her eyes were wet with tears when she returned and settled a dish towel filled with ice cubes on my cheek. "I'm sorry. Somehow I made this about me."

"You didn't," I said.

"I guess you can understand better than most, the urge to come home after a heartbreak."

"I can." I cleared my clogged throat a few times. "Breaking up with Wyatt was nothing like what you're going through, but I know that instinctive pull to come home."

She squeezed my hand, the way I'd squeezed hers earlier. "Is it always like this here now? All crimes and chaos?"

"No." I moved the cold compress around my stinging face, looking for the best angle to leave it.

"I can't imagine what this week is going to do to the crime statistics."

I laughed, then winced.

"Sorry," Judy said softly.

Grady returned a few minutes later with an EMT. "This is her," he said, motioning at me in case the towel full of ice hadn't given me away. "Everly, this is Matt Darning. He just moved out here from the mainland."

I waved in greeting.

Matt knelt before me and eased the towel out of my hand. "Let me take a look," he said, his voice as smooth and warm as melted butter. "You're all dressed up. Did you have special plans?"

I stole a look at Grady, who was watching closely, eyebrows tented. "No."

Matt probed the sorest parts of my cheek and jawline with gentle fingers. "Just bruised," he said. "No broken skin. No need for stitches." He smiled. "Can you follow this light?"

My eyes trailed a penlight with minimal pain.

"Nausea? Light-headed? Dizzy?"

"No."

Matt's smile grew. "Good news, you're only going to hurt for a day or two, and you'll be back to yourself before you know it. Meanwhile, can I interest you in a couple painkillers and a glass of water?"

"Yes, please." I smiled at the sandy-haired man with soulful brown eyes. "Thank you," I said, a bit more breathlessly than I'd intended.

"Don't mention it." Matt dug into his shirt pocket and produced a travel two-pack of aspirin and a business card. "If you need anything else…" He let the offer hang, unfinished.

"All right," Grady said. "I've got it from here." He took the pills from Matt's fingers, dismissing him before ripping the package open.

Judy rose with a smile. "I'll get the water."

"Did you find anything in my garden?" I asked. "Ryan's phone? A lunatic with a driftwood bat?"

"Yes to the phone. No to the lunatic," he said, placing the aspirin in my palm. "The phone is going to the lab. They'll see if they can pull any prints other than Ryan's, then check for anything that might help us locate him."

Well, I supposed it was lucky Ryan wasn't lying in the garden near his phone.

"Could Ryan be my attacker?" I asked. Was the phone a plant to draw me out? Was the phone even his? Couldn't anyone have a *Pink Panther* ringtone if they wanted?

Grady's hopeful expression fell. "I guess that means you didn't get a look at the one who hit you?"

"I did, but it was dark, and the attacker was blurry."

He grinned and cast a look in Judy's direction as she returned to my side with a jar of ice water. "Would you mind giving us a minute? I'd like to speak to Everly privately."

"Of course." Judy passed me the water. "I'll make some hot tea and find something terrible on television upstairs. That's probably our only hope of falling asleep tonight."

"Thanks."

Grady waited for her to leave before lowering his long frame onto the love seat beside me, making it instantly smaller. He slung an arm over the backrest and looked at me carefully. "How are you doing?"

I swallowed the aspirin. "Better than I will be once I've seen a mirror," I guessed. "Did you get a look at the person who whacked me?"

"Dressed in black. Baggy pants. Shapeless hoodie. Whoever it was moved fast."

"Not Mr. Granger, then," I mumbled.

"Definitely not." Grady smiled softly. "You had me scared tonight, Swan. Hearing you scream. Seeing that nut standing over you. I had no idea what condition I'd find you in when I got to the porch. It was terrifying." His voice dipped low as he finished, and my pulse climbed in response.

I refused to let Grady's nearness or fantastic cologne distract me. I'd forgotten to tell him about Ryan's visit to Sun, Sand, and Tea this morning. "Ryan was here earlier," I said. "He didn't stay long, but he bragged about having a big lead on whoever was committing all these crimes."

"Did he give you any hints about who that might be?" Grady asked.

I shook my head. "Nothing."

Grady's expression melted slowly into the blank cop stare I hated, and a shiver rolled down my spine. My muscles bunched in anticipation of what he would say next. "I'd like you and Judy to relocate," he said.

"Why?" Did he know something I didn't? Would he tell me if he did?

"For one thing, your place seems to have become Crime Central. For another thing, I'm circling a few suspects without alibis, and I don't want the guilty one to feel the pressure and do something desperate. If that happens, I have reason to assume the killer would head straight here. It seems to be the location of choice."

I didn't like the idea of being forced from my home or asking Judy to pack up and go somewhere else after all she'd been through. I also didn't want to sit back and wait for another attack. Who knew what would've happened if Grady hadn't shown up when he did tonight? "Okay," I said. "I understand."

"Good." Grady released a slow sigh of relief. "I want to take you to your aunts' house tonight. I'll put a plainclothes officer out front in an unmarked car as an extra precaution."

I flopped against the backrest and yelped at the pain in my head. I hefted the ice back in place along my cheek and jawbone. Out-of-towners wouldn't know how close I was to my aunts or where they lived—though it wouldn't be difficult information to glean. A protective detail out front made me feel a little better about it. At least I'd know my aunts were safe too.

"It isn't a long-term answer," he admitted, searching me with brooding gray eyes, "but it will make me feel better for now. At the very least, it might slow this person down."

"I'll talk to Judy," I said.

Grady stood and offered me his hand. "I'll go with you."

CHAPTER

TWENTY-ONE

My aunts lived in the home where I'd grown up. The same home where they'd grown up, and where their moms and grandmas had grown up. The original structure had burned down once or twice in the early years when dry summers, wooden structures, and a lack of running water were the norm, but the version standing today had hardwired smoke detectors and a fire hydrant on the sidewalk out front, so it was more likely to meet its end via tropical storm than fire.

Neat black trim lined the windows of the Swan homestead, a dark gray colonial saltbox with matching black roof and door. Emerald grass ringed the home and outbuildings where I'd once run barefoot chasing robins and butterflies. Wildflowers pressed against the scalloped wooden fence, and tidy cobblestone paths curled through carefully tended gardens.

I was home.

Grady pushed the gearshift into park at the end of

the driveway, still several yards from the porch, and gave the place a long look.

Battery-operated candles flickered in rows of perfectly lined windows on the home's flat face.

It was just Grady and me in the truck. Judy had opted to go to her parents' home rather than be an "undue burden" on my aunts. I'd insisted that she was never a burden and that my aunts were glad to have her, but she said it was time she quit hiding and spent time with her family. Maybe that was for the best. I just hoped she'd be safe.

Aunt Clara and Aunt Fran sat in red rocking chairs on either side of the front door. My heart lifted as memories rushed in. I'd raced home at the last minute more times than I should have, pressing my luck with curfew after especially fun dates and bonfires. There were three rockers back then, and tears stung my eyes in a slap of unexpected grief as images of my grandma came to mind. Most days, thinking of her warmed my soul and filled me with energy. But sometimes those same thoughts pulled me under me like a tidal wave, and I missed Grandma so much I thought the pain would take me straight to her.

Grady turned his weary face in my direction. "Thanks for agreeing to this," he said, breaking the silence and pulling me back to the moment. "You'll be safe here tonight, and I'll get a patrol car to put Judy's parents' home on a surveillance loop. I know you're worried about Judy, but no one has bothered her. I think she's going to be just fine anywhere she stays."

I studied Grady's eyes. "How did you know where my aunts live?" I asked, realizing he hadn't asked me for directions.

"It's my job to know the people of Charm."

"And their home addresses?" I asked. "You probably looked them up the night you met them, right after you assumed I'd poisoned an old man with my tea."

He smiled. "Maybe, but I also make a habit of knowing as many people as possible when I'm in a small community. It gives me insight when a crime occurs."

"Does it help when half the murder suspects are from Martha's Vineyard?"

"I think your numbers are a little off," he muttered before opening his door and climbing out. He opened my door a few seconds later.

"What are the numbers, then?" I asked. "At my place, you said you were zeroing in on a couple of leads. Do you have a main suspect? Who?"

Grady shook his head, gaze locked on the historic home before us. "It's a beautiful place," he said, taking the duffel bag from my lap and hooking it over his shoulder. "A great place to get your mind off my murder investigation."

I slid to my feet with a huff. Grady was the last person who'd tell me anything I wanted to know about this case, but I decided to be thankful he was trying to protect me in his own way. "The land has belonged to a Swan since the island was settled," I said, going along with the conversation he wanted. "Of course, it wasn't until 1868 that women in North

Carolina could legally own property, so the husbands took our name back then."

He raised a brow. "That was pretty forward-thinking for the average eighteenth- and nineteenth-century man."

"There's always been a price to pay for loving a Swan woman," I teased, "and what makes you think we'd ever marry an average man?"

Grady smiled.

I looked away, focusing on the gorgeous property around us. "The home has evolved over the years. The original was probably a one-room cabin. This one is about four thousand square feet, if you count the additions. A few of my ancestors' husbands were woodworkers and craftsmen."

I leaned against my closed door and looked up at the cloudless black sky and billons of stars winking down at us. It was easy to believe most of the fantastic stories about my family. My legacy. The strong women who'd made a harrowing trek from Massachusetts during the witch trials, who'd founded a town, built lasting businesses, and passed their recipe books down like gilded treasures. Why did there also have to be stories of curses, and why did people in the twenty-first century still have to believe them? I turned my eyes on Grady. "You really don't think there's a chance my family's curse caused Wyatt to stay injured while he and I were together?"

"Zero," Grady answered without taking his eyes off the magical night sky.

"Because curses aren't real?"

"Correct."

I chewed the inside of my cheek, thinking of a way to cover all my bases in case he was wrong. "Do you think that if the curse was real, maybe a strong enough love could break it? Love conquers all? That kind of thing?"

Grady's jaw locked. He pulled his gaze from the sky to my eyes. "Love doesn't conquer all."

Breath caught in my throat. "I'm so sorry," I whispered. I'd been thinking of myself and forgotten about his broken heart. No. Love didn't conquer all. It didn't cure fatal illnesses or stop fatal accidents. Didn't undo things that were already done, and it didn't stop little boys from losing their mothers. *Or little girls*, I thought, hating that I didn't even have a memory of my mother. "I didn't mean to—"

"It's fine," Grady interrupted, repositioning my bag on his shoulder. "I'll walk you up."

Aunt Clara and Aunt Fran stood as we climbed the steps. Their matching red rockers worked steadily behind them in the wind, covered by hand-stitched quilts. Both women were buttoned up to their chins in the usual yin and yang ensembles, cream for Aunt Clara and black for Aunt Fran. Their silk pajama sets were vintage and sleek with coordinating robes tied tightly at their middles. "Thank you for bringing her," Aunt Fran told Grady.

"Anytime." He shook their hands. "If you need anything, call." Grady nodded to each of us, then sauntered his way back down the drive to his truck.

Aunt Clara looped an arm around my shoulders and tugged me against her as we followed Aunt Fran inside.

The kitchen was as warm and inviting as always. I sank onto a three-legged stool at the massive center island and exhaled a week of anxiety. Flames danced in the oversized fireplace, which had long ago served as an oven. A black kettle still hung from a chain above the flames, simmering water with fresh orange peels, cinnamon sticks, and rosemary to sweeten the air.

Aunt Fran unhooked an iron skillet from an overhead rack and settled it on the stovetop. She opened colonial-blue cupboards with black hinges and gathered supplies on the counter beside a deep farmhouse sink.

Aunt Clara poured hot water and delivered a mug of tea to my hands. "I'm glad you're here," she said with a pat on my cheek and kiss on my forehead. "It feels more like home when you're here."

I pressed her hand briefly to my cheek and thanked her for the tea.

Bouquets of flowers dangled from the rafters, handpicked by my aunts and hung to dry. As a child I'd imagined the flowers were part of an upside-down garden, and from their point of view, it was me who was standing on my head. I'd helped pick them back then. I knew all the flowers' names and at least a few practical uses for each. My grandma had made sure of it. The dried leaves and buds would eventually be added to soaps, potpourris, candles, and any number of organic products sold at Blessed Bee. In the meantime, they were just as beautiful and whimsical as I'd remembered.

Aunt Fran poured something into a hot skillet and the warm, buttery scents of my childhood swam up my nose.

I pulled my attention from the ceiling to her face and groaned. "Bedtime pancakes."

She nodded. "They used to be the only thing that would put you to sleep."

My mouth watered. I'd eaten more than my fair share of bedtime pancakes, usually until I was ready to burst or fall asleep at the table from sheer contentment.

Aunt Clara climbed onto the stool beside me, her hands swaddling a steaming cup of tea. "So, do you want to talk about anything?"

"Like what?" I hedged.

"Anything at all," she answered sweetly. "We've got time while the pancakes cook."

I sipped my tea and considered where to start. "I think Grady's mad at me," I said.

Aunt Fran chuckled. "Is that what you think he is?" she asked.

"Yes," I said. "I can hardly blame him. I've ticked off another killer."

"You were always curious," Aunt Clara said. "It's a sign of intellect. You can't help it."

Aunt Fran scoffed, expertly flipping the pancakes with barely a glance. "Don't sugarcoat it. She's put herself in harm's way again. You always coddle her."

"Do not."

"Do too."

"Hey," I interrupted. "Aren't you guys worried that

you could be in danger if I stay here? What if the killer follows me right to your door?"

Aunt Clara smiled around the edge of her cup. "I don't think Grady Hays will let anyone within fifty yards of our property on his watch."

I slid off the stool, setting my teacup aside with a clatter. "What?" I hurried to the kitchen window and pulled the curtain back for a look across the darkened front lawn.

Grady's truck sat at the curb across the street. Only the silhouette of his profile was visible in the night. "He told me he would put someone outside to keep watch. He didn't say it would be him."

Clara joined me at the window. "Who else would he trust with such an important job?"

Aunt Fran poured another round of batter into the pan. "How's your investigation going? You must be close if you're in danger. Otherwise, there wouldn't be any reason to bother you."

"I don't feel as if I've gotten anywhere," I admitted. "Ryan said he had a big lead on who killed Craig, but he wouldn't give me any details. Then I thought I saw him chased down an alley by a speeding SUV, but they both vanished. I heard his phone ringing in my garden, but I got attacked when I went out to see what he was up to." My fingers grazed the bruising along my jaw that throbbed with the memory.

"Interesting," Aunt Fran said, setting stacks of plates and pancakes on the island. "Could Ryan have planted his phone in the garden to lure you outside?"

"Maybe," I said. "I've considered it. I didn't get a look at whoever hit me, but one witness thought they saw an unconscious man in that SUV's passenger seat when it left the alley."

Aunt Fran returned with a tray holding every topping needed for a bedtime pancake feast. "Is Ryan a victim or has he been part of these crimes all along?"

I piled the buttermilk delights on a clean plate and soaked them in homemade strawberry syrup. "I don't know."

"Think about it," Aunt Fran said. "Ask your gut. Which side is Ryan on?"

I paused, fork pressed into one fluffy pancake. "He's smug. Cocky. Presumptuous. His only motive for finding the killer is to give his career a boost."

"But?" Aunt Fran asked.

"I don't think he's a killer," I admitted. "He likes Amelia, which means he can't be all bad, and she likes him, which means he must have some redeemable qualities. Plus, he's offered to partner with me on this from the start, and I can't believe I'm saying this, but he's growing on me as a potential friend. I think he's probably a nice guy under all the false pretenses."

Aunt Clara stirred her tea. "Then it's probably not him," she said. "You've been wildly intuitive from the time you could crawl. If you don't think Ryan did it, then I'm going to take your word on that."

I'd been wrong about Wyatt and I having a future together, but maybe that was a different kind of intuition. The kind I didn't have.

Aunt Fran settled in across from us. "What about Jasper?" she said. "Are he and Judy a couple now? The way he clings to her is mind-boggling. You'd think he was the one she just married."

"They're not a couple," I said, feeling icky just thinking about the way he hung on her. "Judy says they were an item before she left Charm, so there's history and a certain level of comfort and familiarity there. He's obviously thrilled she's back in town, but she's definitely grieving, not dating."

"How far do you think he'd go to keep her in town?" Fran asked, raising her brows.

I didn't know, but I'd considered that as well. Still, I couldn't imagine a scenario where Jasper would intentionally hurt Judy, emotionally or otherwise.

I ate pancakes until I was almost ill, then begged off for the night. "I think I'd better go to bed." I rinsed my dish and loaded it into the dishwasher. "Thank you for having me over tonight. I love my new house, but there's no place like home."

My great-aunts smiled at me. They'd drifted to stand shoulder to shoulder while I cleared my plate. "Anytime," Aunt Fran said. "Sweet dreams," Aunt Clara added.

⁊

I didn't have sweet dreams. I woke repeatedly from the same creepy nightmare where I was being chased through the forest. Everything was green and mossy, cloaked in shadows. I couldn't see the sea. I was toting a giant suitcase, and I was lost. I gave up at dawn and swung my feet over the bed's edge. "Time to start your day," I told myself. "Try to not get into trouble."

I showered and dressed in a haze, trying to guess what the imagery and symbolism in my dream might mean. Then I followed the scents of scrambled eggs down narrow steps to the kitchen.

"Good morning!" Aunt Clara chirped, looking as if she'd had a great night's sleep and was ready to take on the world.

"Coffee." I grunted, patting the counter blindly as I moved toward the pot. Thankfully my aunts had purchased a coffeemaker for my visits, since they drank tea almost exclusively, and I needed black coffee to pry my eyes open.

"How did you sleep?" Fran asked, looking up from the morning paper.

"Okay," I lied, pressing the blessed silver button marked BREW.

Clara spread honey from a little pot on toast. "Your detective is still out there. Fran took him some toast and coffee a few minutes ago when she couldn't coax him in for a proper meal."

I stumbled to the window with my freshly filled mug and two heavy eyelids. "He's been out there all night?"

"Mm-hmm," Aunt Clara hummed.

I rubbed my eyes and returned to the island, unable to bring myself to go out and say hello in my condition. "I'm impressed." And immeasurably thankful. I helped myself to a slice of toast but opted for home-made jam over honey. Illogical or not, I didn't want any bees upset that I was eating their life's work. Bees were smart, and they freaked me out. "Can I use your laptop to check the gossip blog?" I asked. "I'm wondering if there's news about Ryan, or if the cops found a lead in the alley after Grady left to save me from the driftwood-wielding psychopath."

"Use yours," Aunt Clara said. "It's the only one we have. We keep it on the desk in the library."

"My what? My laptop?" The laptop I'd left here was nearing ten years old.

Aunt Fran peered at me as if I was the one who'd said something kooky. "That's the one."

I went directly to the library, and there it was: my high school laptop, complete with vast hodgepodge of stickers pasted all over the lid. I carried the computer back to the kitchen with a smile. "I can't believe it still works."

Fran wrinkled her brow. "Why wouldn't it?"

I didn't know how to begin answering that. "Is it slow?"

"Compared to what?" she asked.

Aunt Clara beamed. "We use it every day to see what's what. We check the weather and the tides. The *Town Charmer* blog. Sometimes we use it to settle Scrabble disputes. It still has all your old files on there. We didn't peek or remove anything."

I booted it up and waited the equivalent of six lifetimes for the internet to appear. First stop: *Town*

Charmer. I skimmed the headlines and articles. "They haven't posted anything we don't already know," I said, feeling unreasonably deflated. "I was really hoping this blogger had heard something more about Grady's investigation."

I minimized the window and ran my fingers over the desktop icons. Shortcuts to my old social media accounts, music files, favorited sites, and personal photos. I went for the photos first and opened the batch marked *Senior Year* as a slideshow. When those made me nostalgic for more, I did the same thing with photos I'd accumulated after graduation but before I'd left for culinary school.

"Why are you smiling?" Aunt Clara asked. "Did you find something good?"

"Just old photos," I said, glancing up at her. "I was so happy. It's hard to understand why I ever left Charm."

"You had to," she said with hushed excitement. "Life handed you a journey. You would have been silly to miss it."

I left the laptop and went to the kitchen table to hug her. "I love you," I said.

"We love you too, sweet girl."

Aunt Fran lowered her paper to the table and removed her reading glasses in favor of watching Aunt Clara and me. "Your grandma would be proud, you know. Your mother too."

The words caught me off guard, and I struggled to find my breath. "Why?"

"For starters, you were wise enough to recognize

when the adventure was over, and you came home. More importantly, you overcame your heartbreak with strength and grace," she said. "And your return has been abundantly fruitful."

I agreed wholeheartedly about my return being fruitful. I loved my home, and still couldn't believe it had gone on the market the moment I was looking to buy. The same house I'd dreamed of one day setting foot inside was mine. Sun, Sand, and Tea was doing well and growing steadily more popular among Charmers. Unfortunately, I also couldn't help thinking about the fact that my mother was unable to get over her own heartbreak, and she'd left me to grow up an orphan because of it. I'd vowed long ago to never let any amount of heartbreak take me away from the living people who still needed me. I would always choose to fight.

"They'd be proud you left the island to follow your dream of culinary school," Aunt Fran continued, "proud that you took a chance and chased love. Doesn't matter if it failed. How could you know if you hadn't tried?"

"They'd be proud you're asking questions about this killer too," Aunt Clara said. "Just like you did with Mr. Paine. You believe in truth and justice, and you fight for both. We're all very proud of that."

"Really?" My aching, worried heart warmed and bloomed in my chest.

"Yes," Aunt Fran said, "but you should probably stay here again tonight. You can't help anyone if you're dead."

"Fran!" Aunt Clara snapped.

Aunt Fran raised her palms. "What? Can she?"

Aunt Clara made a sour face. "Well, no, but have some couth." She sipped her tea, eyes on me. "You handled Wyatt very well, also," she said. "We didn't have a chance to tell you before, but you did much better than either of us would have in that situation."

Fran crossed her arms. "I still can't believe he just inserted himself into your day like that. Then he kept taking his shirt off and fawning over you. What was that supposed to accomplish?"

I smiled. I knew exactly what he'd hoped his presence and behavior would accomplish, but all it had really done was remind me how happy I was without him. "I don't think Wyatt is used to being rejected or ignored, and I'm certain he still thinks there's some angle he can use to get what he wants from me—my attention."

Fran shook her head. "Sad."

I wrinkled my nose. "It kind of is," I agreed. "I guess his need for attention probably drives his need for the rodeo and the spotlight it provides." I would never have been enough for him, because no one person or thing ever would be. And that was fine. *For him.* I wanted more.

I finished my breakfast with a joyful heart and hope for a crime-free day, then rinsed and loaded my plate into the dishwasher. I turned to find my aunts watching expectantly. "What?"

"Are you ready?" Aunt Fran asked. She struck a pose in her vintage black pantsuit.

I took a long hard look at her for the first time that morning. She was wearing makeup and her normally wild, waist-length salt-and-pepper locks had been combed and plaited neatly over one shoulder.

Aunt Clara stood and spun in a little circle, the cream cotton dress fanning around her ankles. Her long silver and blond hair had been wound into a graceful bun at the back of her head, and her normally sun-kissed cheeks were matte with liquid foundation and powder. Her lips were petal pink and mascara lined her lashes. "How do we look?"

"Beautiful," I answered on instinct. *Like airbrushed versions of my actual aunts.* I preferred the originals. It took a moment for my addled mind to catch up. "You want to tape the outdoor portion of your video application while I'm here?"

They beamed.

I went to brush my teeth and dress in my usual T-shirt and cutoffs, bare feet stuffed into unlaced sneakers. I'd learned young to wear shoes in my aunts' backyard, preferably not flip-flops. Bees loved to plot and huddle in the clover.

We met Mr. Butters in the backyard thirty minutes later, an arrangement Aunt Clara had made while I'd gotten ready. Amelia had to open Charming Reads this morning, but I was assured that her extra, Franco, would be along soon. We only needed one background man today, and I couldn't imagine Wyatt willingly donning a mammoth honeybee costume and tights.

I set my phone to record and positioned it on a

tripod, then went to adjust my aunts' hair and clothing. The wind was gentler today, but filming outside meant dealing with nature, including the occasional cloud that wrecked my lighting and sent weird shadows over the set.

Mr. Butters arranged his large wooden flowers on the makeshift stage he'd created. They were works of creative genius Dr. Seuss would surely have approved of. "Here?" he asked, maneuvering a giant yellow blossom across the bright green floor.

"Yes," Aunt Fran said. "That's perfect. Do you have the pollen?"

Mr. Butters gave her a thumbs-up, pointing to several bags stuffed full of what looked like fake snowflakes.

Aunt Clara fussed, dragging hair away from her eyes. "Now all we need is that bee."

Movement caught my eye, and I spun in the direction of a familiar face. "Grady!" I hurried over to see him. "Is everything okay?"

"Yeah. Just checking in on you before I take off," he said. "I need to shower and change, then head out on a lead that panned out about ten minutes ago. Will you be okay here?" He smiled and waved at Mr. Butters and my aunts.

"Yeah. If it's anything like yesterday, I'll be busy a while."

"Good," he said. "Call if you need anything, and I'll come back this way and check in again after dinner tonight."

"Sounds good," I said, smiling as brightly as I could against the relentless Southern sun.

Grady tipped his hat to the others, then leaned in close to say, "Be safe, Swan. I worry." The tenor of his voice knocked me speechless, so I nodded and blushed furiously. He turned away, looking wildly satisfied with himself, and tipped his hat again, this time to the approaching six-foot honeybee.

"Hey there, E," Wyatt said, squeezing a rolled black ball cap in his hands. The rest of him was dressed in a yellow-and-black-striped T-shirt and black pants. The sleeves of the shirt gripped his biceps. "The tights didn't fit," he said.

I stared. "What happened to Franco?"

Wyatt grinned. "Lost a bet." He hooked the ball cap over his head. Two bent antennae stretched forward. "I meant what I said yesterday about making things up to you. I stopped by the nature center after I left your place and spoke with the programs coordinator. I interned there the year we met. Remember?"

"I remember," I said cautiously, still trying to reconcile Wyatt dressed as a honeybee.

"They offered me a position this fall, teaching folks about Charm's wild horses." His eyes glimmered in the morning sun, and his bright smile dazzled. "What do you think of that?"

I was dumbfounded. "That was very nice of them," I said slowly, utterly confused. "They realize you don't live here anymore, right? You travel all year, following the rodeo circuit."

"Not all year," he said. "Rodeo is spring to fall, and I can train anywhere after that." He stepped closer, seizing me with his intense blue eyes. "I didn't realize how much I missed some things about this island until I got here. Now I'm not ready to let them go again."

"But you don't live here," I repeated, hoping the fact had somehow slipped his mind and he'd go back to the nature center and decline the job offer immediately.

"You're right," he said, "and I've still got a couple shows in September, but I told them I'd be back October first to take the job. I'm sure I can find a place to stay in Charm between now and then."

I opened my mouth to say a dozen thing that all began with *please don't*, but a strangled sound came out instead. Irrational panic beat through my veins, and I looked in my aunts' direction for help.

Aunt Fran was already on her way, marching purposefully off the stage to greet the big bee. "Wyatt," she said. "We weren't expecting you. I hope everything is okay with Franco."

"Yes, ma'am," he drawled. "I just hadn't gotten enough of you Swan women, so he took pity on me and let me come in his place."

"Great," she said, forcing a blatantly false smile. "Mr. Butters will show you how to pollinate the big flowers and where to collapse when you're struck down prematurely by pesticides."

His smile widened. "I'm on it," he said, shaking Aunt Fran's hand. His gaze stuck on me. "It's good to be back, E."

I dragged myself to the camera, seeking comfort in the fact that we'd taped more than two minutes of good footage yesterday and there was a three-minute limit on the video. Today's outdoor fiasco couldn't possibly run longer than an hour.

∞

Two hours and twelve minutes later, I'd taped nearly forty-seven minutes of footage that wasn't ruined by wind, forgotten lines, or errant bees from my aunts' adjacent hives that caused the tea-making videographer to scream and run for her life. The day's footage would need cut down by forty-six-and-a-half minutes to fit into the final production copy. Luckily, I'd learned the ins and outs of clipping and splicing footage while I was in culinary school and kept a video blog of my favorite recipes. The blog had been part of my first-year grade, but I'd enjoyed it so much that I'd kept it going until I moved home and opened Sun, Sand, and Tea. Part of me really missed it. The rest of me was too tired to imagine picking up where I'd left off.

I borrowed a spare bicycle from the barn to ride home and kissed my aunts goodbye as they left for work.

The ride home was gorgeous, blessed with the scenery of a perfect summer day. A cloudless blue sky. A warm and gentle breeze. Waving grasses and trees. The whole world smelled of sand and sea, wildflowers and sunblock.

I pedaled along, singing a song from my teen years that had gotten stuck in my head at the sight of all my old music files. The only thing more shocking than the fact that my great-aunts had kept all my old files was the fact they'd figured out how to use the laptop at all, especially to peruse the internet.

Images of my teen years flew through my mind as I belted the chorus to my former favorite song. Broken hearts. First kisses. Truth or Dare. Biggest crushes. Heat scorched my cheeks as another thought edged its way into my head. I'd kept a diary of everything important to me on that laptop. I'd disguised it as homework, but it was still there. I hadn't thought to look for it or I could have erased it. Aunt Clara said they hadn't peeked into my personal files, but if they had, I would die on the spot of humiliation. There were things in there I didn't want to think about again. I surely didn't want my aunts reading about them. I made a mental note to get my hands on that laptop and scrub everything clean, or maybe run over it with Blue a few times and buy my aunts a modern version that ran Windows from this decade.

I parked the borrowed bike at the base of my porch steps and slowed my climb to the front door.

Something intriguing occurred to me, and I dialed Amelia. Maybe I'd been right to think Craig had found something scandalous in the data from Mr. Granger's business. What I hadn't thought about was that the killer didn't have to be Mr. Granger. Maybe someone in his company knew they were about to lose their job, be arrested, or worse when Craig shared his findings with the boss.

"Hello?" Amelia answered.

"Hey," I said. "It's me." Maybe it was time I reconsidered buying a car. I could start by checking out the available selection at Granger Automotive in Corolla. "How would you like to take a road trip?" I asked.

CHAPTER

TWENTY-TWO

Amelia was all in for a road trip, especially when I told her it was to a car lot. She'd been encouraging me to get a car for months, but she hung up before I could tell her I wasn't really planning to shop. Charming Reads was bursting with customers thanks to Summer Splash, and her dad had hourly art demonstrations scheduled all afternoon, so she couldn't get away until six thirty.

I threw myself into the work at Sun, Sand, and Tea, cleaning, buzzing with positive energy. My recipes smelled great, were presented well, and from the looks on guests' faces, they tasted amazing too. That chin-lifting, chest-puffing, float-around-the-room feeling was something I'd been without for a few days, and it wasn't until after lunch when it occurred to me what this feeling was really called: *hope*. I had renewed hope of putting an end to the local crime spree, and now that I had it, I didn't want to let it go.

Grady called to check in as promised. Twice. I assured him all was well both times, and he reminded me he had things handled while I doodled a list of questions for anyone who felt chatty at Granger Automotive.

When the lunch crowd died down, I got to work editing my aunts' video, using every trick I'd learned and perfected while working on my culinary school blog. By late afternoon, the application had been submitted, and the finalized version of our educational dystopian honeybee apocalypse movie was probably the best application Bee Loved would ever see.

Judy slipped into a chair near the window around four, and I went to meet her with some Iced Mint Tea and a smile.

"Hey, you," I said. "How are you feeling today?" She looked pale and defeated. Her simple white V-neck with matching canvas sneakers and blue-jean cutoffs made a cute outfit, but the white top only emphasized the lack of color in her cheeks. Her hair was pulled high in a ponytail, and she'd skipped the makeup, adding to the worn-out, run-down effect.

She turned wide, red-rimmed eyes on me. "I feel like I'm having an out-of-body experience I can't wake up from."

I wished I could tell her I understood, but I didn't, not exactly, and I hoped I never would. "Does this body feel like having something to eat?" I asked. "I can make you anything you want."

"Fruit salad?" she asked, dunking the ice in her tea with a spoon.

"Sure thing." I smiled. "How was your night with your folks?"

"I couldn't sleep." She yawned. "Dad turned my old room into an office years ago, so Mom made up the couch for me. I wound up watching reruns and infomercials until dawn."

I wanted to tell her that we could stay at my place again tonight so she could try to rest, but I needed to talk to Grady first, and I'd promised him I'd be safe. "Do you have plans for the rest of your day?" I asked.

"Not really," she said. "I've made all the calls I can think of for now. Craig's family and I are just waiting for the green light to fly him home and put our memorial plans into action."

"And Jasper?" I asked. I'd rarely seen her without him since the wedding, and I couldn't imagine where he was.

"He had some things to take care of at his office, so he finally left me alone, and all I could think to do with my time was come here. I thought I'd be glad for the silence, but now I'm just lonely again." She turned a listless expression to the sea. "I should probably do something while I'm temporarily without a chaperone, but all I want to do is sleep."

I smiled, thankful to know she realized Jasper was smothering her. Part of me had worried that his leeching would pay off somehow, and knowing Judy was still keen enough to see the situation for what it was would help me sleep better. "Why not spend some time on the beach," I suggested. "Grab a lounger from the carriage house and set it up on the sand. You don't have to be closed up in a room to rest. Get some vitamin D. Breathe the salty air. I've even got a nice beach umbrella for when the sun gets too strong."

Her lips twitched with a little smile. "That sounds really nice."

"Good," I said. "I'll prep your fruit salad to go and pour you a fresh glass of iced tea in a to-go cup."

"Thanks, Everly," she said, turning back to me. "I really appreciate everything you're doing and everything you've done."

"It's no problem," I said. "I mean it. I like to be useful."

"I know," she answered with a bit of a groan. "A little too much."

I wrinkled my brow, unsure of her meaning and whether or not to ask.

"You don't have to keep putting yourself in harm's way to be useful," she said, clearly reading my expression. Her gaze slid to the bruises along my swollen cheek and jawline. "I don't even care who killed him anymore. I just want to forget about it. I want to stop asking why and figure out how to get through this."

I lowered onto the chair across from Judy. "You'll get through it," I promised. "I know you're going to be okay. That's not the reason I'm looking for the person behind all this. I don't think that person is allowed to be okay. That person shouldn't get to just go on with his life after what he's taken from yours." I cast a glanced at the smattering of customers in my shop, then leaned forward. "I think I found a new thread to pull," I said. "I'll know soon."

"What is it?" Judy matched my posture, leaning across the table on her forearms.

"I'm going to visit Granger Automotive in Corolla. Did you know Craig was working for them?"

She lifted her shoulders. "All I've thought about for the last few months is the wedding."

My heart broke a little more at the crack in her voice. I cleared my throat, eager to give her a bit of my hope. "Craig planned to talk to Mr. Granger, the owner of the company, while you guys were in town. He even invited him to the wedding."

Judy stared. "And?"

"Well, it occurred to me that Craig might have found something incriminating in the server data at Granger Automotive, and someone connected to Mr. Granger might've been highly motivated to make sure that information never saw the light of day."

She covered her mouth and let her eyes go wide. "He killed him?"

"No." I shook my head hard, tossing dark curls against both cheeks. "No, I don't think so. I'd originally pinned Mr. Granger as a solid suspect, but Grady said the person who attacked me was lithe and agile. Definitely not Mr. Granger, but on my way home this morning, I realized that someone else in Granger's company might've had information they wanted to hide."

Judy dropped her palms onto the table. "So, you could have had the right motive, wrong guy."

"It would explain why someone tossed your room. I assume Craig kept the information on his laptop or a hard drive of some kind. When his things weren't with yours, the next logical place to look would be his mom's rental. When her place was broken into, the burglar took all of Craig's stuff."

Judy frowned. "Why wouldn't the crimes have ended there? Why attack Pete or keep following you once they had Craig's things?"

"I think whoever is behind this wants to cover their bases. Pete was Craig's partner, so it's reasonable to assume they shared details on clients. If Pete knew whatever Craig had found out, then killing Craig wouldn't end the problem."

"What about stalking you?" she asked. "Why hurt you?"

I held out one hand. "Maybe I've come closer than I realized to naming the guilty party, and that person wants to scare me into leaving this alone."

Judy's curious expression turned heartbreaking. "Ryan the reporter was looking too."

"I know."

Her brows lifted slowly beneath her bangs. "Has anyone seen him since the alley last night?"

My stomach flopped, and a wave of nausea washed through me. "No, but once I take a look around Granger Automotive and talk to a few folks, I'll bet I have a better idea of where he is and what's going on."

"No." She snaked a hand out to grab mine. "Don't. Just tell the detective about your new theory and let it go. I don't want anyone else I know getting hurt this week. I can't take it. I swear I couldn't recover."

"I won't get hurt," I promised, casting a glance around the room. "And I will tell Grady, but you have to promise not to tell anyone what I just told you. I don't know who's guilty, and I don't know who's listening. Neither do you, so you have to keep this to yourself. Okay?" I hoped in vain that she'd listen. Anyone she told could be the killer. I instantly wished I'd kept the plan to myself.

"Do you promise to tell the detective?" she asked. "Someone needs to know where you're going in case you run into the killer while you're out of town."

"I will," I vowed.

Judy nodded, shut her eyes, then lowered her head onto the table. "Fine."

"Great! I'll get that fruit cup and tea," I said, patting her hand before I hurried off.

By six o'clock, the café was empty, Judy was relaxing on the beach beneath a big umbrella, and I was on my way to meet Amelia. Granger Automotive closed at eight, and Corolla was twenty minutes away.

I pointed Blue toward Molly's Market and rehearsed the ways I could segue at Mr. Granger's car lot from talk about upkeep and miles per gallon to how often the sales team used the computer network and what sorts of things they used it for.

I traveled residential roads, taking the long route into town. The street barricades kept pedestrians safe for Summer Splash, but they also made it complicated to get close to Main Street for people who weren't on foot, which I wasn't, per my promise to Grady. I didn't have a buddy to walk with, so I'd taken Blue.

I waved to locals and smiled at unfamiliar faces until I spotted a wide gap between two box trucks with *Mountain Men and a Mandolin* painted on their sides. Blue fit between them with ease, and I patted myself on the back for excellent creativity. Parking was a nightmare within four blocks of Main Street in any direction for cars and trucks. Adorable golf carts were another story.

"Evening, Everly," Mr. Waters rasped as I swept through the door at Molly's Market. "Are you setting up for Summer Splash again tonight?"

"Not tonight," I told him. "Amelia and I are taking a road trip, and I'm here for snacks." I bopped my head to the happy tune being piped through speakers outside.

"Looks crowded already. Is it?" He craned his neck for a look out the shop window.

"It's busy," I said. "I snagged a great parking spot between a couple box trucks around the corner."

"Mountain Men and a Mandolin," he said. "That's them playing now. Best bluegrass band in the state."

"They're pretty good," I said, still bouncing my head slightly. "Loud," I added.

Mr. Waters pointed to the telephone poles outside. "There are more speakers this year. That's your tax dollars at work."

I smiled. "Amelia and I won't be gone long. Maybe we'll be back in time to do a little dancing in the street."

"Let's hope," he said. "Where are y'all headed?"

"Corolla. We're visiting Granger Automotive." I checked the time on my phone. "I'd better hurry if I'm going to get Amelia and get over there," I said, stacking road-trip snacks onto the counter.

Mr. Waters laughed at my pile of snacks. "Have I ever told you how much I enjoy the fact that you make the best food in town, but you come here and buy Twinkies?"

I looked down at the load of junk between us. "I don't have a good snack cake recipe," I told him, "and prepackaging makes for handy travel."

"Don't get me wrong," he said. "I'm not complaining. Your sweet tooth is good for business, and I'm glad to be of service."

I pushed the pile of sugar and carbohydrates in his direction. "I think this will do it."

The door to Molly's Market swung open, and Mr. Waters turned to wave. "Hello, Pamela," he said. "How are you?"

Mrs. Lambert, my middle school health teacher, frowned in response. "Terrible." She came to the counter and glared at my junk food. "Hello, Everly."

"Hi." I tried to look less self-conscious than I felt about her obvious disapproval of my purchase. "It's for a road trip," I explained.

She nodded. "Did you sell out of everything at that new café everyone's always raving about? The one with organic, homegrown foods."

"No."

"So you enjoy contaminating your system with dyes, sodium nitrates, and partially hydrogenated oil?"

"Kind of."

She rubbed her forehead and turned her gaze to Mr. Waters. A heavy group of bangle bracelets jangled as they slid down her forearm toward her elbow. Mrs. Lambert always looked like a television evangelist's wife had done her hair and makeup. Caked-on powders and lipstick, giant eyelashes, even bigger hair that was always stiff from spray. She never left home without triple the average person's amount of jewelry, and her outfits were built around showcasing her cleavage.

Mr. Waters grinned. "What's new?"

She leaned against the counter. "You know that renter I was telling you about?"

"The one who pays by the day?" he asked, bushy eyebrows furrowing. "She's still here?" His voice hitched with excitement, as if this news was more than a little interesting. More like a breaking story he'd been following. "What on earth for?" he asked.

"She won't leave until the body leaves," Mrs. Lambert scoffed. "It's crazy." She tapped long red nails on the counter in a show of impatience. "Completely cuckoo."

The body? A prickly sensation tickled across my skin, and my hand shot up, as if we were in class all over again.

"Yes?" Mrs. Lambert asked.

"Did you say *body*?" I asked. "Like a corpse?"

"Yes. A corpse," she said, pressing a hand to one round hip and staring me down. "The renter is making me half-mad. She was a guest at that wedding you threw, and now she won't leave."

"I only catered the reception," I said, not wanting credit for more than my fair share. "Is the guest a relative of Craig Miller's? I know his family is staying until they can take him home."

"I don't think so," she said. "Her last name is Preston. Do you know her? I'll buy all those horrible snacks for you if you know of a way to get her out of my rental."

"Cynthia Preston?" I asked.

"That's her." Mrs. Lambert lifted a hand over her head. "Tall. Thin. Gorgeous. Sounds like Mary Poppins, but she's a jumbo-sized pain in my behind."

My mouth fell open. *Craig's crazy ex-girlfriend is waiting for his body to be released before returning home.* Hopefully Judy didn't get wind of that. It wasn't any of my business, but I still felt a bit offended on her behalf.

"She's a real pill," Mrs. Lambert went on. "She insists on paying me by the day because she wants to leave as soon as the groom's body is released, but she won't give me a credit card in case of damages or anything like that. Cash only." She shook her head in disapproval. "I don't have another renter lined up or anything, but she's been here a week now and was only supposed to stay overnight. It's just bad manners. Maybe they don't have common courtesy over there in Great Britain or wherever she's from."

I paid Mr. Waters for my snacks and hung the bag

from my wrist. "Good luck," I said, setting a palm on the doorknob. I had no idea how to motivate Cynthia to leave the rental, and I was thankful I didn't have to try. "Wait a minute," I said, turning back to Mrs. Lambert. Her math didn't add up on my mental calendar. "You said Cynthia's been in town a week, but you meant since Friday, right?" Today was Wednesday, so it had been almost a week, but not quite.

"No." Mrs. Lambert puckered her brow. "I meant a week."

"I saw her get out of a cab late Friday night," I said. "She came straight to the reception from the airport."

"Honey, I don't know what she did after she checked in on Wednesday, but I've been getting cash in my mailbox every day since."

Wednesday. The same day Craig, Judy, and his family had arrived in Charm for the lineup of family-merging meals and general prewedding hoopla.

"Thanks," I said, rushing out the door.

A round of cheers and applause erupted from the direction of a stage up the block. The bluegrass band took a bow, and locals showed their enthusiastic approval with a little down-home hollerin'.

I rounded the corner to Blue, tucked neatly between the trucks, and dropped the bag of snacks on my passenger seat. My heart pumped with possibilities as I drove around the block toward the alley beside the ice cream parlor, two doors down from Charming Reads.

If Cynthia Preston had checked into her rental two

days before the wedding, then why had she shown up in a cab on Friday night, dragging her luggage?

I pressed the gas pedal to the floor while I processed the new and peculiar information She'd faked a big rush. Put on a whole façade about her plane arriving late. Took a cab. The whole works. Why would anyone do that?

Unless she'd wanted to cover her tracks, I realized. Unless she'd wanted half the town to see her arrive *after* the murder, thereby establishing her innocence under the guise of sheer geographical impossibility.

I smashed the gas pedal flat to the floor. "Come on," I coaxed the ancient golf cart. "Hurry." I grabbed the phone from my bag and dialed Grady before the next intersection.

"Detective Hays," Grady answered.

Music poured from speakers on either side of me, and applause erupted from the next block where half the town had gathered to enjoy the bluegrass.

"Hey," I said, projecting my voice past a lump of pressure building in my chest. "I think I know who killed Craig Miller."

"What?" he said. "I can't hear you over the music."

"I said I think I know who—"

The roar of an engine stalled my words and drew my attention to the cross street at my side, where a black SUV barreled down on me.

"Everly?" Grady demanded, his voice tight with fear.

I screamed.

CHAPTER
&

TWENTY-THREE

I woke to the steady roar of an engine vibrating my chest and the distinct new-car smell overwhelming my senses. I tried and failed to part my sticky eyelids beyond narrow slits. A profound headache seemed to have sealed them closed. Pain emanated from every muscle in my body and nausea pooled in my gut. *What was happening?*

Had I been in an accident?

My body jolted and my stomach lurched as the rumbling tires of whatever I was riding in rolled along beneath me. *When had I gotten into a car? Why was I lying down?* I pressed my eyes shut once more and prayed for the continuous jiggling of my world to stop.

When I came around again, it was thanks to a blast of sweltering heat that stole my breath and pried my eyelids apart. I turned my face away from the blazing orange light of a setting sun and fought the urge to be sick.

"Time to go," a woman said.

I grunted, unable to find my voice and still wondering what was going on. My limbs were leaden, but I moved anyway, involuntarily sliding forward as if by conveyor belt. The itchy material of an old blue tarp crinkled around my ears and limbs as something dragged me forward.

"You're heavy," the woman's voice came again. She heaved, and I slid forward once more.

"Cynthia?" I croaked.

Her accent rattled in my head. Not southern. Not local. Not the R-less dialect of Mrs. Miller or the other guest from Massachusetts. The distinctly British sound I'd once loved.

"What are you doing?"

She pulled again, and I fell.

My body hit the ground with a hard thud, forcing air from my lungs and popping my eyes fully open. She pushed my bound legs back onto the tarp, then repositioned her grip on the material and began to drag me away from the SUV's hatch.

"Stop," I pleaded, uselessly wriggling as my tarp slid over twigs and rocks on the hard-packed earth. My wrists and ankles had been tied with thin strips of satin material, probably scarves or belts from her fancy dresses. The tarp smelled like something she'd found in a dumpster. "You don't have to do this."

Cynthia stopped to wipe sweat from her brow before pulling me into the tree cover. The sun blinked out, and I batted my eyes, allowing them to readjust.

"You could stand to lose a few pounds," she complained. "At least thirty, maybe more."

My brows knitted together. "Let me go," I demanded.

I worked my feet and wrists as clarity firmly returned and adrenaline flooded my limbs. "You're not going to get away with whatever you're doing," I said.

Cynthia shot me an angry look. "Shut up," she said, her face red with heat and exertion, her eyes wild with rage. "I didn't want to do this, but it's like you're all determined to drive me mad." She made a sharp turn, lugging me deeper into the lush maritime forest.

"I don't know what you're talking about. I didn't do anything to you." I swung my bound feet over the tarp's edge to slow us down and complicate her work. "Why are you doing this to me?" I worked hard at the ties that bound me, certain that whatever happened when the tarp stopped moving wouldn't be good.

She shot me another venomous look. "Why do you think? Or are you really as dumb as you look?"

I wasn't sure how I looked to her, but I was getting plenty tired of the insults. "I suppose you killed Craig because he didn't love you," I said. "You probably tried to kill Pete because he knew too much. You killed Ryan because he knew what you did."

Cynthia hacked a humorless laugh. "You don't know anything.

I closed my eyes against the raging nausea. Memories of the black SUV crowded my mind. She'd driven it into Blue as I raced to tell Amelia what I'd learned from Mrs. Lambert. The bluegrass band had drawn a crowd on the opposite end of Main Street, and I'd been heading away from them. I pressed my lips shut against a building whimper as a red-hot flash of pain arrived with the next memory. I'd been ejected by the impact of her vehicle against mine, tossed onto the street. I'd rolled and bounced against the curb. My skin began to sting and burn as the memory ignited the pain.

Blue had been crushed against the face of an historic brick building.

"You don't have to do this," I pleaded as the tarp came to a sharp stop.

Cynthia trudged forward. "You're an idiot," she said. "A big, chubby idiot."

I gritted my teeth and jerked wildly against the ties at my wrists. "Then make me understand. Tell me your story," I said.

"You already think you know my story," she snapped.

"I know you didn't get into town late Friday night."

Cynthia hooked a left, pressing impossibly deeper into the woods. "You're right about that. I got into town on Wednesday with the rest of the wedding party," she said. "I followed Craig here to stop him."

"You spoke to him before the wedding?"

"Of course I did!" she shouted, moving dangerously close to the edge of a small drop-off. "I met him in this infernal forest and tried to talk him out of marrying that stupid island girl, but he wouldn't listen. He told me to go home, as if I was a child in need of correction, as if him marrying another woman was none of my business." She repositioned her grip on the tarp. "I told him not to do it. I warned him that he'd be sorry." She gave the tarp a swift yank, and I rolled off it, spinning roughly over fallen limbs, rocks, and tree roots. My muscles roared in pain. My vision blurred. I cried out as I came to a crashing stop at the base of a tree.

Cynthia tromped toward me, looking like she might prop me up and strangle me with her bare hands. "Craig said he didn't love me, but he wore his bracelet!" she screamed. "To their wedding!"

I squirmed upright, bracing my back against the tree trunk. "The braided hemp thing?" I asked, kicking my feet back and forth where my ankle bindings had all but given up their duty on that last tumble. I tried not to think about what sort of creatures or snakes might be hiding in the undergrowth where I sat.

"That was our memory," she said, charging in my direction, arm extended, ugly hemp bracelet on display. "When I saw it on him *at his wedding reception*—" Cynthia paused. Her already red face grew darker. Her chest rose and fell in deep, hysterical puffs. "I lost it," she seethed. "He was taking a piece of *us*"—she pounded a fist to her chest—"of *me*, into a marriage with *her*." She belted out a feral scream, and I winced.

The pain in my head ratcheted up until dark spots swam in my vision. "I'm sorry," I said, begging my harried brain for some kind of plan. "I didn't have anything to do with any of that. I only spoke to

Craig a few times this week, and I hadn't seen Judy in years. Please just let me go. I won't tell anyone about this."

"Yeah, right," she scoffed. "You're just like him. All you care about is getting answers to things that aren't any of your business."

"Just like who?" I asked, following her gaze to a man, lying on his side a few feet away. "Ryan!" My heart lodged painfully in my throat. "Is he dead?"

He was covered in mud and leaves, as if she'd attempted to camouflage him.

"Not yet." She stared blankly at Ryan, detaching mentally and emotionally from the situation. She'd clearly lost her mind, killed the man she loved, probably almost killed his partner too, and now she had to kill two more people to cover up the first.

"You don't have to do this," I said again, as calmly as I could manage. My pulse rose, and my heart hammered harder with each word. "Please." My mind reeled, and I felt myself reaching hysterics, but I couldn't afford to lose control now. It wasn't just me anymore. Now I had myself and a six-foot reporter to save.

"You wouldn't leave it alone," she said, her voice cracking. "I tried everything I could to scare you off the case, but you wouldn't be dissuaded. You were getting closer by the minute, and I had to do something. Not to mention you're so chummy with the detective who's been breathing down my neck since Saturday morning. You left me no choice."

"There's always a choice," I said, extending my bound hands in her direction. "You chose your actions every step of the way, and you can still choose now."

"Shut up," Cynthia said, digging wild fingers into her hair and pulling hard. The ugly bracelet slid down her thin wrist.

"You were the one who broke into Judy's room," I said. "First my place, then Mrs. Miller's rental. You didn't find Craig's things in a dumpster. You put them there." I kicked myself mentally for not insisting Grady arrest her on the spot. I'd let myself believe she was crazy but harmless. "Why would you go through all that trouble looking for a stupid bracelet? Why didn't you just rip it off his dead body after you stabbed him and shoved him in the ocean?"

"Stop talking." She pointed her crazy eyes back at me. "I suppose they'll bury him in the bracelet now, and I'll never have it."

I twisted my face into a knot. "Lady, you're going to jail. You're not going to have that bracelet or anything else for a very long time."

Cynthia tossed her head back and laughed. "Jail? Really? And who's going to make me?" she asked, craning her head to look around. "You? Him?" She pointed to Ryan, eyes closed on the ground. "I don't think so. I'm going back to London. There's nothing left for me here now."

"Except jail," I muttered, twisting and tugging my wrists, now covered in dirt on my lap.

"I'm not going to jail!" Cynthia yelled.

"Why did you attack Pete?" I asked, hoping to keep her talking until I could free my wrists.

"Accident." She frowned, sliding her gaze back to Ryan. "I thought Pete was Ryan. They practically wore the same outfit to that pitiful vigil you threw. I'd followed Ryan all evening, waiting for Mr. Chatterbox to take a minute alone, then I spotted him in the surf, and thought the whole scene would be poetic. Until it wasn't, and I'd knocked out the wrong man. Though, to be honest, that was probably for the best. Pete hates me, and he knew I met with Craig the night before the wedding. It was only a matter of time before he wondered if I'd finally taken matters into my own hands. And if he took those suspicions to the police, I'd be in big trouble." She focused on me, jaw tight. "Why wouldn't you just leave this alone?" For a moment, she looked less crazy and significantly more sober. "I didn't want to have to do this."

"You were stalking me," I said. "I had to catch you before you killed me. I couldn't just sit back and wait to be killed."

"I wasn't going to kill you. I just wanted you to be afraid. I needed you to stop so I could go home."

I kicked my feet free from the bindings and stilled, hoping she hadn't noticed. My hands were nearly free as well. The moment she left, I'd get Ryan on his feet and head for the road. Cell reception wasn't great in the maritime forest, but I knew the area well, and she wasn't getting on a plane home as long as I was breathing.

Cynthia sighed deeply, digging into her bag. Hopefully for her car keys.

"You're just going to leave us here?" I asked, hoping to sound panicked. "We're both hurt. We need help."

"You won't," she said, pulling a gun from her bag and pointing it at my head. "And I won't just leave you here. First, I'll shoot you. I had to make a trip to another town to buy this gun today. It's an unnervingly simple process, but efficient."

My lungs seized, and my eyes crossed. "Why do you have a gun? Are you crazy?"

"I'm moving on," she said. Her hands trembled slightly. "I'm putting this mess behind me, and I'm going back home where people don't break my heart and insert themselves into my business."

"You don't want to do that," I said, desperately trying to come up with a reason why not. "The gun will echo when it goes off. Everyone will hear. Hikers will come running. They'll call the police. Someone is always nearby on an island like this."

"Not today," she said. "Not with that weird art party in town. Besides, no one has found him yet." She pointed the revolver at Ryan. "He was here all night." Cynthia moved another step closer, closing one eye and gauging the shot.

"Wait!" I lifted my adjoined hands. "At least tell me why you killed Craig," I said. "He married another woman. So what? Move on."

Cynthia pressed her hands to her ears, moving the gun's barrel skyward and allowing me to breathe.

Ryan exhaled audibly beside me.

I jerked around to find him staring at me. *Ryan was awake.*

"I met Craig in college," Cynthia said. "I was new to the States, and he was new to dating. He thought no one would ever see past his nerdy persona. That was one of the reasons we broke up. I wanted something serious, and he'd been burned too many times to think marriage was a possibility for him. We stayed friends until he met Judy." She stopped to clench her jaw and gaze at the thick greenery overhead. "All of a sudden he was serious about a future with another woman. Someone he barely knew. I'd waited for that for four years, but she came along and he starts talking about marriage." Cynthia pressed a hand over her eyes, wiping tears away. "He kept me at bay for a while, then he showed up on my doorstep a few weeks before the wedding. Cold feet. It was what I'd been waiting for."

My heart broke for all of them: Craig for being so low he'd go back to an ex-girlfriend instead of working through his doubt with his fiancée *like an adult*; Judy for being cheated on weeks before her wedding; and Cynthia for finally getting what she'd wanted, only to have it ripped away again.

"I comforted him in all the ways he'd ever asked me before," she said. "It was beautiful, and I woke the next morning with renewed hope. I thought that night had been a turning point in my life. I thought I'd finally get everything I'd ever wanted. I didn't think twice about it when he was gone before dawn. That was just how he was. So, I made a nice brunch and took it to his house in a picnic basket. Judy answered the door."

I frowned, feeling her pain. "I'm sorry."

Cynthia bobbed her head, tears falling fast and thick. "The wedding was still on. Nothing had changed. I thought maybe he wanted someone to intervene and save him. Maybe our night together had been a cry for help."

"So you followed him here."

She sniffled. "I was wrong. It's over." Cynthia cocked the trigger back. "And now, I'm done sharing."

Ryan clutched his stomach and rolled onto his side with a wail.

Cynthia turned her eyes on him. "What's wrong? What's he doing?"

"I don't know."

He pulled his knees to his chest and curled into the fetal position. Cynthia marched closer, gun pointed low as she leaned over him.

Suddenly, I realized Ryan was staging a distraction!

I grabbed the nearest fallen branch with my still partly bound hands and whacked Cynthia across the backs of her ankles, using my fear to power myself. She wobbled and screamed. Her arms shot out for balance, flailing.

Bang! Her gun went off skyward, scattering birds from the treetops.

Cynthia toppled onto the edge of the drop-off at our side as I scrambled to my knees, diving at her with both hands outstretched for a powerful shove. They connected with her back, and Cynthia went rolling.

I rubbed my feet against the slackened ties and forced the material off of me. "Come on." I grabbed Ryan by the arm and tugged.

He wobbled upright, bumbling like someone who'd been drugged or had a serious head injury. "I can't," he said. "I think I have a concussion. Go without me. Get help. I'll be here."

"You can't stay here," I said, pulling harder and willing him to comply. "You just saved our lives. Stop being stubborn and let me return the favor."

Bang! The gun went off again, and dirt flew into the air.

"She's still got the gun!" I yelled. "Run! Now! Hurry!"

Together, we stumbled through the underbrush, shortcutting toward a place I knew well—a place with a cell signal and walls. The abandoned cabin had been a treasured escape for Amelia and me as children. We'd played a thousand games there. Spent hours unloading our greatest fears and heartaches there. Best of all, it was nearly invisible in the green foliage this time of year. If Ryan and I could make it there now, we had a chance at survival. I could call for help. Rally the cavalry.

Branches cracked and snapped behind us as Cynthia climbed back up the hill I'd shoved her over.

Bang! The gun went off again, and Ryan fell to his knees with a start.

I dropped beside him and grabbed him under the arms. "We can't stop now. We've got to move!"

He got back to his feet as another shot rang out.

We cut through some limbs and scrambled away with effort, me out of breath and Ryan looking as if each ragged inhalation might be his last.

I pulled my cell phone from my pocket and dialed Amelia. Amelia would know where we were with little explanation. She could get Grady to us before it was too late.

The call connected, then cut out as the single bar on my phone vanished.

I gritted my teeth and stopped at the next live oak for cover. "We have to get a little farther for signal," I whispered, raising the phone overhead.

Ryan leaned against the tree and pressed one big hand to the opposite shoulder. His pale face grimaced with pain.

I lifted a finger to my lips, tracking Cynthia in the distance. She was headed back toward the road where she'd left the SUV, wrongly assuming we'd gone that way as well.

I tugged Ryan's hand off his shoulder and folded my fingers around his. "This way," I whispered. "You can make it."

Ryan wagged his chin infinitesimally. "I can't."

Blood poured from the shoulder where I'd pried his hand away. "Oh my gosh. You were shot." My stomach dropped. That was why he'd fallen, not because he was unsteady from a previous injury or because the sound of a firing gun had frightened him off balance.

It was up to me to make sure he lived.

CHAPTER
❧

TWENTY-FOUR

Ryan moaned and tipped sideways.

I braced him up with one arm. "Shh," I whispered, scanning the forest for signs that Cynthia had doubled back. I needed a plan, fast. The problem was that Ryan had been moving insanely slowly since I'd first seen him on the forest floor, and that was before he'd been shot. He'd been in the elements all night and hadn't escaped. He'd probably taken a big blow to the head like Pete, and he was surely dehydrated, along with who knew what else?

I craned my neck to peek around the tree in every direction.

Twilight filtered through the thick, leafy canopy overhead while sinister-looking shadows writhed and stretched across the ground with each balmy breeze. My senses heightened to maximum capacity, and my muscles tensed to spring at the slightest of sounds. I jerked my gaze left, then right, half expecting Cynthia to pop out from a cluster of shrubs or from behind the live oak. *Think,* I scolded myself. *Concentrate.*

Clouds raced across the sky, sending us into momentary blackness.

I squeezed Ryan's hand, as much for his reassurance as mine. We would be okay. Somehow.

My phone rang, and I nearly screamed.

I flipped it in my palm and answered before it could ring again. Amelia's face and one bar of cell service lit the screen "Hello?"

"Where are you?" she asked. "Did you call and hang up on me? I've been waiting at the store for you. Why weren't you answering your phone?"

A gunshot rang out, and I held my breath in fear Cynthia might hear me.

"I heard that!" Cynthia screamed, her voice echoing through the dark woods.

"Oh my goodness!" Amelia squealed. "Was that a gunshot?"

"Yes."

"You won't get far," Cynthia yelled. "I know I hit the reporter. He's too big to carry, and you're not the kind of girl to leave him behind, so you might as well come out from wherever you are and let me finish this."

I cupped my hand around the phone, hoping to hide the light of the screen. "We're in the maritime forest," I whispered, my mouth dry and my throat thickening with fear. "Send Grady to the cabin. Tell him it's Cynthia Preston. Don't call back." I hung up and peeled Ryan away from the tree. "Come on. We've got to move," I told him.

He shook his weary head, eyes drooping with fatigue and blood loss.

"You're going to be okay," I promised. "You're strong, and you can do this."

His eyes slid shut all the way, knees buckling.

"No!" I gasped. "Wake up." I pulled one of his arms over my shoulder and tilted forward. I imagined dragging him. Leaving him. Carrying him. None of it would work. He had to help.

"Wake up." I pulled his arm and elbowed his belly. "No sleeping until we get to the cabin." I hooked my free arm around his back and took a painful step forward, weighted by his nearly useless frame. "Come on," I whispered harshly. "You have to try. If you live, this will be the byline of a lifetime. Now let's go." I jerked him forward another step, and he swung a leg in cooperation. If Ryan didn't quit on me, I would get us there.

Relief washed through me as the cabin came into view. The structure looked less stable and more decrepit than I remembered. Formerly a one-room log cabin, the place had been abandoned more than a century back. Now, green moss climbed the slick, dark logs and vines wove through the gaping windows like creepy organic curtains. I hoisted Ryan inside and pressed the door shut behind us, disturbing a nest of spiders in the process.

"You did it," I whispered, lowering Ryan onto the rotting floor boards. "Can you scoot back?"

Ryan inched his long, filthy frame across the questionably sound floor littered with holes and debris. He pressed his back to the cabin's far wall, blending seamlessly into the shadows.

"Let me see your shoulder," I said, pulling the fabric away from his bloody skin. My cheeks flared hot and my stomach roiled at the sight of the angry wound. I blew out a long stream of air to keep from passing out.

"Bad, huh?" he asked.

"I think so," I admitted. I'd dealt with all kinds of injuries from a lifetime of hiking, surfing, and kitchen work. I'd even accompanied Wyatt on dozens of ambulance rides following particularly bad rodeo experiences, but I'd never seen a gunshot wound, and the fact that Ryan was covered in dirt didn't help. "There's a hole here, and she shot you from behind, so the bullet went all the way through. I think that's good, but you're losing a lot of blood."

"Bad," he said.

"Yeah." I looked around us. "I don't know what to do," I admitted. "Can you cover it with your hand again? Add pressure while I find something better to help stop the bleeding?"

Nothing in sight was clean enough to use on an open wound. Honestly, his hands weren't either, but it gave him something to do while I tried not to have a complete breakdown.

"Where are we?" Ryan asked. "Somewhere in the mountains?"

"No. Still Charm," I said. "This is the maritime forest near where Judy grew up. Cynthia said Craig brought her here the night before the wedding and told her to go home. She didn't like it."

Ryan chuckled. "I accused her of killing him. She didn't like that either."

"She chased you down the alley, didn't she?" I asked. "She was driving the same SUV last night that she used to bring me here today."

"She tricked me," Ryan said. "I told her I thought she killed Craig, but she assured me she didn't. Then she said she knew who did, and asked me to help her prove her theory to get justice for Craig. I agreed to meet her in the alley, and here I am."

"Did she hit you with her SUV?" I asked, assessing his injuries. Was he moving slow due to broken bones? Fractures? Internal bleeding?

"No." Ryan grimaced. "I got in willingly. We were going somewhere to talk, but she whacked me on the head and I woke up in the woods."

I let my mouth hang open. "You willingly got in a car with someone you thought was a killer?"

"Why not?" he said. "She's a girl. I didn't see how I could be in danger."

"Good job," I said flatly. "How'd that work out for you?" I looked out the window, listening closely to the sounds of the forest and trying not to panic. "Most of the Outer Banks were covered in forests at one time," I said, trying to stay calm. "People cut a lot of it down in the name of commerce, but pockets of ecosystems like this one are still scattered over the islands." I turned to check on Ryan when he didn't respond.

His eyelids had fallen to half-mast, and his hand had slid away from his wound.

"Hey." I ducked back to his side. "Wake up, okay? I don't know what happens if you fall asleep because I don't know what's wrong with you."

"I was shot," he said, "and a bunch of other stuff." His eyes closed, but his lips curled into a lazy smile. "I'm sorry I told you what your ex said."

"What?" I stared at his fading smile.

"He shouldn't have said you were cursed, and I shouldn't have repeated it. It was mean of us both and untrue. I watched some online footage of his bull riding. He was really bad."

I laughed. "You should be quiet. Save your energy for the big rescue."

"Why? Is Amelia coming?" His smile brightened briefly.

"I certainly hope not," I said. I didn't want anyone I loved to come anywhere near this place with crazy Cynthia on the loose.

Ryan's face went slack.

"Ryan?" I crawled closer, careful to stay below the window's edge. "Hey," I whispered. "Ryan?" I patted his cheeks. "Wake up." My heart clenched with the thought that he might not wake. Ever. I pressed two fingers to his throat.

A faint pulse tapped back.

"Oh, thank goodness." I slid onto my backside and gulped air. I could still get him out of the forest alive.

"Fee. Fi. Fo. Fum," Cynthia's voice trilled outside the window. The snapping of her feet on twigs carried through giant holes in the cabin's walls and elevated floorboards.

Fear beat in my heart and head.

She's here.

I gave Ryan a long look. He wasn't dead yet, but he would be if she got inside the cabin. I couldn't protect him from a gun, and I couldn't carry him out in my pocket. I wrapped my fingers around a narrow piece of broken board and pulled it to my chest. The rotting edges crumbled under pressure from my grip, but it was all I had.

I slid my feet through a broad hole in the floorboards and lowered myself down, praying not to land in a den of snakes or on an alligator's back. I crawled carefully through the dirt, moving toward the front of the cabin, prepared to do whatever it took to keep Cynthia out.

I stopped short when a distinct pair of legs formed from the shadows.

"Come out, come out, wherever you are," Cynthia said, heading straight for the door. She pointed her gun at the cabin, then swept the door open with her free hand.

I crawled out from hiding a few feet away and hefted the wood onto my shoulder like a baseball bat. My next footfall landed on a cluster of dried leaves.

Cynthia whirled to face me, gun extended. "There you are," she said, a smile blooming on her lips. "Where's your sidekick?"

"Dead," I said, hoping she would take my word for it. If I didn't get away, maybe Ryan could still live to tell the story.

Cynthia's smile vanished. Her lips turned down at the corners, either sorry for his death or regretting she hadn't gotten to see it, I wasn't sure. Her thumb grazed the top of her gun, cocking the hammer and preparing to send me to meet Ryan on the other side.

"Wait," I pleaded, raising my hands in surrender. I scrambled mentally for something else to say but came up empty. The broken plank wobbled in my grip.

"Freeze!" Grady's voice exploded nearby. A sudden and blinding light flashed onto Cynthia's face, and she turned on instinct.

I swung the wood until the sound of its connection with her head echoed through the trees, and she dropped like a sack of potatoes.

∽

September was as beautiful in Charm as any of the summer months, with the bonus of slightly cooler temperatures and the hint of turning leaves. I sat in the gazebo, sipping tea and enjoying the sweet sights and scents of my rose garden, along with the comforting sounds of the sea. I'd added time for reflection into my daily routine after surviving the business end of Cynthia Preston's handgun. As a result, I felt more centered, more at peace, and more like myself. I'd even taken the plunge and ordered the new furniture for my café. Judy had assured me it was not only an investment in a business I believed in, but an investment in me, my family's recipes, and our legacy of strength and fortitude. So I went for it, and it felt amazing to take a chance on myself again. Hopefully there would be many more opportunities to do the same in my future.

"Sorry we're late," Aunt Clara said, hurrying to the gazebo with Aunt Fran in tow. "She's been on the phone for so long, I threatened to leave without her. Finally she decided to tell her story walking."

I patted the seat beside me, motioning to the small table of drinks and treats I'd set up. Evening tea time in the garden wasn't just a new habit of mine—it seemed to be something a lot of important people in my life could get behind.

Aunt Clara held a giant yellow sun hat to her silver and blond hair as she took a seat. Wind blew her long locks around her shoulders. "I don't think I'll ever get used to the beauty here," she said, a clear note of admiration in her tone. "I doubt there's anyplace as beautiful on earth."

Grady climbed the hill before me, slowly interrupting my view of the ocean and sun on the horizon. "That makes two of us," he said.

I blushed, senselessly hoping the view he was thinking of had me in it. "How was your walk?" I asked, letting my gaze travel behind him to where Denver and Denise normally appeared.

"Good. Collecting stones. They'll be up soon." Grady took a bottle of water from one of the ice buckets on the table and cracked it open. "Seems that ending our evening walks at your place is becoming a habit," he said. "I always feel like we're intruding on your calm."

"Nonsense," Aunt Clara cooed. "You're always welcome. The more the merrier."

I smiled. "I look forward to it."

Grady grinned. "Me too." He pulled in a deep breath, then turned to survey the scene. "What's going on with her?" he asked, homing in on Aunt Fran, pacing several feet away.

I shrugged.

"Politics," Aunt Clara said. Her smile waned briefly before spreading once again. "I got a call from Bee Loved this afternoon," she said.

My heart leapt in my chest. "You did?" The application deadline had come and gone without an update on the Bee Loved website. My aunts' video had blown all the others away in terms of quality and fun, but the most votes had gone to a man dressed as a bee and acting like a clown. The site had been abuzz for days with beekeepers awaiting the announcement of Bee Loved's winner.

Aunt Clara nodded slowly. "We won!"

I threw my arms around her. "That's wonderful! Congratulations." I kissed her cheek and pumped a fist in the air.

I turned my eyes to a very quiet Grady and went still at the shock on his face. I tracked his gaze to a new arrival.

"Ryan?" I said, smiling wider. "Hey!" I dashed to his side and pulled him into a hug. "How are you?" I still couldn't believe how happy I was that he'd survived. Severe dehydration, a concussion, and a gunshot wound hadn't kept him down long. Not when he had a major story to write and pitch.

He hugged me back. "I'm good, thanks to you. I came to say so in person."

I hadn't seen Ryan since he'd left the local hospital to recover someplace closer to his home. I hadn't expected to see him ever again.

Ryan released me to shake hands with Grady and kiss Aunt Clara's cheek. He helped himself to a glass of iced tea and a slice of lemon cake. "Nice job putting Cynthia behind bars," he said to Grady, immediately mentioning the name I'd gone out of my way not to utter for weeks. "I've been meaning to ask what made you let her go after you initially questioned her," he said, taking a seat opposite me and fixing his gaze on Grady.

Emotion flickered in Grady's clear gray eyes. *Regret?* "Cynthia was on my radar once I found the discrepancy between her real and stated arrival times, but lying isn't grounds for an arrest or motive for murder. I started digging, but at first it just looked like she'd wanted to hide the fact she'd been with Craig before the wedding."

"You knew that?" I asked.

He dipped his chin in one stiff nod. "Yes, but she'd been forthright about why she was here, and I couldn't place her at the crime scene. It wasn't until I discovered she'd had restraining orders and charges from menacing to domestic violence filed against her following three previous breakups, including Craig Miller, that I went looking for her. When I couldn't find her, I called the car rental companies at the airport and asked about vehicles fitting the make and model of the SUV that followed Ryan into the alley. It occurred to me that taking a cab to the reception might've been one more part of the smoke and mirrors she'd set up, and maybe our intrepid reporter here had managed to upset her more than you had."

I wrapped my arms around my middle, feeling myself go cold. I could still see her wild expression as she leveled her gun at me.

"My hunch was right," he continued, "and I was out looking for the vehicle when I got Amelia's call saying Cynthia had taken you to the forest."

I swiveled at the sound of a vehicle nearby, heart pounding.

A red convertible stopped near the front of my home, and Amelia climbed out. She had a stack of papers in her hands and Judy at her side.

I hurried to meet them. "I'm so glad you're here," I said, hugging each of them.

Judy held on for an extra few beats. "I'm going to miss these evening tea times," she said. "I had to squeeze one more in before catching my plane."

"Are you sure you can't stay another few days?" I asked.

Judy had gone home for Craig's funeral and to tend to the legal matters of his estate, then traveled back on the notion she might buy a home in Charm and stay. Ultimately, the bad memories were more than she could bear, and Jasper's affection had been a bit intense for a newly widowed woman. So she'd settled on buying her family a modest home close to town where her aging folks had easier access to friends and necessities like a pharmacy and grocery. The place had a guest room over the garage where she could stay anytime.

"Maybe once I've had time to figure things out," she said.

I nodded. "If you change your mind, or if you ever need anything…"

Judy pulled me back into a hug. "Oh," she said. "I have something for you." She dug into her purse and handed me an envelope. "It's the final payment for the rehearsal dinner and reception. I added a little extra to help with the costs of your café expansion—or kitchen updates or even a new golf cart for deliveries."

"No," I said. "I can't accept that." I pushed the envelope back in her direction.

She stopped me with an uplifted hand. "I have lots of money now, and I've been advised to make sizable charitable donations," she said. "Consider this an investment in your soon-to-be-famous iced tea shop."

I smiled. "If I keep this, it comes with free food and tea for life."

She extended a hand for a shake. "I've got to get back before Pete takes on another client he's not prepared to handle."

"You're keeping the business going?" I asked. I'd been under the impression the company couldn't go on without Craig. He'd been the brains. Pete was just the face. A lucky face who'd woken from a trauma-induced coma about a week after Cynthia's arrest. His body had already healed from the physical injuries, and from what I heard, he was seeing a therapist about the emotional stuff.

"I'll keep it going as long as I can," she said, "as long as I'm able to recruit qualified data scientists from other companies and colleges, we'll be okay. None of the new employees are as talented as Craig, but they get the jobs done."

I smiled. "Good. I'm sure he'd love to know you're keeping his dream alive."

"I'm trying. Running a tech company has been a lot to get my mind around, but Pete's really stepped up," she said. "He told me recently that he knew about Craig and Cynthia, which was completely humiliating, but he also said it was part of the reason he'd been so mad at Craig, and that helped me understand why he vanished after the wedding."

I rubbed her arm. I'd heard that story too.

Judy squinted against the sun and hooked flyaway hair behind her ears. "Did Detective Hays tell you it was Cynthia who called Craig at our reception? Craig told us it was Pete, but the phone records showed it was Cynthia. First, she called. Then, she showed up and killed him."

"I'm so sorry."

Amelia approached next, having gathered lidded drinks and snacks in pairs. "Take these papers," she urged.

I took the thin stack of copy paper she'd pinned beneath one arm.

She passed half her treats to Judy. "We're headed to the airport now, but I'll be back tonight to see what you think about the story."

I looked at the paper in my hands. "*The Case of the Missing Pony,*" I read. "Is this your mystery? You're really writing it?"

"I figured out why I couldn't get started," she said. "I'd been trying to put our new adventures into words, but sometimes we do scary things, and I didn't want to share my nightmares." She gave a nervous chuckle.

I flipped the pages in the stack. "This is about the collectible colt figurine I lost in third grade."

Her brilliant smile ignited. "I'm going to write children's books. All our old adventures with a new inspiration." Her gaze moved to the horizon.

The sound of giggling turned my head in that direction.

Denver ran full speed for Grady, chased by his intrepid au pair. "She's a sea monster and she's going to eat me!" he squealed.

Grady lifted his son into the air and spun him around, hanging him upside down for Denise to tickle.

I turned the page of Amelia's manuscript. "A little

boy named Denver visits two third-grade island detectives in search of his missing colt." I smiled up at Amelia. "This is perfect."

She tipped her head. "Thanks. Now we've got to go, but I'll be back for movies and ice cream later."

"Deal." I gave Judy and Amelia one more good-bye hug.

Ryan appeared a moment later, arms open for a hug of his own.

Amelia blushed, and I rolled my eyes. "Did you get the byline you'd hoped for?" she asked him. "Were you able to sell your story to the *Times*?"

Ryan gave his trademark cheesy grin. "I did, and it generated so much buzz I got an agent to negotiate a potential television movie deal."

Grady groaned behind me. "That ought to keep you humble."

Ryan winked. "I'll be sure to get a solid Barney Fife look-alike to play you."

"Funny," Grady said.

Amelia turned to Ryan. "We have to go, but you could ride with us to the airport if you want," she suggested. "Maybe we can get dinner on the way back."

"That sounds like a date," he said. "I like it."

I rubbed my forehead as the trio climbed into Amelia's little car. "Remind me why I saved that guy."

"Because you're a hero." Grady's voice was low and gravelly. "I should have held Cynthia the moment I suspected she was more than just an obsessed ex-girlfriend."

"Don't start that again." I nudged him with my elbow. "We got her. That's what counts."

He stared down at me, head shaking. "I should have had her sooner."

"You know what I think," I said. "I think we make a great team."

"No. We aren't a team. We're a detective and an iced tea–maker."

I headed for the treat table and sliced a piece of lemon cake for Grady. "Try this." I knew he loved my lemon cake, and I wasn't ashamed to make it every time I knew he was coming.

He accepted the cake with a mischievous look. "It's illegal to bribe a lawman, Swan."

"I'm not asking for anything," I said sweetly. I followed Grady to a grassy spot where Denver and Denise had taken their treats and had a seat.

Grady watched his son's happy face, streaked with sand and icing. "He really loves it here," he said. "With everything he's been through, he could be a mess right now, but he's doing okay. Just like you said he would."

I tapped a finger to my temple. "I know things."

"Yeah?" He forked a bite of cake between his lips, watching me closely as he chewed. "Is there anything else that I should know?"

I considered a number of corny and potentially sappy things I could say but decided to keep them to myself. "Not at the moment."

Aunt Fran raised her hands into the air and shook

her cell phone in one tight fist. "That's it," she said, heading for Grady and me. "It's done."

"What's done?" Aunt Clara asked, a hint of alarm in her voice.

"That infuriating Mayor Dummy and Bracie Gracie have given me no choice. I'm running for mayor next year," Aunt Fran said. "I won't see this town fall apart because those two want to make Charm some uptight, no fun, rule-lover's paradise. Charm should be a place people want to live, raise children, and retire."

"You're running for mayor?" Denise asked, suddenly looking concerned and turning her attention to Grady.

He pursed his lips.

"That's right," Aunt Fran said, "and I'm going to announce it at the big Christmas party."

"Fun." I smiled. "What big Christmas party?"

Aunt Fran rubbed a palm up and down my arm. "The one we throw at Sun, Sand, and Tea?"

I hugged her. "Whatever you need."

"Excellent." Aunt Fran pressed her phone back to her ear, immediately beginning to make it all official.

Grady lowered his head to mine when she walked away. "Remember how I told you my mother-in-law feels like she's losing Denver by being so far away from him?"

"Yeah." I tried to gauge his strange tone and expression but couldn't. Was he worried? Did he think whatever he said next might make me angry? Sad? I faced him. "What's wrong?"

He watched Aunt Fran. "I mentioned my mother-in-law loves politics?"

Saying a U.S. senator loved politics seemed like a significant understatement, but I nodded. "Yeah."

"She put a bid on a home in town the last time she was here," he said.

"That's great news." I gave his hand a squeeze. Sure, Grady was probably concerned about rebuilding a relationship with his wife's mother after their joint loss, but they'd likely find comfort in being near someone who knew what they were going through, and it would be great for Denver. I couldn't imagine what my life would have been like without my grandma in it. "This is wonderful," I said. "Why do you look upset?"

Grady turned away from Denver. "She's leaving the senate, but she's not done with politics."

I searched his eyes for the thing I was clearly missing. "What are you saying?"

"She plans to run against Dunfree next fall."

I lifted my gaze to Aunt Fran, wildly happy as she spoke on the phone. "Uh-oh."

"Yeah," he said, returning to the refreshment table for a second, fatter slice of lemon cake. "This should be an interesting Christmas."

I grabbed a spare fork and lifted a bite from his plate. "Probably," I agreed, "but Christmas in Charm is always interesting."

Grady hiked a brow. He didn't ask for specifics, but curiosity danced in his eyes.

"You'll see," I said.

And as for my beekeeping great-aunt challenging the current mayor, my childhood nemesis, and a state senator to an election by the people…well, that was something I didn't want to miss.

Blushing Bride

Enjoy this delightfully refreshing hibiscus recipe with a splash of lemon or garnish of lime. Also known as the J. C. Miller or the Summer Splash Special, iced tea enthusiasts are guaranteed to call this tea delicious.

Prep Time: 20 minutes
Yields: 2 quarts

8 cups cold water
1 cup dried hibiscus leaves
2 cinnamon sticks
1 cup sugar
Lemon zest or lime wedges (optional)
Ice

Bring water, hibiscus flowers, and cinnamon sticks to a boil in a large saucepan. Remove from heat and stir in sugar until dissolved. Cover and allow to steep for 20 minutes.

Strain. Add lemon zest or lime wedge to taste. Refrigerate until ready to serve, and pour over ice.

Pineapple Chicken Wraps

Nothing says lunch at the seaside like these signature pineapple chicken wraps pulled straight from the chalkboard at Sun, Sand, and Tea! Serve with a fresh fruit salad and tall glass of sweet tea, then dig your toes into the sand and enjoy!

Prep Time: 15 minutes
Yields: 4 sandwiches

1 tablespoon canola oil
4 pineapple spears, sliced ½ inch thick
1 tablespoon olive oil
2 chicken breasts, thinly sliced
Salt and freshly ground black pepper, to taste
Juice from 1 freshly squeezed lemon
Juice from 1 freshly squeezed lime
Juice from 1 freshly squeezed orange
4 tortillas
4 large lettuce leaves

Heat canola oil in a sauté pan over medium heat, add pineapple, and heat until golden, turning occasionally.

In a grill pan, heat olive oil over medium heat. Season both sides of the chicken strips with salt and pepper, add to the olive oil, and cook through, turning once.

Splash chicken with the lemon, lime, and orange juices. Cover and remove from heat.

On a serving tray, arrange 4 tortillas. Place one leaf of lettuce in each tortilla. Then, arrange pine-apple on top of lettuce. Top with chicken strips, roll tortillas, and serve.

Sweet Tea with Jasmine

Looking for a gentle afternoon pick-me-up to enjoy on the back-porch swing? Try a little sweet tea with jasmine to ease your weary mind.

Prep Time: 20 minutes
Yields: 4 servings

5 cups water, divided
4 heaping tablespoons Chinese jasmine tea leaves
2 tablespoons black tea leaves
2 cups sugar

Bring 4 cups water to boil in a large saucepan. Add the tea leaves, reduce heat, and simmer for 1 hour.

In a separate saucepan, bring remaining 1 cup water and sugar to a boil. Once the mixture boils, remove from heat.

Strain the jasmine tea, and pour into a one-gallon pitcher. Add the warm sugar mixture to the tea, then add enough cold water to fill the pitcher, and stir. Serve tea over ice.

ACKNOWLEDGMENTS

Thank you, sweet reader, for taking another adventure with Everly and her crew. You make my dreams possible, and I am forever grateful.

Thank you, Anna Michels and Sourcebooks, for the amazing opportunity to be part of your team. I'm still pinching myself because you not only took a chance on my stories, you gave them life and you made them better. Enormous thanks to Jill Marsal, my literary agent extraordinaire, who never lets me get bored and always gives me hope. You had no idea what you were getting into when you took a chance on me three years ago, and I appreciate that kind of bravery in a leader. Thank you, Jennifer and Keri, my critique partners and friends. Thank you, Ann Swain, for sharing your delicious jasmine sweet tea recipe. Thank you, Judy and Craig Miller, dear neighbors and friends. I've borrowed your names but could never replicate your likeness. Finally, thank you, family: Mom, Dad, Darlene, offspring, and husband. Without your continued career support and encouragement, I'd probably be micromanaging your lives as a creative outlet, so I think we're all winners here.

ABOUT THE AUTHOR

Bree Baker is a Midwestern writer obsessed with small-town hijinks, sweet tea, and the sea. She's been telling stories to her family, friends, and strangers for as long as she can remember, and more often than not, those stories feature a warm ocean breeze and a recipe she's sure to ruin. Now she's working on those fancy cooking skills and dreaming up adventures for the Seaside Café Mysteries. Bree is a member of Sisters in Crime, International Thriller Writers, and the Romance Writers of America.

"The coastal town of Charm makes me want to walk the beaches and find a real, Sun, Sand, and Tea shop. Even with the murders…"

—Lynn Cahoon, *New York Times* bestselling author of the Farm-to-Fork Mystery series

PRAISE FOR
LIVE AND LET CHAI

"A charming cozy debut with characters as sweet as the titular tea, a mystery with numerous attractive byways, and a budding romance waiting to be explored."

—*Kirkus Reviews*

"A smart and likable protagonist, a vividly rendered setting, a suitably twisty plot, and some colorful supporting characters are the ingredients for a concoction as appealing as any of Everly Swan's specialty sweet teas. I can't wait to try out some of her recipes and to visit this delightful series again."

—Livia J. Washburn, national bestselling author of the Fresh-Baked Mysteries

"Bree Baker's seaside town of Charm has everything readers could want: an intrepid and lovable heroine who owns an adorable iced tea cafe, a swoon-worthy hero—and murder. Fast-paced, smartly plotted, and full of surprises, it's as refreshing as a day at the beach!"

—Kylie Logan, bestselling author of *French Fried*

"Fun and intriguing, *Live and Let Chai* is filled to the brim with Southern charm."

—Kirsten Weiss, author of the Pie Town Mystery series